"Angels have never been fiction."

He was right, of course, but had Cassandra ever imagined she'd one day be standing in an angel's arms? Yes, she had. It had been a blissful, sensual dream of a warrior.

Sam stroked her shoulders and bent before her, as if to kiss her. But he only lingered there, their mouths inches apart, breaths dallying, eyes searching each other's.

She wanted the kiss. It was wrong on so many levels, but she needed it. Yet she sensed Sam would not give it. Could not. Because they were both fearful of the Pandora's box their desire could open.

But at that moment all she heard was an insistent voice inside her head. *Kiss him. It will be dangerous…but how can you resist?*

Dear Reader,

As with most of my Nocturne™ books, this story stands alone but is set in my Beautiful Creatures world. I've created Club Scarlet online so you can look up characters and learn more about them. Stop by and check it out at clubscarlet.michelehauf.com.

I'm pleased that the novella *The Ninja Vampire's Girl* is included with this release. It features Coco Stevens, the sister of Cassandra (who is the heroine of *Ashes*). If you want to read events in order, that novella takes place about five months before *Ashes of Angels*, so I suggest you page to the back of this book and read the novella first. (But you won't be mixed up if you choose not to; I promise.) I hope you enjoy the stories. I had an amazing time creating them.

Michele Hauf

ASHES OF ANGELS

MICHELE HAUF

All the characters in this book have no existence outside the imagination of
the author, and have no relation whatsoever to anyone bearing the same name
or names. They are not even distantly inspired by any individual known or
unknown to the author, and all the incidents are pure invention.

First published in Great Britain 2011
by Mills & Boon, an imprint of Harlequin (UK) Limited,
Eton House, 18-24 Paradise Road, Richmond, Surrey TW9 1SR

© Michele Hauf 2011
The Ninja Vampire's Girl
First published in Ebook form by *Nocturne Bites*
© Michele Hauf 2010

ISBN: 978 0 263 88016 8

089-0911

Harlequin (UK) policy is to use papers that are natural, renewable and
recyclable products and made from wood grown in sustainable forests. The
logging and manufacturing processes conform to the legal environmental
regulations of the country of origin.

Printed and bound in Spain
by Blackprint CPI, Barcelona

Michele Hauf has been writing romance, action-adventure and fantasy stories for more than twenty years. Her first published novel was *Dark Rapture*. France, musketeers, vampires and faeries populate her stories. And if she followed the adage "write what you know," all her stories would have snow in them. Fortunately, she steps beyond her comfort zone and writes about countries she has never visited and of creatures she has never seen.

Michele can also be found on Facebook and Twitter and michelehauf.com. You can also write to Michele at: PO Box 23, Anoka, MN 55303, USA.

Prologue

Cassandra Stevens stepped back from the finished silver sculpture to admire her handiwork. She had formed the male body from silver sheet metal, and worked with various shaped anvils to capture the smooth muscles and lithe structure of the male form. For the wings, stretched back and out from the body, she had used a lost-wax casting method to achieve the intricate barbed vanes.

A month's work glistened under the bright light that hung over her workbench.

When she wasn't working afternoons at the Central library as a research assistant, she spent her evenings designing silver objects d'art and jewelry. Her dream of forming an elite jewelry design business were going much slower than planned since arriving in Berlin two years ago, but better to be meticulous and careful than to rush into things. At least regarding business.

In life, rushing into things was always the better option. Danger did not sit back and wait for a person to weigh their options. One must always be ready.

Yeah, you go, Action Danger Girl, she chided her silent thoughts. Thinking she was ready was much easier than actually *being* ready. She'd never be sure. Never.

The silver sculpture had known its form the moment she'd begun to sketch a flat image on paper and had then transferred it to a sheet of silver.

"An angel," she murmured, knowing, as she'd been working on it, how telling it was she sculpted an angel.

Fascinated during the process, her fingers had worked of their own volition, as if they instinctively knew what her subject should look like. That had never happened with any of her previous projects.

Tossing her hair over a shoulder, loosely bunched at the middle with a ribbon to contain the thick, wavy tresses that hung to her elbows, Cassandra stroked a finger down the abdomen of the figure. She sighed. This was the closest she'd been to six-pack abs in months. Lately, her social life had been suffering for her art.

What social life? You forgot to get yourself one of those, remember?

Another sigh would just be redundant.

The silver wings stretched out behind the sculpture about a foot, and the whole work was heavy, but not delicate, for she'd riveted and soldered the wings in place.

Cassandra had dreamed of winged men most of her life. Winged nightmares had visited her sleep, as well. But her hopeful heart emerged during that flicker of wakefulness following a nightmare and, as a result, the dreams overcame the nightmares.

Most of the time. Doom remained the overwhelming common theme in her dreams.

Angels were...not good. The Fallen ones Granny Stevens had taught her about were downright evil. They were as spiteful, selfish and dangerous as some mortals.

But one angel managed to rise above the dire warnings and tease her admiration. She'd never imagined his face—until now.

Studying the tiny face about the size of her thumb, Cassandra offered him an approving nod. "You are a handsome bloke." No halo sat above the sculpture's head, but that made sense to her. He wouldn't have one.

A dangerous thrill giddied over her skin. She'd created an effigy of something others believed could harm her.

Danger teased, and she always responded. "Will I meet you someday?"

She carried it into her bedroom and placed it on the pine dresser opposite the end of her bed. Sitting on the bed, beneath the violet mesh canopy, she marveled that the angel looked down over her. She hadn't planned it that way.

He's the furthest thing from a guardian angel.

"I pray to survive when finally you come for me," she said to the sculpture. "I can feel it. You'll be here soon."

Paris—Underground

"We've intercepted sensitive information between a muse and a hunter." Bruce Westing handed the tribe leader, Antonio del Gado, a computer printout of conversations. "Cassandra Stevens is located in Berlin. She's the contact point for what I estimate to be at least three muses traveling to Germany. And, I can't verify this, but I think a pregnant muse is also on her way to Berlin via unknown escort."

Del Gado slapped the paper on the desk before him. "She's pregnant with a nephilim?"

"Fingers crossed."

Bruce winced when he realized that should have been a more exacting reply. He was doing the best he could with the technologically inept staff provided for him. Tribe Anakim was one of the most clichéd groups of vampires around. They lurked in darkness due to their extreme sun affliction, and Bruce was never surprised when one developed the Bela Lugosi sneer and creep.

The tribe leader rubbed the heel of his palm

over an eye. The man was ancient, and had big dreams, but Bruce supported his wacky idea. Being denied the sun for centuries would try any man's nerves. "How many more names do we have?"

Bruce tapped the laptop keys. Antonio del Dado didn't know how to use a computer any more than the other tribe members, so Bruce was the tech wizard for tribe Anakim, as well as the chief angel tracker. The latter was much less taxing on his patience.

"Only three," he reported, turning the laptop so Antonio could read the names. "You want me to prepare the summoning room?"

"Yes, immediately. If any number of muses are congregating in Berlin, then we'll have to bring the Fallen to them. And check with Rovonsky. He's been preparing equipment for capturing and securing the nephilim. The equipment is easy enough to move. I say we leave for Berlin before daybreak."

Bruce lifted a brow but didn't comment. Anakim's entire tribe lived by the night. They had slaves to do their day work. Like him.

Not a slave, but a well-paid employee.

"This is finally coming together, Bruce. I can feel it. Soon, tribe Anakim's bloodline will be infused with the blood from our nephilim ancestors. We will finally become daywalkers. Do you know, I haven't seen the sun for three centuries?"

"That's a long time, boss. You could use a tan."

Antonio's expression remained sober.

Reminded of the boss's lack of humor, Bruce closed the laptop. "I'm on it. And I'll send a man after the muse, Cassandra Stevens, to keep an eye on her."

"Excellent. Soon, Bruce, soon, a plague of dark divinity will stalk the earth."

Yeah, whatever. Always so dramatic, the boss man. Just as long as that plague stayed away from him.

"When this is over," Bruce muttered as he strode down the torchlit walls of Anakim's lair, "I'm going topside for good."

Coco Stevens listened to the phone ring endlessly. Her boyfriend, Zane, waited in the doorway, one of Coco's pink suitcases in hand. Outside in the cab sat Ophelia O'Malley, her pregnant belly ready to burst from the seams of her stretchy sweater dress.

"No luck?" Zane asked and glanced outside. "You can try calling your sister again when we reach the airport."

"I forgot to charge my cell phone, and you don't carry one."

"They do still have pay phones, love."

Sighing and hanging up the landline, Coco melted into her boyfriend's embrace. That Cassandra trusted her enough to handle this mission meant the world to her, but that also meant she couldn't screw it up, or there'd be no future missions. Coco was all about the adventure.

"I wanted to let Caz know we were on our way. She's been uptight about us informing her on every leg of this mission." She peered over his shoulder. Berlin was getting a snowstorm, but here in London it was raining. "Is Ophelia all right?"

"The muse is fine. Craving a pint, or so she says. But I don't think alcohol is safe for a pregnant mother, eh?"

"She's due any day now. I'd say a little beer isn't going to hurt a thing. We'll get her something at the airport." She closed the door to her flat behind them and locked it. "Cassandra must be out skiing or free-running, or doing something dangerous. She's been into the danger-play lately. I worry about her, Zane. She's not indestructible, yet she thinks she is."

Zane wrapped an arm around her waist and led her to the cab. "She's got a lot on her shoulders, love. I think it's her way of spitting at the big bads and challenging her less-than-rosy destiny. Of course, Adventure is not her middle name."

"It's mine," Coco said with a gushing smile and kissed her lover. "I hope she's out partying. Living it up before, well, you know."

"Don't worry your pretty head, love." He helped her into the back of the cab, then went around to put the suitcase in the boot. "Off with Adventure in hand," Zane muttered. "Never a dull moment with the Stevens sisters."

Chapter 1

The halo hunter's shoulders hit the wall, the back of his skull thudding rather loudly from impact. Samandiriel held him with ease—and one hand—about the neck. The hard knob of an Adam's apple gulped against his palm. Mortals were startlingly delicate.

To the hunter's favor, he didn't kick at him, but merely hung calmly. The mortal's pulse banged beneath his palm. Quite a unique feeling. Samandiriel had no pulse.

"You're...second...seen..."

"Stop mumbling, human," Samandiriel said. A leather messenger bag strapped over one of the hunter's shoulders revealed its contents. He sorted through the dozens of clanking halos in the bag, but couldn't resist asking, "Second?"

"A-angel," the hunter croaked.

"That you've seen? Well, aren't you lucky? Most mortals never get to see such a thing. Do you marvel over me?"

"Uh, sure. M-marvel."

One halo glowed, but before Samandiriel could touch it, he felt a prickle of awareness, brought on by an intruder approaching from behind.

Turning, and keeping the halo hunter pinned to the wall, he thrust out a hand to stop the person who approached. The simple gesture slammed the intruder against the opposite wall. Apparently more willful than the halo hunter, this one dropped to her feet and came at him again. The tiny female flashed a sneer and wielded ineffectual fists before her.

"Vinny…okay…"

The woman stood straight, dropping her fists, evidently understanding the hunter's abbreviated reassurance.

Before she could dodge, Samandiriel placed the heel of his palm against her forehead. A flash of her memory assaulted his brain and he grasped a very pertinent detail about her.

"Vampire?" He made a fist to swing—

"No!" The hunter squirmed and now he did kick, but only managed a knee to Samandiriel's thigh. "She's not dangerous!"

Bouncing on her fancy high heels as if ready for the next swing, the vampire in question quirked a brow and huffed, disagreeing with the assessment of her lacking danger. "Another angel?"

"Others have been here before me?" Samandiriel asked the hunter. "That's right, I'm the second." He loosened his grip to allow the man to slide to the floor and stand of his own volition. "Where is the other? What was his name?"

"Zaqiel. He's dead now. But the vampires—"

"Are summoning the Fallen?" Samandiriel spoke the knowledge he'd pulled from the vampiress. "You can verify that is true?"

"Yes, tribe Anakim," said the hunter. "But she's not with the bad vampires. She's with me."

Samandiriel assessed the twosome. He read the mortal hunter's confidence, yet the man maintained a healthy respect for the divine. While the female, who seemed to match his cockiness, possessed an innate fear of him that held her at a distance. He did not fault her vampirism. Hate was not in his arsenal. But he would be cautious. He'd not dealt with a fanged one in the short time he'd walked the earth.

Shoving his hand into the messenger bag, Samandiriel claimed the one halo that glowed blue and held it before him. "This one is mine."

"I can see that."

"Luck in your quest, mortal. And you." He turned to the vampiress, who backed against the wall. He placed a palm against her forehead and strained the details of the angel summonings

from her. She knew much. It was information he
needed.

Vampires had summoned him to earth?

His original goal to stalk his fellow Fallen in
order to win his return Above remained. How-
ever, with vampires in the mix, now he'd have to
change tactics.

The hard-driving rock anthem blasted a sexy,
moaning chorus that enticed Cassandra onto the
dance floor of club Schwarz. She didn't understand a lot of German, but the lyrics didn't matter.
The beat thundered in her heart. Warm bodies
dancing close by brushed her skin and, at times,
matched her rhythm with a sexy rotation of hips.

The club decor was black, covering everything
from the walls, tables, ceiling, glasses and gob-
lets (including the drinks in clear glass) and bath-
rooms. The lighted floors flashed white squares
and illuminated most, and the sparkles in the
black paint shimmered as if it was a midnight sky.

She loved this club, and it had been too long
since she'd been here. After completing the angel
sculpture something had compelled her to get
out of the flat and let loose. It was high time she
kicked her lacking social life into gear.

She'd lost track of her date but wasn't overly
concerned. Marcus wasn't exactly a date. The guy
down the street had asked her out a dozen times
and she'd finally succumbed. A little too tug-
the-tie for her—though she did find his glasses

sexy—he was probably at the bar nursing a vodka neat. He was a computer tech at MasterSysteme, yet it was apparent Marcus had no idea how to let loose after hours. He refused to dance, telling her to go off and enjoy herself.

Constantly on guard was her normal MO, had been since she was a teen, so learning to let loose once in a while had become a necessity to her survival.

Flipping her long black hair over her shoulders, she toyed with the red-and-white ribbons her hairdresser braided within the strands every other month. She didn't like the idea of dreads, so the ribbons added that *something extra* she wanted in the style.

Sashaying sideways, a gorgeous dancer with dark stubble that emphasized his square jaw followed her gyrations. They spun and bumped hips and shoulders in fun play. He had a sexy smile, but she'd seen him making out with a blonde earlier beneath a black steel nude bent over the archway that led to the *private* rooms. She couldn't abide double-dipping.

The beat changed, relaxing, and the dance floor sighed as couples paired up, while lone figures swayed to their own design.

Not ready for a break, Cassandra danced closer to the edge of the floor where the lighted tiles flashed. It was cooler here, and she knew she'd worked up a good sheen of perspiration, because she could smell her spearmint body lotion.

Smiling, because she smelled like a stick of spearmint gum, Cassandra realized this particular let-loose night had been a long time coming. It felt amazing forgetting…everything.

There was so much to forget. Dark things. Evil things. Impossible things. But only for the night. After a decade of training, she'd never completely let down her guard.

Casting her gaze about the shadows lining the dance floor, she stopped herself from surveillance with a mental slap to her wrist. *Just dance. Enjoy some mindless fun!* But her vision landed on a man who stared at her.

The hungry look wasn't new. She caught men staring at her all the time across the stacks or a research table in the library. So the Stevens sisters were hot—as she'd often heard men comment—so what? What she looked like on the outside was vastly different from her insides because, Glory Hallelujah, no one wanted to deal with her baggage.

Still, she'd never refuse interest. And tech guy would understand. Hell, Marcus was still nursing that vodka. And was that a bespectacled redhead with whom he was conversing animatedly?

"Ditched so soon?" It was difficult summoning irritation. They looked like a great couple. "Go for it, bloke."

Moving along the dance floor, she noted her observer continued his intense task. The man gave new meaning to chiseled features. Every part of his face—square chin, straight long nose, smooth forehead, pale yet strong mouth—called for notice, and then combined to form an overall captivating result.

Sexual allure spilled from his pores like pheromones she could actually see. The melting look in his eyes oozed over Cassandra's skin. All he was doing was standing there! Had to be a celebrity. The club was famous for them, though normally the celebs did not turn her head. She wasn't into paparazzi or the materialistic lifestyle.

A crisp white dress shirt strained across the man's chest like tight sheets on a bed. Cassandra imagined running her fingers across the white fabric and putting a few wrinkles in it for good measure. Wrinkled sheets sounded inviting tonight. Because seriously, she'd known she and Marcus wouldn't mesh the moment he'd suggested the opera as his first choice for the evening.

Crooking her finger, she invited her mysterious observer to join her. He navigated the crowded dance floor with an ease that belonged to fictional characters, like the brooding vampire in a Gothic novel, and matched her slow, sensual dance moves as if trying to mirror her. A little awkward with the hips, but he was at least on the beat.

Obviously not a dancer, but she didn't care. His focused attention shimmied over her skin, feeling like warm rain. And he was all hers. No one else in the room stood in their air.

Mercy, but she'd been too deeply enmeshed in

her own projects and worries lately. The world was putting out men who resembled Hollywood warrior gods? She'd been missing out.

But not any longer.

Turning and swaying before him, she invited his hand to her hip and held it there with hers. He leaned in to smell her hair. Vanilla shampoo, combined with her spearmint body lotion, mixed a sensual combination. He stroked her hair and drew out his hand, trailing a red ribbon along his forefinger. A tilt of his head and a sweet smile displayed his wonder over the decoration.

Cassandra shrugged and winked. She wanted to nuzzle her nose against his neck, divine his scent and whisper an invitation, but she wasn't pushy, and she wasn't a tease.

All right, so maybe a bit of a tease. But she'd come here with another man; she would not ditch him. That was just plain rude.

Unless Marcus and the redhead developed plans of their own.

Suddenly itchy, Cassandra rubbed the heel of her palm over her wrist. This new dress was some kind of wool blend, though very thin. It exposed her back to midspine. The short skirt dropped mid-thigh, and her thigh-high boots were tied up the backs with red ribbons to match those in her hair.

She touched her sexy dancer's forearm, clasping it. *Too intimate, Cassandra.* But she didn't heed her intuition. The dancer's arm was cool, and the difference in their temperatures increased his allure.

The music switched to a fast rocker beat, one of her favorite songs about dangerous beauty, snarled out by a sultry female singer. The guitar riff in this one was insane. Bouncing before him, she performed a sexy shimmy and hip shift while he observed. He'd catch the beat. He seemed to learn quickly.

"What's your name?" she asked over the blast of music.

"Samandiriel."

She hadn't caught the last name—Darrel?—but the first had sounded like Sam. She loved that name. Had dreamed about it…

Shimmying close to him, she spread a palm up the front of his crisp shirt and leaned up on tiptoe so he could hear, "You in town for the convention across the street or sightseeing on the Spree?"

Please don't be a mortician. There was a convention at the Radisson Blu across the street. She'd already talked to two body pokers since arriving at the Schwarz.

"I'm here for you, Cassandra."

Her? Well. That was some kind of all right. It wasn't every day a chick found her own personal—

Wait. She hadn't given him her name.

"Rather a nice distraction," he said over the din. "Hadn't expected to meet you so quickly."

Cassandra stopped dancing. She also stopped

midscratch. She tugged up the dress sleeve, dreading what she would see. The sigil on her wrist, which was normally a reddish-brown color and shaped like a spiral, glowed blue.

It had never done that before—yet that didn't mean she didn't know exactly what it meant.

"Oh, hell, no."

The sensual heat flushing Cassandra's face chilled faster than it would've stepping outside into the freezing winter weather.

Shaking her head, she moved away but was rudely bumped by a dancer. The man's eyes—Samandiriel, now she remembered his name from a dream—were bright and designed from many colors.

"Kaleidoscope," she whispered, choking on her breath.

Years of preparation, of knowing what her destiny would bring, sent her into action.

The time had come. Here stood danger.

Fisting her hands, she assumed a defensive stance. "Come on, buddy, I am so ready for you."

The man's dark eyebrow quirked and his perfectly sculpted lips compressed.

Amidst the ruckus of dancers and ear-thrumming music, Cassandra realized she didn't want this to go down in such a public place. Probably he didn't care, and would use the crowd to his advantage.

Protect the innocents, Granny Stevens had always warned. *At all costs.*

Darting off the dance floor like a banshee called to the grave, she pushed through the crowd of dancers, lovers and chatterers. A swing of her elbow spilled a drink, and someone swore at her in hearty German. She couldn't bother to apologize.

Without looking to see if the stranger would follow she headed down the dark hallway toward the back exit door. Pinpricks of light spattered the walls like a constellation, but did not serve illumination for any more than a careful stroll to find the restrooms.

She shoved a man out of the way. He called back, wondering if she was okay.

She'd worn her thigh-high boots today. The heels were only two inches, but slippery as hell on the tiled floor, which was wet from people entering with snow on their shoes. Grabbing the door, she swung it open and glanced back. The man followed.

It was *him*. Samandiriel. Her dream man. Her destiny.

Her danger.

Her wrist would not itch were it any other man in the universe. And the sigil glowed! Granny Stevens had said it would. She'd always wondered how that would work.

There was only one reason a muse's sigil glowed: it was near another sigil that matched it. Playing angel-to-muse sigil matchy-matchy was not a game Cassandra had signed up for, but certainly, she was prepared.

"Right," she muttered to herself. "You went all kick-ass on him for two idiot seconds!"

Wishing she'd had the time to swing by the bar where her now ex-date sat to put on her leather coat, Cassandra cursed the wicked cold air as she plunged into a wall of prickly snowflakes. A burgeoning storm swirled relentlessly. A drift consumed the bottom step and swallowed her boots ankle deep.

She kept another coat in the boot of her car, along with gloves, hat and other necessary items. No one drove around Berlin in December without the essentials.

The club door smashed outward, cracking the outer brick wall. The stranger marched down the steps, his pace determined. He wore no coat, and appeared unaffected as the bitter wind buffeted his chest and face.

Cassandra's teeth had already begun to chatter. Slipping her hand inside her boot, she claimed her car keys from the inner pocket. She'd parked five rows back and in the corner.

Slipping on the icy surface, she slapped a palm on the closest car to steady herself. A hand grasped her by the shoulder and swung her against the hood of a vintage BMW.

"Where are you off to in such a hurry, Cassandra? I was having a fine time dancing with you.

Were my moves not correct? I thought to follow your direction."

Seriously? She kicked his knee, landing her toe hard, but he didn't register pain with a wince. In fact, he instead winked at her.

"Let go of me! I'll scream."

He slapped a palm over her mouth. His square jaw pulsed and his eyes flashed a mad array of colors at her. "You are—" he trailed his gaze over her face and down her body "—mine." The words came out in a wondrous gasp.

Oh, bloody hell in a handbasket.

She kicked and managed a boot toe behind his knee. "Let me go!"

"Calm, Cassandra, I'm not going to hurt you."

"Oh, yeah? You call having sex with me against my will not hurting me?"

"I—no, I won't do that. I admire you. You're like nothing I have ever imagined beauty can be. Your voice is the color of happiness. It is gorgeous."

The guy was actually trying to flirt with her?

Chill wind whipped across her face and cut off another scream. Cassandra kicked and shoved, but he was too strong. "I'm ready for you, buddy. I know what you want, and no matter how you phrase it, it's not going to happen."

"Please listen to me, Cassandra—"

This time a kick to his inner thigh, so close to the family jewels, managed to present her with freedom.

Dashing for her car, Cassandra said thanks for the Walther semiautomatic pistol she kept stashed in the car's boot. It was over-the-top, but it had been easiest to obtain, and was as easy to use. It wouldn't stop the guy, but it should slow him down long enough for her to escape.

The man who chased her was a Fallen angel. Yes, a real bloody angel. She didn't need an ID card or divine beam of light to convince her. And she, being a muse, wore a sigil that matched only one Fallen. And his idea of *admiration* was not in alliance with hers.

Everything Cassandra had been taught about angels and their muses was falling into dreadful place.

She'd been born a muse, a female mortal who would ultimately attract a Fallen angel. Said angel would one day come for her, impregnate her, and she would give birth to a vicious, giant nephilim. Or so, that is how Granny Stevens had related it to her.

Slamming her palms to the boot of her car, she skidded and hit her knees against the chrome bumper. Struggling with the key, her icy fingers inserted it into the lock and the boot popped open. She grabbed the pistol and turned as the angel slid up to her. His chest met the barrel.

"Back off," she commanded firmly. Holding the weapon gave her a confidence she'd never expected to need. This adrenaline junkie knew how to use nervous energy, yet her dreams of angels had always been merely dreams. "Or I blow you back to the Ninth Void."

He raised his hands in surrender but did not relent by stepping back. Wind blew his dark hair across his face, underlining his eyes. "You've not the power to do so. And please, that place was miserable. I've only been out a day. Won't you allow me a holiday?"

He was trying to charm her? Did he not feel the menacing semiautomatic she held against his chest? One squeeze of the trigger would—well, it would damage him, but not kill him. Only an angel could kill an angel. Unless the nonangel was armed with a divine weapon.

Coco should have mailed the halo to her. What she wouldn't give to have that in hand right now!

"You step back," she directed in a surprisingly calm tone.

"*Nein*. We need to talk."

She chambered a round with a metallic click.

"Try it, beautiful one. But you'll only piss me off. And splatter your pretty dress with my blue blood."

So it really was blue? Bloody hell, it was all true. In a moment of utter bewilderment, Cassandra looked aside, her mind fighting to grasp her new reality.

The Fallen grasped the pistol and turned it on her. "Get in the car. Through the driver's side."

Teeth chattering, she was shoved inside the midsize coupe. Probably her brain was already half frozen, which was why she'd been overtaken so easily. She wasn't able to remain on the driver's seat because he slid in right after her.

"Don't hurt me, you...you monster." *Oh, nice, Cassandra. As if begging will help.*

He grabbed the keys from her numb fingers and shoved them in the ignition. "You're calling *me* a monster?"

No, he was some kind of male model with gorgeous eyes and a sexy smile. Cassandra blinked. *Idiot!*

When she tried to open the passenger door he pressed the automatic door lock on the steering wheel. The lock tab fit flush into the door so she couldn't pry it up.

"Yes, a monster! You're a freakin' Fallen angel who wants to rape me."

The car swung out of the parking spot, swerving on the ice. "Don't use that word. It is an awful mortal word for a cruel act. I would never profane a woman. You are sacred to me, Cassandra. I want to protect you."

He smiled at her. Actually smiled as he navigated the lot with starts and stops and some wild swerves. Did the guy even know how to drive? He said he'd been on earth only a day.

A shake of his head flicked off the heavy snowflakes from his thick, dark hair and shoulders.

Sacred? Is that what he labeled the woman he wanted to get down and dirty with, and without asking first? And *protect* her?

Had she gotten a damaged one? This Fallen must have hit his head upon release from the Ninth Void and landing on earth. Everything he said to her was the complete opposite of what she'd been taught.

Twisting on the seat, she wondered if the backseats would pull down to open into the trunk. She'd never tried it before. The angel had tossed the semiautomatic in the snow back in the parking lot, but she had another pistol in the boot.

The car spun onto the main street, swerving, but he quickly got it under control. He drove right through a stop signal, riding the brake but not slowing. Passing cars honked at them.

"You're very pretty, Cassandra. And the ribbons in your hair. So interesting."

"Is that your idea of foreplay? A few awkwardly random compliments? Buddy, I'm not interested."

"You were interested on the dance floor. Your eyes took me in, sized me up and decided to like me. You touched me." He stroked his forearm where she had placed her hand. "I've never been touched by a mortal woman."

"Yeah?" She had touched him, had even imagined wrinkling the sheets with him. *Oh, Cassandra, get smart. Right now!* "The only touch you'll get from me is a punch or another kick. Want one right now?"

"No, thank you."

Man, but his eyes were incredible. When she

thought they were blue, she noticed the violet, and then, brilliant gold. Wow— "Pay attention to the road. The light is red!"

He drove through the intersection without causing an accident. Cassandra clutched the seat and tensely put her heels to the floor. "You don't know how to drive, do you?"

"No, but I'm learning," he said proudly.

She itched the sigil, which still glowed blue. "Hell."

"Matches mine." He tugged up his shirt and leaned forward to reveal the sigil on the back of his hip. The spiraling dark brown line resembled a tattoo.

The sigil was not a tattoo, but an indelible mark. Cassandra had been born with hers. It was the reddish-brown color of henna, but it never faded, as henna did. "Yours isn't glowing," she remarked.

"Only when I'm in half form."

Cassandra's heart dropped to her gut. The only way a Fallen could get his mortal muse pregnant was in half form. They assumed the wings of an angel on top, yet remained human in every way, including all the essential sexual organs.

Samandiriel.

She had known his name since Granny had found it in the book of names and sigils. Neither had spoken it out loud to the other. Yet after everyone had gone to sleep, and Cassandra lay in her bed staring at the sky through the oak tree near her window, she'd whisper it. Because that's what teenage girls did.

The name had become a sort of mantra, and at the same time a death toll. Samandiriel, the one angel who existed to find her. Samandiriel, the angel she had sculpted in silver. Samandiriel, her death.

A dizzy wave washed through Cassandra's brain. She had to remain alert. *Stay strong.* As soon as he stopped, she'd open the door and run, never mind her lack of coat and gloves. They were only blocks away from a busy restaurant area; she could find help before she froze to death.

"So you're taking me somewhere, and then you're going to shift shapes?"

"No. Cassandra, I would not assume you'd be so enamored with me you would allow such an intimate act so quickly."

She could only gape at him.

Was this one for real? The Fallen were supposed to be focused on getting their muse pregnant. She'd never thought the Fallen would have a sense of right and wrong.

"Seriously, did you land on your head when you Fell to earth?"

He chuckled. "Actually, I originally landed in a shallow stream. I almost drowned, were it not for a couple of village children who pulled me out. But that was a long time ago."

Uh-huh. Like during Biblical times. The angels originally Fell way back when, and God decided to punish them for Falling and swept them all to the Ninth Void courtesy of the Great Flood. Water and angels did not mix; they couldn't swim.

She had to do something. She couldn't let this go further. Opening the glove compartment, she shuffled through the manuals and parking tickets. Yes! She knew she'd put that in there last month.

The Fallen pulled the car to a sliding stop against a snow-stacked curb. Ice slicked the tarmac. The snowplows had not been out since the storm had begun earlier in the afternoon.

"You live close," he said, "but I'm not picking up your heat trail. Can you give me directions?"

"To my place? Not bloody likely."

Gripping the Taser in the glove compartment, Cassandra swung her arm around and landed the angel aside the neck, under his chin. He jerked, his hand releasing the steering wheel. His torso stiffened, unable to fight the high voltage.

A thrusting fist bent the steering wheel. He let out a sound that crackled in her eardrums. It sounded like myriad languages all at once. Gritting her teeth at the pain of the noise, she held firm on the Taser.

And he cried out as if struck through the heart by a blade. Something creaked and then a flash of thick silver *something* moved out from between his shoulders. Whatever it was, it cut through the car roof and smashed out the rear window.

Panicking, Cassandra dropped the Taser and kicked open the passenger door. She scrambled out onto the foot-high snow packed along the curb and looked over the destruction.

Wings had grown out of the Fallen's back, bladed, thick wings that had cut through the car like butter. They looked like…silver? She was a silversmith; she knew her metals. The entire structure of wings looked forged from silver, yet appeared soft as feathers, for the downy barbs fluttered in the brutal cold.

Trapped, the Fallen looked at her and growled.

Not about to stick around, Cassandra took off across the street and headed in the opposite direction of her apartment—only a quarter mile up the street—and one very angry Fallen angel.

Chapter 2

Samandiriel shook off the vehicle from his wings. Metal creaked and split. A tire rolled up against the snowbank. The backseat wobbled and fell from the passenger half of the vehicle.

He eased a hand over his shoulder. That little misadventure had taxed his mortal muscles to weary bands. Though his wings were of silver—indicative of his mastery over the silversmith art—they were adamant and indestructible. Yet there was only so much damage this mortal body could take, even in its half form, which was as close to his original ineffable form he could get while on earth.

He glanced at the mangled car. He'd had to rip his wings out sideways to get free. "Bitch," he muttered, but the anger that had spurred his shift subsided quickly.

It had been a common human reaction to fear. Yet the muse had known what to expect. She had known he would come for her. And it appeared the petite bit with the big brown eyes and beribboned hair could handle herself in a threatening situation.

With a smart cock of his head side to side, he then unfurled his wings completely and followed with a whole-body shake that flexed muscles and tested mortal bones for endurance. Nothing broken.

Thing is, he had no intention to hurt the muse, as she suspected. Cassandra Stevens was a beauteous creation to admire. He could look at her ever after, admire her fine bone structure, the soft brown flesh and long hair that seemed alive with depth. Her voice spoke to him in vivid pinks and violets, bathing him in a luscious sensory oasis.

But once in this form, and if he were near Cassandra, he would feel the compulsion, the need to mate with the muse.

After his original Fall, Samandiriel had observed his brothers. The Fallen went after their muses with sanguine intent and did not care that they harmed, hurt or damaged the muse psychologically and physically. Their only focus was to mate with them, to experience the carnal pleasures that had tempted them to Fall.

Yet after that initial Fall, the Great Flood had

washed over the lands and swept his fellow Fallen from the earth. Samandiriel had been imprisoned in the Ninth Void, awaiting release. He'd had much time to think.

He wanted nothing to do with the wicked pact he'd joined in with his brethren. All he desired was to return Above. But to do so, he suspected he must prove his worthiness, which necessitated his current mission.

A mission to ensure his Fallen brethren did not achieve their goal. And for the other reason, once a Fallen mated with a muse a nephilim would germinate, be born, and destroy all living things in its path.

Yet that mission had been altered after learning about the vampires. So much work to do. And here he stood, having been defeated by an odd electronic device wielded by a tiny woman.

"Bloody bunch of good you've done so far."

He'd walked the world upon arrival on earth yesterday. His kind could move swiftly over the land and sea, taking in knowledge of all things, places, ideas and emotions. He now knew all languages, cultures and history. He knew the modern world, and admired it as much as he worried for it. It was clean and beautiful and ugly and devious. Children suffered and adults wallowed in self-important luxuries. The pious existed right alongside the profane and psychotic. What an ugly yet necessary mix.

Once he had achieved his goal, he would not remain long after.

During his walk around the world, he'd only picked up flickers of knowledge regarding the Fallen. The vampiress with the halo hunter had provided the most curious information. He'd been summoned—by vampires.

Vampires and the Fallen? He suspected it had something to do with the nephilim but couldn't piece that together.

Shaking his wings down, his mortal muscles screamed in protest. He'd not felt such pain, ever. But he did not condemn the pain. It indicated he was part of this world now. Not completely mortal—he intended to retain his angelic half at all costs—but appreciative of all The Most High had given the creatures of the earth.

With a shuffle of his shoulders, he assumed complete human form. His leather trousers and boots were intact, but the shirt was a loss. He picked off shreds of torn white fabric from his arms and shoulders. Snowflakes landed on his skin but did not melt. Due to his cold blood, he didn't feel the winter chill as a human.

Fascinating how the tiny flakes fluttered down from the clouds. There was much to marvel over as he learned the world. Samandiriel cautioned himself not to get lost in wonder when the greater task demanded his complete focus.

A shirt was in order—he had to fit in. But first

he must find the muse. If Cassandra Stevens knew so much, she could prove an ally on his earthly quest. And, he simply wanted to bask in her presence. Because she was his. And he wanted to be near her. To touch her and hold her and—not harm her.

He took two steps across the slick, snowy tarmac. A female scream spun him about, eyes tracking the unremarkable building fronts in the darkness. "Cassandra?"

He'd thought her long gone after witnessing his forced shift.

Again, she screamed, from somewhere in the vicinity a few blocks behind him. Samandiriel's boots dug into the packed snow, and he took off running.

The thugs had knives, and Cassandra had left all weapons in the car with the angel. Samandiriel. Too weird that *her* Sam had finally found his way to her, yet why should she think it weird? She'd been expecting him all her life.

One thug sporting a huge diamond earring, but not resembling an NBA all-star, had demanded her purse, which she didn't have—it was in the car. The other thug, who bore a closer resemblance to an all-star, only because he was so tall, waved a chipped blade menacingly. She could guess they weren't going to leave her without getting something.

Yeah? She had an expert roundhouse kick she'd

give them both. But the first smart line of defense was to run. So she dodged to the right and raced toward the chain-link fence blocking off the alley. Hooking her fingers in the frozen links, she pulled herself up, yet a boot toe slipped on the icy metal, causing her to drop.

Hanging from the fence by numb fingers, Cassandra struggled for hold. Her attackers did not come after her from below. One jumped over her head and landed a precarious balance on top of the fence. An impossible feat. How had he—?

He grinned down at her from his gargoyle post, revealing long, pointy fangs.

Shit. Her fingers slid from the chain links, and Cassandra dropped to the ground.

Vampires were not something she'd trained to defend herself against. Only recently her sister, Coco, had alerted her to the vampires' involvement in the frazzled mess she called her life. She'd been doing research and had secured a weapon, but hadn't expected them so soon. Or ever.

Straightening, she drew in a breath. When life gave her surprises, Cassandra snapped to all-systems-ready mode.

The fence vamp dropped and backed her up against a garbage bin in the dead-end alley. Snow swirled in from the street, and she was starting to feel some serious freeze on her thighs where her boots ended and didn't meet her dress. Never mind the chill against her bare back that made it difficult to stand still.

Stupid to have abandoned her car in this weather. But it wasn't as if it was drivable with an angel literally embedded within it.

Times like this she wished for superheroine powers. She'd often wondered what her muse powers were. Shouldn't she have some? Granny Stevens had always shaken her head and smiled wistfully.

Her wrist itched and the sigil glowed. That could be very bad, or possibly a lifesaver at a moment like this one.

"You got some kind of funky tattoo?" the one with the blade demanded. He did not sound German, but rather Russian, though he spoke English well enough.

"Wait," the not-all-star, diamond-earring thug said. "You know what that is, Russell?"

"Haven't a clue. Some kind of club stamp?"

"I think we found her." The biggest thug crushed her petite body against the wall with his two-hundred-fifty-plus-pound frame, most of the weight in his gut. "Go keep watch," he said over a shoulder to his buddy.

"If she's one of them, we have to bring her to the boss."

"We will. Isn't that right, pretty little muse?"

Now Cassandra screamed. It was involuntary, her body reacting against her brain's better judgment.

The one who'd went to keep watch soared over her and her aggressor's heads and landed on the top of the garbage bin with a dull thud. The blade dropped from the tossed man's hand and landed in the snow.

"What the hell?" The vampire holding her switched his attention to the tall, shirtless man standing not ten feet from them. He held a Taser in one hand and wielded a cocky grin like a switchblade.

"Hi, honey, I'm home," the angel said.

"What took you so long?" Cassandra spit. The vampire still held her by a shoulder, but if he twisted farther to look at the angel...

"Sorry. I had to shake a car off my wings."

"Your wings?" the vampire asked. "What, are you some kind of faery?"

The angel straightened his shoulders and narrowed his eyes. "I say wings, and your first guess is faery?" He shook his head and made a come-and-get-me gesture with the fingers wrapped around the Taser.

The vampire released Cassandra and turned to the angel in time to catch the Taser's copper hooks with his thighs.

Sam preened over the powerful device and nodded. "This is nice. I gotta get one of these for myself."

The vampire ripped out the hooks from his legs and growled. "Try again, you bloody faery."

"You shouldn't use foul language in front of a lady." Tucking the Taser into a back pocket, the Fallen then held up a palm, fingers tight together, and pointed them toward the vampire. "You ready for this?"

"Ready for—"

The angel shoved his spaded fingers through the vampire's chest, pulled him forward and slapped his spasming body onto the ground. A hot, meaty blood scent assaulted Cassandra's nose. The angel roared in myriad tongues like he had in the car. And in one hand, he held a bloody mass from which a puddle of crimson rapidly formed around his boots.

"Mercy." Cassandra's knees wobbled. She was on the verge of hypothermia, too out of sorts, and she'd just watched an angel rip out a vampire's heart.

"Too bad there aren't any witches in the area," the warrior angel commented to the blubbering vamp. "I know they have a use for vampire hearts. Keeps them immortal."

The angel tossed the heart behind him, then made a gesture with his fingers that sent the vampire, seemingly weightless as a pillow, onto the garbage bin atop the other attacker.

He bent and plunged his bloody hand into the snow to clean it off, and Cassandra noticed the flesh on his back was seamless. No sign wings had been there. It was broad and burnished from the sun and it would probably warm her if she clung to him.…

Just need heat.

"Shall we?" Sam offered an arm, glistening

with fresh-fallen snow and vampire blood. "I don't think these two are the sort you should be spending your time with, honey."

"D-don't honey me."

"It is a mortal endearment. You prefer sweetie? Perhaps *mein* little cupcake?"

"Please, spare me your pitiful attempts at charm." Cassandra stumbled past him, but turned and grabbed the Taser from his back pocket. "Give me that. It's mine."

The angel slapped a hand to her wrist, easily winning the weapon from her frozen grasp. He tilted the stubby barrel against his shoulder and eyed her calmly. "Take it from me, and it's yours. Cupcake."

Like that was possible.

And what was with the endearments? If he thought to win her over, the guy needed to take off and never return.

Cassandra turned and marched away from the one man on earth she knew wanted to do her harm. And it wouldn't be by chance, like the two idiots piled on top of each other at the end of the alley.

Sam hooked an arm in hers and walked her swiftly down the snowy street. Cassandra struggled to keep up. All parts of her felt heavy and burned, but the sight of the mangled car made her pause. Cut open and the steel carapace peeled back, it looked as if someone had taken a giant can opener to it. "You think that looks bad, you weren't the one trying to get it off your wings," the angel said. "Clever trick, though."

"The T-Taser is mine."

"I'll keep a hand on it for a bit."

"Where are you taking me?"

"To your home. You need to get supplies."

"F-for what?"

"In case you hadn't noticed, Cassandra, vampires are after you."

"As well as a Fallen angel!"

"I'm not after you. I've already found you, dear one. The vampires, on the other hand, are on the hunt for muses. I'm sure you've plenty more weapons at your home, and probably some nasty angel spells, too, eh?"

"Spells that'll repel you from me. If you think we're going t-to g-get busy—"

"I've already explained I've no intent to harm you. Convincing you will have to wait. You're shivering madly. Your skin is colder than mine. Frostbite is a real danger. I won't have that."

"You'd pass up a ch-chance to nab some nasty vamps to get me warm?"

His eyes grabbed her the moment they connected. Cassandra could not resist the warmth in them, the utter dazzle of colors. Did he possess some kind of mind control? Some means to see into her thoughts? Transfixed, she swallowed.

"I would do anything you ask, Cassandra."

"Anything? Then let go of me. I can walk myself."

"You can barely stand." He lifted her into his arms, and the thought to struggle did not come to her fuzzy mind. "I can find your home."

"Can you read my thoughts?"

"Now that I've you in my arms, I can read your heat trail."

That sounded nifty, but she didn't say so as he marched her south. She allowed him to do so because she wasn't thinking straight and she needed to conserve her energy so she could think once she got home.

"So…you're S-Sam?" *My Sam,* she thought. Then she mentally kicked herself. Hard.

"You know much. I had expected you would initially be quite surprised by me."

"My Granny Stevens taught me everything she knew about angels and demons and me being a muse," she said.

They turned west. Her apartment was just up the street. She was not leading him, but her shivering limbs homed on it like a beacon and he probably sensed that.

"You know angel names?"

Time to shut up. If he wasn't going to tell her his name again, it didn't matter to her. As soon as she got home, she'd perform an angel repulsion spell and kick his ass back to the Ninth Void.

After she warmed up. Would she ever warm? Her blood had stopped moving, she felt sure. And her skin burned with frostbite.

"Samandiriel is my name," he finally confirmed. "And please, release your worries regarding our connection. I Fell with a greater purpose than merely tupping mortal females."

"Right. You're holier than holy then? Tell me another one."

"Have I tried to attempt you yet?"

"No, but you are taking me home. What are you going to do with me once we get there?"

"That's up to you, Cassandra. It's all up to you now."

Sounded ominous, and like a cop-out. She couldn't control anything but keeping her own ass safe. She'd done it for twenty-seven years. She had sacrificed a lot over the years. Intimate relationships, for one thing. It was always difficult explaining why she spent all her time studying angels and martial arts to a boyfriend who preferred her to focus on him.

For the same reasons, good friends also fell by the wayside.

But that sacrifice meant she was now prepared for the worst—doom. And doom had just come knocking.

Though she hadn't been prepared for Sam's conflicting behavior. He *didn't* want to have sex with her? She'd been taught that was the Fallen's principal purpose for walking earth.

Coco should leave for Berlin tomorrow with a pregnant muse in tow. Ophelia O'Malley hadn't been so lucky avoiding her Fallen. Cassandra wasn't sure what they could do for her, since she was but days from delivery.

Now that Sam had landed on earth she might have to call off the gathering of muses she'd convinced to join her. It wasn't safe with a Fallen in Berlin. Right next to her, actually. Carrying her. Which her shivering limbs appreciated right now.

The best she could do was to kill Sam before Ophelia arrived.

That was a plan she had covered. Although it would come off much easier if he were not carrying a Taser and not seemingly able to read her mind. The man knew too much about her already.

"You l-learned the world after you were summoned?" she wondered.

"Yes, it's an interesting place, I must say. I imagine the earth is a Sinistari's pleasure dome."

The Sinistari were demons forged specifically to slay the Fallen. She could really use one of them right now.

"So vampires summoned you?"

"I learned that truth from a vampiress who was in love with a halo hunter."

Cassandra would not allow him to see her gulp. She knew exactly what couple he was talking about. She'd developed a network of muses and, as a result, others in the know, like halo hunters.

Sam marched her up a snowy path and kicked open the door to her building. "The vampires want you and me to get together much more than you or I do, trust me on that one."

He set her inside and she stumbled forward, but hit the stairs at a run. It felt like a run, but was actually a laborious climb up four steps. Her limbs bent with great difficulty. Icy fingers didn't properly grasp the iron railing.

He beat her to her apartment door. Cassandra huffed with exhaustion, stunned she hadn't seen him pass her up. The angel flashed her his cocky grin, and—was that puppy-dog look admiration?

Wrong time; wrong guy. If only Marcus had been more romantic, she might have avoided this date with destiny.

Wrong, Cassandra. The angel would have found you. Be thankful Marcus hadn't revealed a hero complex when that happened. Protect the innocents.

She leaned against the wall, thankful for the support. One thing she never minded about this building was that the landlord blasted the heat out into the central hallways. Already she felt melty and the tingling in her fingertips had stopped.

"My house keys are in the car. You owe me a car. I'm not rich, and I just paid that thing off."

"You won't need a car to do what we've to do."

"I don't need your help to stop the apocalypse, buddy."

"I prefer your shortening of my name to Sam over some senseless nickname," he offered. "And who said anything about the apocalypse? I want to slay the Fallen and annihilate the vampires. That's far from end of days."

"You really hate the Fallen, eh?"

"I do not subscribe to hate. I don't know how. But I will do whatever is necessary to make things right."

He didn't know how to hate? Made sense in the greater spirit of angels and divine goodness, but the Fallen were not the good guys, so why couldn't they hate?

He gripped the doorknob and twisted it hard. It splintered the wood around the lock and he opened it and walked inside. "Don't worry, you won't be returning."

"Like hell I won't. You are not the one who gets to tell me what to do," she said, feeling her energy return in spurts of warmth rushing through her veins. "Why wouldn't I return? This is my home."

"Because as of right now, you are on the run."

"Yeah?" Rubbing her hands together, Cassandra soaked the loft's toasty warmth in through her pores. "Generally the person one runs from does not accompany them on that escape."

"You're not running from me."

"Oh, right, the vampires. I forgot."

She lived in a vast third-floor loft that stretched the building's width. The highly glossed cement floors flashed with moonlight, and at the south end gray velvet furniture nestled before the floor-to-ceiling window. Tiny blue spotlights—she always left them on—in the ceiling tracks to her right lit the kitchen with what she'd always called an ethereal glow.

The angel strode about and sorted through her things, lifting the couch cushions and tugging open the drawers on the coffee table. He found the pistol in the coffee table and tucked it into the waistband of his pants, next to her Taser.

Shaking first her left foot then her right, Cassandra worked the blood back to her extremities. She wasn't completely warm yet, and sensed her blazing cheeks may have developed a touch of frostbite.

Sam turned to her, too sexy in only leather pants and boots. In the midst of a winter storm, he had marched her home wearing nothing but that. Stunning.

His shoulder-length dark hair, scruffed this way and that, spoke more of the bed-tousled look than angry warrior. Muscles and, well—who could disregard those guns? And since when had a man accessorized with deadly weapons appealed to her? She liked danger, but not the sort that could kill.

"Where is the rest of your arsenal?"

"In the bedroom," she offered sweetly.

He stalked down the hallway.

Cassandra made a beeline for the shelf of cookbooks above the stove. She pulled out the red leather-bound grimoire Granny had given her and paged to the spell designed to put a force field of white light around her to protect her from angels.

She found the dog-eared page and began to chant the Latin verse.

A hand slammed the book shut, pinching her fingers in it. An overbearingly sexy male leaned over her shoulder, whisking her bare back with the hard curve of his pectoral muscle. "No, sweetie. You don't want to keep me at a distance."

"I'm pretty sure I do." Mostly. Yes, she did! "Back off, will you?"

"And what will you do when the vampires come? How will you protect yourself?"

"If you'd stop raiding my arsenal, I'd give 'em what-for with a bullet to the brain."

"Won't kill a vampire. You need a wooden stake."

"That's Dracula movie stuff. The stake doesn't need to be made of wood, and that's definitely not the only way to kill a vampire. A bullet will slow a vamp down, and I've a machete to slice off their heads, and..."

And something special she wasn't going to reveal to anyone. She had to keep at least one ace up her sleeve.

"That'll probably do the job." The angel slid a hand along her jaw, and when Cassandra thought he was feeling her skin, deciding if she were soft enough for him to have his way with her, he abruptly tipped up her chin. "You want a repulsion spell against me? I'll give you a simple one. A means to put me back and give you space.

You can use it if I ever feel the compulsion come upon me."

"The compulsion?" She knew what he was talking about, but wanted to hear it from him.

"To have sex with you."

She swore at the back of her throat and her body sank against the stove. Granny had explained all this and had made Cassandra and her sister repeat it until they'd known it by rote. But until now she'd never felt the implications of what it would be like to stand before the man who wanted to ruin her life.

Why must he be so handsome? And his eyes. All angels had kaleidoscope eyes, but she'd never imagined the mix of colors could be so utterly captivating. She didn't want to run from him, she wanted to put her arms around him, and—no!

Snap out of it, Caz. The moment you start thinking you're a muse—an object that an angel seeks to use—then you've lost the battle. You're more than that. You are strong. You've trained for this!

"Listen, Cassandra." He lifted her by the elbow to stand straight and she met his eyes. It was peaceful there. His voice soothed her too sweetly for a man she should fear. "The word is *agothé*. Try it."

"Agothé."

As if struck by an invisible force, the angel was slammed against the kitchen wall, his arms pinned out and his feet dangling above the cement floor. His bare chest, impossibly strapped with muscles of steel, heaved.

He smiled. "See?"

"How long does that work for?" She slunk along the counter, backing away from him.

"Not long."

Not long was long enough for her.

Cassandra raced down the hallway and into her bedroom. Kicking off her wet boots, she grabbed a pair of black wool leggings and slipped them on. Pulling out of a drawer a thick red sweater she knew she was going to need to stay warm, she first put on a tank top, then yanked the sweater over her head and tugged it over her hips.

Because the angel was right. She couldn't stick around here any longer. Not now that the Fallen knew it was her home.

Her computer flickered, and she grabbed the flash drive from the USB port. It was on a nylon lanyard, which she pulled over her head. Next important item was her rosary, which she slipped on next to the lanyard, then thought about it and tucked it under the sweater. Granny had given it to her; she didn't want to lose it.

Another Taser from the bedside drawer she fit into her back pocket. The pocket-size Ruger she kept stuffed between the mattresses wasn't there. The angel must have found it during his swift reconnaissance.

She ran out of the bedroom and slammed into a solid object. Her palms slapped against hard, muscled flesh. For a moment, she stared at his skin, nicely tanned and stretched like silk over steel. How could a body be so hard? And why did a flash of her tongue tracing between his nipples disturb her thoughts?

"Told you it only works a short while," he offered with a wry grin.

She began to say the word again, but he pressed a palm over her mouth. "It was just for you to try. Hear me out before you turn the word into a Tourette's tic."

She nodded.

"What's this?" He grabbed the flash drive and pulled it from the plastic cover.

"Nothing. Just important papers. Financial stuff, you know. If I'm not returning..."

Pushing her back into the bedroom, he inserted the USB in the computer drive, and Cassandra was so shocked at the angel's actions she stumbled to sit on the bed. It was as if he knew her every secret. Or had been given a clue to finding each one. Could their sigils have something to do with that? She just didn't know.

She averted her gaze to the silver angel posed on the dresser. The face resembled the live angel poised before the computer. Had she brought him to life by invoking him in silver?

She caught her head in her palms. The silver rings she wore reminded her of another time she'd tried to invoke danger. Would she never learn?

The monitor beeped, prompting her attention, and a list flashed on the screen. Sam turned and eyed her. "Financial stuff?"

"It's just a list," she murmured. "My grandmother gave it to me."

"A list of all the Fallen ones' names and…their sigils." He whistled, impressed. "Honey, you do not want this to fall into vampire hands."

"It's not going to."

"No, because I'll make sure it doesn't." He dragged the computer file to the trash.

Cassandra dove for the flash drive and tugged it out. He gripped her wrist. *"Agothé!"*

The angel was forced against the wall again, arms spread. He struggled futilely. "Fine! Keep it," he said. "But you make sure it is erased from the computer and any other copies you have are destroyed. Your home will be searched, I can guarantee it."

She thought about it. He seemed to know what was up in this whole war between the vampires, Fallen and muses. Double clicking the trash icon, she emptied it.

"Where's the original?" he asked.

"I burned it after transferring it to the computer."

"Don't lie to me, Cassandra."

"I'm not."

Okay, so she was, but he didn't need to know she had the original book and was still in the process of scanning all the pages into digital files. Granny had suggested she be very careful with the last page; it wasn't to be scanned—ever.

She made a concerted effort not to look out the bedroom door to the bathroom as she grabbed the Taser and marched out, leaving him pinned to the wall next to her *X-Files* poster and the angel sculpture.

He met her in the living room poised casually near the couch, hands on his hips. How did he do that? It was as if he could move at supernatural speed—ah, yes. He had the ability to walk swiftly, hundreds of miles an hour. It is what he'd done to walk the world and gain knowledge. Because he couldn't fly. Once an angel's feet touched earth, they lost their divinity, and their...

Cassandra noticed the object hooked at his hip for the first time. "Your halo?"

She clamped a palm over her mouth. He had his own halo? But he should have lost that when Falling. It was a powerful weapon in the hands of its owner.

He tapped the circlet, and it clinked dully. "Found it in the halo hunter's bag. It is mine." He stroked the curved blade and it glowed as blue as Cassandra's sigil had.

Despite her dread, an innate curiosity nudged to the surface of her mind, and Cassandra leaned toward the marvelous device. "Can I touch it?"

He snapped it against his chest. "I don't think so."

"Why not? You afraid I can use it? Mortals can't kill angels."

"In theory."

Really? Well, that went a ways in answering a few of her questions. Perhaps a mortal could kill an angel; in fact, she knew that one had. He wasn't about to hand over something she could use as a weapon against him. Smart angel.

"It holds your earthbound soul," she stammered. "Why don't you claim it? Then you don't have to…" *Hurt me,* she couldn't say.

"Don't want it. When I'm finished here…" He looked aside, apparently unwilling to complete that statement.

So the angel had a few secrets of his own. Which meant he wasn't entirely undefeatable. If the enemy had a secret, it was most certainly his greatest weakness.

"You ready to rock?"

"I'm not going anywhere with you. Where is a Sinistari demon when I need one?"

"You know more than I expected," he said.

"What were your expectations? A stupid woman who would swoon at your feet and beg you to take her to bed?"

He smirked. "I am pleased you are not as you describe. Do you have a spell to summon the Sinistari?"

"I do." Cassandra eyed the grimoire, lying open on the black granite kitchen counter.

The angel took it and the book sparked into

flames. He held it until the flames began to lick at his flesh, then dropped it in the sink.

"Now you don't. So here's the plan. We will go after the vampires. Kill them all. That'll take care of their interference. And if we encounter any Fallen along the way, we'll take those out, too. That's what this will come in handy for." He tapped the halo.

"And why do I need to come along? Wouldn't it be safer if you tucked me away somewhere?"

"I need to protect you. I can't do that unless you're with me. You've already seen what can happen if you go off on your own."

"That was a coincidence. They intended to rob me—"

"Oh, really? And since when are vampires more interested in robbing than biting?" He lifted a querying brow. "This will be dangerous for you. Are you willing to risk everything, Cassandra?"

"For what? To save the world? To end some kind of apocalypse?"

"It's not the apocalypse, but it is the beginning of a very dark time. Should the vampires succeed in breeding more nephilim—I am aware one is soon to be born, and nothing good can come of that—something very akin to the end times could result. We'll need stakes."

"What about the Sinistari?"

"What about those metal-brained misfits of angeldom?"

"A Sinistari can kill you, thus ending your grand plans to save the world."

"You put your faith on the wrong side, Cassandra."

"I don't believe in faith."

"Ah? You do have faith—you just don't want to believe in yourself."

"I suppose an angel would say something like that. Sort of your creed, eh? If it works for you. But it doesn't work for me."

"Please." He extended a hand. "Trust me?"

She shook her head and took a step away from him. "I trust no one."

"Your grandmother teach you that? Smart old lady."

"She'd kick your ass if she was still alive. She was black belt karate and a judo master."

"Impressive. I'm guessing she taught you that defense jazz you attempted against the vampires?"

Cassandra nodded.

"I have those skills and more. The strength of a dozen mortal men, surely. Can you at least agree I may have the ability to protect you?"

"You may. But I'm not sure I wouldn't be safer hitching the train to Siberia."

"The Fallen walk all parts of the world. You know about them seeking their muses. If the Fallen has attempted his muse, then he goes on to the next muse, and the next. Which means not only are the vampires pursuing you, but also frustrated Fallen."

Again he extended his hand.

Danger? She was all for it. But she worked alone.

Cassandra made to slap her palm onto his, but instead, she shoved him toward the center of the living room and recited the ancient spell, "Letencious! Tricurcious!"

A triumvirate of angel sigils drawn with invisible ink on the wall behind the television, the front door and the wall in the kitchen connected, trapping the angel in the center of the living room.

Sam slammed a fist against the invisible wall. A kick of his boot proved as ineffective. "Oh, this is rich. You think you can keep me in here while you go play with the vampires?"

"I'm not going near the bloodsuckers." Cassandra stuffed her feet into knee-high boots lined in fur that she kept by the door, then scrounged for her leather gloves, which should be in the drawer at the end of the kitchen counter. "And you're not coming along to protect me."

"Don't do this," he said calmly, so quietly she paused and looked at the icon of a man who stood trapped but inches away. "Cassandra, please."

"Don't use my name," she said. "You have no power over me!"

"Cassandra Stevens, muse mine. We have been bonded since the beginning. Since before you were born." He rubbed a palm over his bare chest. "Do you think this is easy for me? To deny the compulsion?"

"You said you didn't feel it unless you were in half form. Easy, or not easy, don't you think it's safer for me to keep you under lock and key? What if this compulsion does hit you? Will you be able to stop yourself from attacking me?"

"I hope so."

"Hope? Oh, brother. More angel babble."

"In this human form I am not a threat to you," he protested.

"I know the drill, buddy. Only in half form— what the hell were your wings made from anyway?"

"Silver. Interesting, isn't it," he noted, with a nod to a silver plate on the wall, "that you are a silversmith?"

She lifted a brow. Manipulating the metal gave her a sense of control. It was the most natural thing when she crafted silver to her will.

"I didn't pick the craft because of you."

"I'd be surprised if you had. On the other hand, it makes perfect sense you'd choose silver. Let me out and I'll show you some new tricks with the metal."

"I'm not in the mood for creating tonight. It's late, and I'm out of here. If you manage to escape, you can have the place. There's food in the fridge. I'm not sure if angels eat."

"Don't go out on your own, Cassandra!"

She opened the front door to a black metallic creature with horns and glowing red eyes.

Chapter 3

Cassandra stumbled away from the demon in the doorway, her thighs colliding with the couch. The thing gleamed like a polished black sports car—wearing armor. Its red eyes were the only part with color.

She made the obvious guess. "Sinistari?"

With a confirming nod, it said in a sepulchral voice, "I've come for the Fallen."

She gestured with a shaky hand toward Sam, trapped in the center of the room. As if the demon couldn't plainly see him.

Smarten up, Cassandra. It's happening. Deal with it.

The demon stalked into the room, each footstep clanking metallic on the cement. The exposed flesh on its face, neck and hands appeared hematite, yet moved like muscle. Ebony horns curled at the side of its head, and it wore black armor over legs, arms and torso.

It was beautiful, and she wanted to touch it, to connect with the impossible—but she wasn't stupid.

If she could inch toward the door...

"Release the wards," the demon commanded.

Halfway to the door, Cassandra spun about. "You can't get at it like that?"

"It?" Sam scoffed and crossed his arms. "I'm standing right here. I can hear you."

"You won't hear much after I've ripped your head from your neck," the demon said on a toothy snarl. He had mastered menacing nicely.

Sam tutted an admonishment and shook his head at the demon. "Apparently," he said, "you're not up on angel-slaying techniques."

"You're supposed to protect me!" Cassandra cried.

The Sinistari swung a look toward her and snorted. "I am not charged with your protection, mortal female, only to slay this wicked one."

Sam chuffed. "Me, wicked? Look who's sporting the black metal like some kind of satanic death cult worshipper."

"Satan has no dealings in our situation. I possess divinity," the Sinistari hissed. "Unlike you."

Sam shrugged, offering a dismissive splay of hands. "So my feet have touched mortal soil. So have yours."

"Not before I was created," the Sinistari corrected.

Cassandra knew the Sinistari had been forged from the Fallen. Twenty angels were caught as the original two hundred Fell and were made into something dark, dangerous and set only to the one task—slaying angels. While the Fallen had been imprisoned in the Ninth Void awaiting summons, the Sinistari lived Beneath. Cassandra had never imagined what the place was like, and now she didn't have to because a part of it stood before her.

"This won't even be a fight," Sam taunted. "You can't slay me unless I shift. And I don't intend to do that again for a while." He shrugged a bare shoulder, wincing. "Hurts like a bitch when I'm wearing mortal flesh."

"You will shift if challenged," the Sinistari answered confidently.

Cassandra had made it to the doorway, gripping the now-loose doorknob, when the Sinistari reached around and slapped her against the kitchen counter.

"Don't touch her!" Sam roared. He beat his fists against the invisible walls. "Let me out, Cassandra. I will kill him for touching you!"

"Sweet," she managed. "Commit murder for me?"

"Anything for you, cupcake. And I prefer the word *smite* over *murder*."

She quirked an eyebrow. Was he joking or actually being serious? It was impossible to determine with him.

The Sinistari growled at her, exposing sharp teeth. On second assessment she decided it was ugly and not at all beautiful. But if he had it in for the Fallen, then she may be able to escape while the two engaged in battle.

Never one to shun opportunity, Cassandra spoke the reversal spell, then dodged to avoid Sam as his release sent him plunging forward.

The Fallen charged the demon. Metal clashed with solid muscle and might. They soared backward into the door, which splintered and spit out the tangled opponents into the hallway.

They exchanged punches that sounded like heavy sacks of sand hitting metal. Neither appeared the least injured, nor reacted with pain. They faced off before the door, spoiling Cassandra's escape plans.

One of Sam's fists missed the Sinistari's face and knocked out a section of door frame.

Eyeing the Taser lying on the floor, Cassandra crawled out from behind the kitchen counter and grabbed it.

The demon kicked high, and his faltering equilibrium teetered him backward. Sam lunged and the twosome tumbled down the stairwell, damaging the plaster walls and bending the iron railing as they went at it, wrapped together in a death clutch.

But Sam had spoken correctly. The Sinistari,

who possessed a blade capable of entering the Fallen's glass heart, could only slay the angel if he was in winged, half form. She wasn't sure why, but that was how it worked. So he was safe—

"Or not."

Cassandra clasped the uppermost railing and watched as the angel shifted, releasing those deadly silver wings. The hallway was tight and his wings could not stretch out completely, but a full unfurl wasn't required. He swung them as weapons toward the Sinistari.

The demon's only purpose for walking this earth was to slay the Fallen. But from the looks of it, this angel slayer had met his match.

Thrusting high the hand that clutched the halo, Sam let out a deafening cry. Cassandra stumbled backward, slapping her palms to her ears and tucking her head against the wall. Sharp and piercing, the angelic cry heated her veins. She thought her blood would boil and bubble through her skin—

And then it stopped. And she heard nothing, only muffled thumping noises—her heart. The angel's cry had affected her hearing.

Gripping the railing and pulling herself to a wobbly stand, she gasped, which succeeded in popping her ears and restoring some sound. A swirl of dark glitter fluttered about the shirtless angel. Arms extended out, wings stretched high along the wall and ceiling, the angel was bathed in the demon's ashy remains. The halo dripped with black tar, the demon's blood.

The angel had defended her honor. Go, Fallen one!

Yet Sam's wings were out.

That shocking realization shifted her instincts to overdrive. She started for her loft then paused. That choice would trap her.

She raced down the hall to the door that led to the roof. Without stopping to see if Sam followed, she grabbed the stairwell door. With luck, he would be so enthralled by his kill she could slip away unnoticed.

Samandiriel shook off the demon ash from his arms and with a flick of the halo to shed the demon blood, he replaced it at his hip. He toed the pile of ash.

"I was quicker," he muttered. "But you gave good fight. Rest peacefully, brother."

Briefly, he wondered if the soul bringer would arrive for this one, but wasn't sure if the Sinistari possessed a soul. If he had indeed Fallen the same time as he had, that meant the Sinistari's halo had fallen away, too. He did not possess a soul. And Sam knew for certain the demon did not hold souls captive in his heart, as he did.

That was a hazard of teaching mortals the craft of silversmithing. An act he could hardly regret, even if those souls had been imprisoned inside him for countless millennia, never allowed to move on to either Above or Beneath.

Stretching back his shoulders, he worked his wings along the walls until he found a comfortable position for them. He'd not intended to bring them out, but seeing the Sinistari shove the muse had bruised his resolve. The wings felt heavier while here on earth. Or perhaps it was that weaker mortal flesh and bone could never serve him as well as he required.

The slayer was dead—just punishment, after his cruel treatment of the muse—but Sam bowed his head in reverence for his Fallen brother.

Footsteps scampered nearby, and Sam glanced up to see a pair of boots, attached to a very desirable female, swing around a corner and up a stairway.

"The muse."

He caught a whiff of her luscious perfume. Mint entwined with vanilla spice. The scent permeated his pores and swirled within his being, winding deep into his core. Want emerged as a powerful burst of desire.

He wanted to taste the muse. To wrap his hands about her soft skin and pull her close to his body. To experience the pleasures only she could give him. For the Fallen could experience pleasure only with his muse; no common, mortal female would serve.

Inhaling, he drowned his senses with her teasing scent, spritzed over skin the color of crushed cacao. He wavered, slapping a palm to the wall to steady his dizzied senses.

This is what you Fell for. Take her. Receive the mortal flesh.

"Must...have."

Darting up the stairs, his wings dragged along the ceiling, cutting a jagged line in the plaster. He rounded the corner and sighted the boots again. Jumping the steps, he pounced onto the square landing between the two levels of stairs and swept up a wing to block the muse from running higher.

She screamed and punched at his jaw and chest, delivering a random yet skilled defense that made him chuckle.

The sigil at her wrist glowed brightly, and he knew his own did as well for it flared hot at his hip. He moved in closely, trapping her against the rough cinder-block wall. The Taser dropped to the floor.

Her brown eyes grew wide and fearful. She tried an open-palmed punch with her free hand and landed it sharply on his chin. He smirked and slammed a wing tip aside her body, pinning her in on the left. And with his other wing, he coved her into a cozy trap.

"This is not you, Sam! It's the compulsion."

Silly chit. She thought to know his nature? He desired her, and he would have her.

Flicking a single silver feather under her chin, he savored the soft heat there. The muse's heady scent filled his pores. He read her nervous fear, and it heightened the desire with a dangerous twist. Truly, the Fall—and his resulting imprisonment—had been worth the sacrifice for this moment.

"Agothé!"

His shoulders jerked back, his spine following. Forced away from the muse's teasing flood of desire, he was slammed against the ceiling, wings bending painfully along the walls to fit into the small stairwell.

The muse took off up the stairs, while he struggled for release.

That damned spell! Why had he given it to her? In full human form his brain had apparently favored the muse's safety over his desires.

He flexed his feeble mortal muscles, but it was as if he were glued to the wall and could only wiggle the very ends of his wing tips. "Curse it all!"

Grunting and struggling, he decided if he shifted to human form completely perhaps he could loosen from the spell's hold faster. The shift liquefied his wings and shimmered them to particles that segued to nothing. His shoulders pulled away from the ceiling, tearing out the plaster in chunks—and he dropped to land on his knees and palms.

Blinking, Samandiriel gasped in breath. He needed to breathe like the mortals, and it startled him at how difficult it was at this moment.

Why had he chosen this punishment? Walking

earth? It could never match the paradise Above offered. Had his passion been so unrelenting? Or had he merely joined the pact with his brothers out of common need to belong?

We had only wanted what He gave man.

A bit out of sorts, Sam searched his recent memory to piece together why he knelt in the stairwell. A glint of black demon ash floating through the air reminded him he'd just slain a Sinistari. Over a woman.

"Cassandra." He'd held her against the wall. Had desired her so strongly. "No, I did not. I could not."

He scanned down the stairs. If his heart could beat, it would thunder right now because he feared what he may have done to her. He'd never wanted to scare her, to make her feel fear.

He raced up the stairs and kicked open the roof door.

Snowflakes bruised his cheeks and eyelids as they swirled and shifted in the conflicting winds. Across the roof, the muse stood at the edge, looking down, her arms stretched out for balance. Her boots stepped closer to the sky....

"Cassandra, no!"

At her side in an instant, he clasped her into his arms to keep her from jumping. The delicious warmth of her burnished his cold heart.

Saved her. Don't want to lose her.

She struggled and kicked. He didn't want to release her, but her scream registered the same scream he'd heard when he'd been in half form. She'd been utterly frightened then.

Humiliated by his own uncontrollable impulse, he released her and stepped away, slapping his arms across his chest. "I'm sorry, Cassandra. That wasn't me back there. Please, you must realize that."

She slunk down against the cinder-block border edging the roof, nodding profusely but not looking at him. She tucked her head into her palms. "I know. But you scared the crap out of me."

"Is that reason to jump? To end it all?"

"There's a huge snow pile from plowing out the parking lot below. I'd have landed safely."

"I see. It still saddens me that I frightened you. What can I do to earn your forgiveness? Tell me, please, and I'll do it."

Cassandra, gasping and hugging herself against the cold, bent forward, long strands of hair and ribbon spilling over her face. She put up a hand to keep him away, and he respected the silent yet shaming request.

She'd just witnessed a Fallen one slay a Sinistari. Quite a lot for a mortal to take in, even one trained to expect just that thing. *What, you think the vampire heart didn't scare her?*

"Oh, Sam." Her tiny voice filled his vision with soft violet waves the color of bright summer fields. "This is all a bit crazy. I'm sure I'm not thinking right, but…bloody hell."

She lunged forward, slipping her arms over

his shoulders and hugging him tightly. "You're the one person in this world I should stay away from, yet at the same time I want to remain next to you. It's like I feel a compulsion of my own. It scares me."

"Don't be frightened." She felt so good pressed against his bare chest. So real. "You're strong. Trust your instincts."

"But my screwed-up instincts tell me we need to stay together."

"To accomplish what I've set out to do."

She nodded against his neck and shivered. "Kill the Fallen."

"And vampires, too."

"The Sinistari were not part of your plan."

"They are expected. When a Fallen walks the earth a Sinistari is dispatched. I don't believe that's the last we'll encounter. Let's get you inside to warm up." He lifted her into his arms, and she allowed it.

"The way you looked at me," she said. "It was…"

"I know. Do you have a spell against horny angels?"

She smirked and shook her head. "Just the one that traps you between wards I've placed in my home. But, Sam…?"

He stepped inside the stairwell and brushed aside the hair from her eyes. It felt like fine silk, too valuable to set a price to. "What is it?"

"If you did have sex with me while you were

in that...form..." She winced and flashed a teary gaze at him. "Well, you know, would you try not to hurt me?"

"I will never hurt you. I vow it, because I will not again shift in your presence, demon or no demon."

And that was all he could give her, because he didn't know the truth himself.

Would spending more time with Cassandra build on the violent compulsion to attempt her? He must strive to remain true to his word. If he sensed the compulsion coming on, he would sooner take his own life than harm her. Yet who would save the world then?

And beyond the world, all he really wanted was to leave it and get back home.

Chapter 4

"We've made contact with a muse and a Fallen," Bruce said.

"Samandiriel?"

"My men did not get the Fallen's name, but I would assume so since that is who you recently summoned. They encountered them both on the way to set up the warehouse in Berlin."

"A Fallen together with a muse? Was he attempting her?"

Bruce winced. Such a heartless euphemism for the vicious act of rape. His man, who had witnessed it all as a lookout on a nearby rooftop, reported to him, but hadn't interfered because he hadn't wanted to become ash. Or to lose his heart, which, apparently, one of them had.

"The angel was defending her against my men."

"That's to be expected. She is the one woman on this earth who can give him pleasure. Where are they now? In custody?"

"My man is on it."

Which meant, they'd let them get away and now Bruce was scrambling to pick up their trail.

"The pregnant muse is Ophelia O'Malley," he said, deciding to change the subject. "She has only been pregnant three months, but my spies say she's waddling about like a full-term mother."

"The nephilim's gestation is rumored to be very short," Antonio clarified. "As is its growth period. It's likely the muse will give birth soon. Have you taken her into custody?"

"Working on it. Have my best team in London, where she was last seen. The muse's sister is escorting her. And that officious Zane. Traitor." Bruce intended to stake that bastard soon.

"He never did fit in," Antonio muttered. "You know this is my greatest and only desire, Bruce? To walk in the light."

"Yes, sir, I'm aware of that."

Antonio steepled his fingers thoughtfully before him. "I remember my mother used to tell me about the daylight. We lived below even before puberty gave me the blood hunger, so I have never, ever, known what it was like to feel sun on my skin."

That had to suck, big-time, Bruce thought.

Even bloodborn vampires, like Antonio, didn't come into their vampirism until puberty, which meant they were basically mortal, and could eat and walk in the sun, until the blood hunger changed them completely.

"So many vampires can walk in the sun," Antonio continued. "Why should I be denied light simply because my bloodline is ancient and revered? Am I damned? Are we not all damned?"

He held up a silver chain, from which dangled a silver coil. It caught the torchlight and flashed brightly. Antonio closed his eyes, as if soaking in sunbeams.

Bruce silently backed from his master's office. At times like this, when he went all introspective and waxed on about his damnation, it was better to leave him to sulk.

But his determination was renewed. No man should be denied the simple pleasures of life. Even if the sun would probably burn him after a few seconds, Antonio did deserve the pain of it, just once.

Cassandra stepped down the stairs outside her loft in the building stairwell. Metallic flake demon ash sifted over her hands and cheeks as she did. It tingled and felt hot, as if real ash from a flaming fire.

"It's too pretty for demon remains."

Sam swiped the back of his hand across his chin. A blue line dashed where a cut had opened his skin. "If you know things about us, then you know the Sinistari were forged from the Fallen."

"I do. So he was originally an angel who Fell with you?"

"Yes, but he was taken before his feet touched earth and was forged into Sinistari."

"That's so sad, that something divine was made—" She stopped before saying *evil*. Because the truly evil ones were the Fallen. The Sinistari were the good guys.

But how to label Sam? An evil angel bent on destroying his own? That sounded accurate, but when she caught more demon ash on her palm, she couldn't decide if evil had just vanquished the real good.

And only moments earlier she had stood in his arms because she'd wanted to. She had needed to feel safe. In the arms of her destroyer.

The night could not get any stranger.

It must be close to morning. She should be standing in the shower right now, washing away the day's simple trials, like stressing over which silver piece to next work on and about leaving her date at the bar. She should not be thinking about running from angels, demons *and* vampires.

Marcus would be pissed she'd left the Schwarz without him. Or maybe not. He had been talking up the redhead.

"I'm tired." She sat on the bottom step and toed the metallic demon ash. It glowed bright red and dispersed to talcum fineness, resembling a big pile of dust rather than ash. "Can we put off the vampire hunt until I've gotten some sleep?"

"We'll have to. The Anakim tribe doesn't walk in sunlight."

"Just let me stay here and sleep a few hours. You return after you've killed all the vampires, Fallen and Sinistari." She yawned. "Promise I won't ditch you."

"I will give you energy."

"I don't know how you can do—"

Sam pulled her to stand and clutched her against his chest. He was so solid and *there,* and yet, not warm. Not cold, either. Almost as if he were a sculpture crafted from silver. Weird but strangely appropriate.

Strong arms slid up her back and firmly caressed her against him. For the muscles strapping his body, she had expected any hug from him to hurt, but he held her as if she were fragile, delicate.

He was doing something to her. She felt him radiate through her body. Not exactly heat or a tingle, but a feeling of satisfaction. No, not exactly that, either. She felt positive, and suddenly perceived an outcome that would see her the victor. Was it hope? If the halo was supposed to give a mortal hope, as her sister believed, then perhaps an entire angel could do the same.

For the first time since this night had gone crazy, Cassandra thought about the sigil and real-

ized it didn't itch. Why was that? Did their closeness negate the irritant power of the sigil?

Sam had come after her with mad lust in
his eyes after he'd killed the demon. His silver
wings...they had been gorgeous. Something she
could never duplicate though she had tried. The
sculpture in her bedroom was a pitiful replica of
the real deal.

Gorgeous, and yet a sign of very real danger
she couldn't defend herself against no matter what
tricks she pulled out of her pocket.

"How's that?" he said against her ear.

"Huh? Oh, great." She pulled from him, following the skim of her fingers as they marked his
smooth, tanned chest. "Ready for action, I guess.
But do you intend to stalk about the city without
any clothes? I mean, the no-shirt look works on
you, but it's snowing out, buddy. We don't want to
attract any more attention than you already do."

"I will need a shirt, yes. But you are not so
tired now?"

Cassandra assessed her muscles and bruised
body, and realized she did feel kinda peppy. A
flex of her shoulder didn't sense the heavy exhaustion she'd just experienced. "What did you
do to me?"

"We have a connection, Cassandra, like it or
not."

"Raising my hand for *not*. It's a connection I
don't wish to complete, if you get my meaning."

"I understand there are reasons you cannot trust me."

"You got that right. You said you wouldn't come after me, but then your wings popped out and—wham! I've never seen such malevolent lust in a man's eyes before. You really scared me, Sam."

She tried not to meet his eyes, because she knew she'd find a pleading puppy-dog pout there. But it was impossible, and the moment she connected with his gaze, she fell into wonder. The true magic lived there, in his eyes. She felt powerless against it.

"I understand I must earn your trust. I cannot simply demand it. And I will, I swear to you. But that does not discount me from the desire to mate with you. You are a beautiful woman, Cassandra. I would not be a man did I not recognize that."

"Good thing you gave me the repulsion word."

"The more often you use it, the weaker it becomes, so use it sparingly."

"If you keep your eyes on the vampires, and not me, maybe I won't have to use the word ever again."

"It won't be that simple. But I thank you for your trust, cupcake."

"You haven't earned my trust yet, buddy. And what's with the cupcake? Name's Cassandra."

"I like the endearment. It is a common practice between mortals to name each other with sweet nicknames."

She rolled her eyes, realizing it was fruitless to get him to stop with the silly names.

"Mr. Nelson on the first floor is about your size. Not quite so firm. He has a tendency to leave his clothes in the laundry room dryer for days. I'll slip in and borrow a shirt."

Cassandra grabbed two button-up shirts and a pair of jeans, but felt squicky about taking a pair of Mr. Nelson's boxers. She guessed Sam probably didn't do underwear anyway. Or was that a secret hope?

While the angel changed in the bathroom, she dialed up her sister.

With vampires and Sinistari roaming the city, she did not want to endanger Ophelia, the pregnant muse her sister planned to escort to Berlin.

It always lightened her heart to hear her sister's voice. Cassandra had moved from London two years ago, and though they talked all the time, they only saw each other half a dozen times a year. It was never enough.

"Coco, when does your flight leave?"

"Ohmygosh, I tried to call you yesterday afternoon, Caz. We're here!"

"What? I thought it didn't leave until tomorrow?"

"Nope, last night. We landed at Hamburg four hours ago. The flight was redirected due to bad weather. We went straight to the hotel for breakfast—"

"You and the muse?"

"Me, Ophelia and Zane."

"Right, the sexy new man who helped you slay the angel." Her sister had been oddly tight-lipped about Zane, other than to wax over his gorgeous muscles and how she loved to kiss him for hours. Ah, love. "You bring the angel ash?"

"Yes, it's in my suitcase, safe and sound."

After they'd slain a Fallen, Coco had been smart enough to gather the crystallike ash left behind. It was a necessary weapon should the worst occur.

"But, Cassandra, I've lost something else. Oh… you're going to freak."

"What?"

The pause over the phone line felt like forever creeping over Cassandra's skin. She bit her lip and met Sam's eyes as he strode into the living room to display his new attire. The jeans fit snugly and low at his square hips. The shirt, unbuttoned at the chest and sleeves, would probably be too tight, but really, she didn't mind the casual look at all. And look at those cut abs. Yikes, they were hard and firm.

She gave him a thumbs-up. The angel beamed, turning to display the clothes as if a child with new things.

She gestured to the phone and then winced, because the silence was still there between her and her sister. She and Coco never lied to one another, and Cassandra sensed this one was going to be tough.

Coco finally said, "We lost the muse."

"What? How?" Cassandra sank to sit on the sofa. "Where is she?"

"I don't know. I left her for five minutes to go with Zane to get a skinny vanilla latte in the shopping gallery. Ophelia was complaining about back pain and said the latte would relax her. I think she's close to giving birth, Caz. We've searched the hotel. No sign of her. It's as if she's disappeared from the earth."

"She couldn't have gone far. You said she was huge."

"Like she's ready to give birth to quadruplets."

"You have to find her. She can't be alone. The poor woman." And what if she went into labor and couldn't get to a hospital? Or worse... "Coco, there are vampires in Berlin."

"Oh, my God."

"You must be careful. You don't have protection against vamps—"

"I do. I mean, I know how to kill them, Caz. Stakes and beheading."

Cassandra stared at the phone. Really? When had her sister done all the research on vampires? *She* was barely getting her feet about the creatures.

"Zane thinks he can track her heartbeats," Coco continued, "so we should be okay."

"Wait. Her heartbeats? What does that mean?"

"Oh, uh…oh, here's Zane. I need to go, Caz. We can't lose the muse's trail. It's only been twenty minutes since we lost her. I'll stay in touch."

The phone clicked off, and Cassandra stared at it. That the muse was missing was cataclysmic. But something else bothered her more. "She said Zane could track the muse's heartbeats?"

Sam, who fumbled with the tiny shirt buttons, cast her a lifted brow.

"How is that possible? I don't understand that."

"Is he vampire?"

"What? No! My sister would never…"

It occurred to her Coco had been pretty tight-lipped about her new lover of late. But a vampire? No. *Nein*. Impossible.

Hell, lately Cassandra had been insane with learning all she could to protect herself and save the world, if it ever came to that. Okay, she'd always been like that. All focus went toward learning everything she could about angels and how to keep them away from her (like that was working). Coco had always stood in the background, going to martial arts classes with her yet sitting on the sidelines doing school homework for the two of them.

When they were teenagers Coco had originally been the adventurous one, wanting to travel the world and climb every mountain. Cassandra had always wanted to be an artist, living the celebrity lifestyle like the rich and famous.

Until Granny Stevens had sat them both down and forever altered their destinies by detailing impending doom.

Now Coco worked at a travel agency, because she never had time for adventure and, truthfully, Granny had put the fear of danger into Coco's heart.

And Cassandra now sought danger as if some kind of drug. And damn, didn't the man who'd just sat on her sofa exude danger. He held out his wrist, and she buttoned the sleeve cuff then gestured for the other wrist.

Of course she hadn't found time to chat with her sister about her new man. But could he be…a vampire? He had slain an angel. Normal mortal men weren't capable of that feat. Not without the proper weapon. Coco had said Zane owned a Sinistari blade. That may allow a mortal such strength and skill. *Hmm…*

"I can't think about this." She finished with his button, then stuffed the phone in a pocket and stood to pace. "The pregnant muse is missing. Her name is Ophelia. We've lost her, and she's to give birth any day now."

Sam caught her in his embrace and, in lieu of a much-needed sisterly hug, she allowed the unwarranted touch. He was much taller and more solid than Coco. Standing in his arms made her feel a little less small, supported, and not so close to the edge.

It is what you want. Safety. Take it.

"We'll find Ophelia. We'll find the vampires. We'll stop it all," he said reassuringly.

"You have grand plans, angel. Don't you know it takes more than two of us to stop an army?"

"How do you know it's an army?"

"Tribe Anakim must be many. They have to be if they expect to capture a nephilim. And just because you took out the Sinistari doesn't mean another won't be summoned. Isn't that their job? The demons will pursue you relentlessly. Too bad we can't get them on our side."

"Their alliance would help. Yet, the Sinistari are too lustful. One minute they're focused on the Fallen, the next they're following the shifting hips of a sexy looker. They are easy enough to distract."

"You were easily distracted by my shifting hips at club Schwarz."

"I, er, hmm…" No way to deny that one.

"How did you find me, by the way? Were you looking for me?"

"I was not. I do have a mission. But when passing the club, I felt the heat of the sigil on my hip and sensed you were inside. You know how it goes from there."

The angel bowed over her and pressed the crown of her head with his lips.

"I can't fathom this," she said.

"But you can accept it. You believe in everything you were taught does not exist. That goes miles toward your strength, Cassandra."

"Not like I have much choice. I would love it if vampires had remained fictional characters."

"Angels have never been fiction."

"True."

And had she imagined she'd one day be standing in an angel's arms? Taking comfort from a supernatural being? And not at all frightened of their preordained connection?

Yes, she had. It had been a blissful, sensual dream of a warrior.

Sam stroked her arms and bent before her, which brought them eye level. As if to kiss. But he only lingered there, their mouths inches apart, breath dallying, eyes searching each other's.

She wanted the kiss. It was wrong on so many levels, but she needed it. Yet she sensed he would not give it. Could not. Because they were both fearful of the Pandora's box their desires could open.

Kiss him. It will be dangerous. How can you resist?

Cassandra tilted onto her tiptoes and pressed her mouth to his. He pulled away, his eyes flashing at her as if to ask whether this was okay.

"Yes," she murmured, and touched her mouth to his again.

He was cool, but he did not stay so for long. Heat blossomed at the point of their connection. His firm mouth remained unmoving against hers. He allowed her to explore with a soft brush of her mouth over his, to direct the kiss in the manner she desired.

Then she realized he might have never before kissed a woman. Sam had only been on earth two days. And she had no idea what he'd done after his original Fall, but surely after millennia of imprisonment in the Ninth Void, whatever sensual technique he may have possessed had gotten a little rusty.

The idea excited her, and also gave her concern. She might be his first experience.

Sensing his tension, she smoothed a hand over his jaw, measuring the pulse of his muscles once, twice, beneath her spread fingers. "Relax," she said, "I'm not going to hurt you."

He smirked, both of them aware that he'd said the same earlier, but in not quite the same context.

"This is new," he started, then looked aside and chuckled. "I've not done this before. With any woman."

"I guessed that."

"Because I botched the kiss terribly?"

"Not at all. You kiss well. Your mouth is, um, it's soft but firm. I like it. You willing to follow my lead?"

"I would follow you to world's end, Cassandra."

"All right, but I'd rather not stand at the end, if you know what I mean. Especially with all that's going on right now. Let's just keep it right here and now."

His mouth softened to hers when she kissed him again, and he pressed gently, opening slightly. She caught his breath on her tongue, sweet, ethereal, unnamable. Yes, really something like that, perhaps even angelic.

Clasping his hand, which was planted at her hip in deference to politeness, she glided it around her back and higher. Taking direction, he pulled her closer without breaking the kiss. He assumed the mien of a seducer with ease. Perhaps he assimilated this experience as easily as he'd assimilated the world. It made sense to her.

If falling felt like this—a soft flutter of wings in her heart—Cassandra was all for it. Kissing Sam made her feel light, weightless. Unencumbered. It was a kiss like no other, because while it was new and experimental, it fed her danger addiction. She kissed the enemy. It didn't get more dangerous than that.

Yet the longer the kiss lasted, the quicker she forgot the bad stuff threatening to bring down the world around her. And danger segued into passion.

Opening her mouth, she traced his lower lip with her tongue and slashed a quick flick over his white teeth. He moaned an agreeing tone and caressed her petite curves against his lean, hard body. Her feet left the ground, and he held her easily, his tongue matching hers.

Cassandra raked her fingers through his soft,

dark hair and broke the kiss to stare into his eyes. "How are you able to do this?"

"I think it comes naturally. And you have a great method of teaching."

"No, I mean, kiss me and not want to, you know…"

"Oh, right. I don't think I'm capable of feeling the relentless compulsion to mate unless I'm in half form."

"So we can do this, over and over, with no repercussions? No wings, no worry?"

"Over and over sounds spectacular."

"It does but—" It sounded *too* good. Nothing ever came so easily. Not without a devastating price. "Set me down."

He did, shoving a hand over his hair and wincing with concern.

Cassandra exhaled deeply and offered the nervous angel in the tight shirt a weak smile. It was disconcerting being in the room with a man who sucked in all the air merely with his overwhelming presence. By simply *being*. He was a warrior from another realm. A mythological creature. A divine creation!

And yet he looked perfectly mortal waiting for her to make the next move.

"I just kissed an angel," she offered with a nervous chuckle. "How weird is that?"

"I just kissed a mortal. I think I've matched you on the weirdness scale."

She laughed and twirled a long strand of hair

and ribbon about her forefinger. Dipping her head, she looked up at him. "Truce?"

"Most definitely. Though I never had reason to name you my enemy in the first place."

"Still, I'm going to keep one eye over my shoulder. I don't believe you're completely trustworthy."

"I'm probably not, since I'm focused on a specific goal. I will do what must be done to ensure it is achieved. You're a smart woman, cupcake." He teased his tongue over his lip. "And your mouth makes me want to fall to my knees and worship a new god. Make that a goddess."

"That sounds blasphemous."

"Don't tell the big guy." He averted his eyes heavenward, and Cassandra realized he'd just made a joke.

But laughter eluded her. "Speaking of gods and goddesses, what is your relationship to Him now that you've Fallen?"

"He is my Father. I love Him. But as children are sometimes wont, we wish for things denied us and rebel. Forbidden fruits, and all. I pray He can still love me after my rebellion. I could not go on should The Most High abandon me."

"So you plan to go back someday? To Heaven?"

"Above."

"Right, you call it Above and Beneath." A detail Granny hadn't cared for. As a good Catholic, she had preferred the traditional Heaven and Hell.

"If it is possible, I want to return Above, with all my soul."

"They why Fall in the first place? It couldn't have just happened like that. You want to Fall, and you do it. You had to have considered it, planned it, thought about it."

"Exactly."

"And yet, you've changed your mind about that decision?"

He nodded. "I serve no purpose here on earth. I wish to get back to my real work Above."

"Which was?"

"I led the ranks of the Seventh Kingdom. We, well…we did a lot of smiting."

"Is that so?" It sounded like a band of warrior angels, slashing at things with swords. A guy thing. No wonder he wanted to return. "You do serve a purpose here."

"Which is?"

She wasn't exactly sure, but he'd not yet harmed her, so that made his presence seem… right. But what a pitiful explanation.

She glanced to the halo hooked at his hip. Granny Stevens had explained how it worked, what it meant and what it contained. "What about that soul?" The halo held the Fallen's earthbound soul.

"It will remain unclaimed. Earth is no place for one such as me."

She shrugged. "I don't know. You seem to fit in well. You look like the average guy, er, well, maybe not. You look like some kind of fitness model with perfectly tousled hair. But you look human, is what I'm trying to say."

"Good thing, too. It would be difficult to walk the land with thirty-foot wings sweeping behind me all day."

"Remarkably, no one would take notice."

"I understand that. Your world is filled with dreamers, actors, thespians and what are those others…? Ah! Role players. They dress like orcs and Klingons—"

"And angels. That's why the wings wouldn't shock anyone. Only a few would know your truth."

"Children. They are pure of heart and can see more truths than adults could ever fathom."

"Truths we adults grow out of, like faeries and vampires."

"Exactly." Granting her a delicious smile, Sam asked, "Can we kiss some more?"

Not a bad suggestion. And yet… "I thought we were to hunt vampires?"

"The sun is high in the sky. We won't find them now."

Cassandra yawned.

"You should get some sleep. I forget mortals require rest."

"I should if I'm going to stake vampires later." She sat on the sofa and patted it for him to join her. "Do you need to sleep?"

"Nope." He sat beside her and took her hand

and kissed it. "But I'd like to lay beside you while you doze off, if you are okay with that."

To lie in the arms of a protective angel? Who could ask for their guardian angel dreams to get any better?

She tilted a kiss against his mouth, and pulled him to lie beside her.

"Tell me the truths you've forgotten, Cassandra."

Cassandra sighed and closed her eyes. "I wasn't allowed to forget for very long. Granny told me and my sister about the Fallen and muses when I was twelve and Coco was ten. I think I had stopped believing in Santa Claus right around then."

"You mean the man in the red fur suit? You know he's not the meaning of Christmas. At least not for a good Catholic girl like you."

"How do you know—you know everything about me?"

"Not at all. But I saw the statue of the Virgin Mary on your bathroom sink when I was looking for weapons."

"That belonged to my mother. There are days I'd like to stop believing in it all. But I don't. How can I? You're right here in front of me. Looking so—" *sexy* "—angelic."

"That's called faith."

"Call it what you will, but it's not faith to me. Just…belief." She yawned and closed her eyes.

* * *

It didn't take long for the muse to fall asleep beside him. Sam looked over her as she breathed softly, captive to sleep's unavoidable grasp. Of all His creations, mortals were the most exquisite. Each one different from the next and endlessly compelling in design.

Cassandra's red lips were like soft petals. They'd felt like fire against his mouth. A sweet fire he wanted to consume. Her skin was light brown, not tan, but of a mixed heritage that fascinated him. The soft sweater rose and fell with her breath, and he couldn't stop watching her breasts rise and fall with it.

"My muse," he muttered. "Until I leave."

He must return Above. It was where he belonged. He'd made a mistake Falling, and he'd meant it when he said he had no purpose here. He would correct that mistake.

Chapter 5

After supper at a nearby McDonald's, and Sam's declaration that fast food was very odd—one presses meat and bread together and eats with their fingers?—they decided to case the park across the river Spree from the Schwarz, since they'd been in the vicinity when Cassandra had been attacked by vampires. Where there had been two bloodsuckers, there could be others.

The sky was overcast, as usual in the wintertime, and the park lights had already flickered on and cast a circle about their steel bases that glittered on the bright snow. Sam had insisted they set onto the hunt early, while the vampires may not yet have emerged from hiding.

Casting a glance across the river, Cassandra sighted the patina domes of the Berlin Cathedral.

The area was a tourist hot spot, but the park was empty. It was winter, and tourists usually preferred shopping to playing in the cold.

She tromped across the park grounds, which were laden with six inches of fluffy snow. Fur-rimmed winter boots hugged below her knees. Black wool leggings and a long, chenille sweater kept her warm beneath the stylish Gore-Tex parka that was thin but made of material that repelled the cold like a dream. Leather gloves and a rabbit-fur hat with flaps over the ears topped off the unsexy look.

Sam followed close on her heels, quiet, but she thought she felt his breath at the back of her neck. Impossible, because her hair spilled from under her cap over her coat and down her back. And he wasn't that close.

She'd be okay with him walking beside her companionably, but she suspected she would have to teach him that bit of relationship etiquette. Interesting. A man with no sexual history whatsoever, and yet, he could wield sex against her as a weapon.

It made her feel powerful and, at the same time, weak. She didn't like the contradiction. She shouldn't want what she'd been thinking, a connection between the two of them. She was a big girl and could take care of herself.

Yet a little protection from a warrior angel would feel great. A relief, after years of always being alert and ready.

Not that they were in a relationship, by any means. But she did partially trust him, which made him more than a stranger and a little less the enemy.

A *thwump* startled her. Cassandra spun to spy another Fallen across the park. It strode purposefully toward them. She knew it was an angel because black wings spread out behind his shoulders and he wore only jeans and biker boots.

These angels and their lack of winter clothing. Shouldn't they want to blend in?

But seriously? Another Fallen was not a good thing. And those wings were not black feathers, they were—she couldn't tell what they were fashioned from, but they looked like shards of coal.

"Stay back," Sam directed curtly. "Behind those trees."

Taking orders, Cassandra tromped to the blue spruce trees lining the edge of the city park. By the time she slapped a glove on the cold bark trunk, the angels were circling each other in the fresh-fallen snow. Sam did not bring out his wings, but his height and build matched the other in power and strength.

He'd made a promise to her. Would he be able to stand against one of his own without wings?

"Nazariah," Sam said. "What brings you to this neck of the mortal realm?"

The burly Fallen rolled his shoulders forward in a classic wrestling intimidation move. "Same thing that brings you here, Samandiriel. I've been summoned."

"Tribe Anakim. Vampires," Sam confirmed. "They're up to foul deeds."

"Vampires are easy enough to crush. But I do appreciate the release from the Ninth Void." The new angel nodded toward the trees where Cassandra stood. "She yours?"

"She is," Sam answered confidently. His fingers moved over the halo at his hip as if he was a gunslinger anticipating his opponent's flinch.

Nazariah chuckled. "Haven't gotten down to business with her yet, I'll wager."

"I'm not going to—"

"That's right. Samandiriel is all about *admiring* the muses. 'We should respect the mortal muses,'" he said mockingly, "'not use them as we please.' Idiot outlaw angel."

Nazariah charged Sam, catching him about the shoulders. The two soared through the air much farther than normal men engaged in fight were capable. The Fallen's wings flapped, and when Sam landed in the snow on his back, Nazariah's wings caged him in with feathers of stratified anthracite.

A *shing* of metal hummed the air. Blue blood spattered in a line across the snow. Halo in hand, Sam had cut a line across the Fallen's forehead.

Snow flew and their tussle blurred into a blizzard. Cassandra stood at the tree line, silently urging Sam on and wanting to help him, to jump into the fray, but knowing he didn't need her intrusion. He may be in a form less strong than the half-shifted Fallen, but he held his own.

Still, she slashed a hand through the air, delivering a smart chop and an angled kick. Smacking a fist into her palm sounded in the still air. Cassandra winced as Sam took a wing tip to his solar plexus. Ooh, that one had to hurt. Would have knocked the wind out of a mortal man.

Nazariah had the advantage of wings, which, with a flap, swept him away from the physical clutch and briefly suspended him in the air. The Fallen could not fly, though they could apparently use wind currents to move about. He dive-bombed toward Sam.

With a shift of his hips, Sam stepped aside. The Fallen's landing, heels skidding over the icy ground, pushed the snow into a half crater before him.

Go, whispered a voice in Cassandra's head. *Now is your chance. Get away from them both!*

Abruptly ending a punch in the fight she wasn't a part of, she looked over her shoulder. Car headlights rolled by not two blocks south of the quiet city park. She could insinuate herself into the busy metropolis nightlife and return—no, she couldn't go home. It would be the first place Sam, and other deadly creatures, would look for her.

And did she want to leave him? The man was an innocent concealed behind the mask of the enemy. But he didn't feel like the enemy now. The enemy never kissed so sweetly, did he?

"You are not like us!" Nazariah yelled.

Cassandra's attention returned to the battling angels.

"For that I am glad," Sam answered. He wavered, his stance wobbling. Blood dripped from a cut on his cheek and blue streaked his white shirt.

"Do you think to win your return Above with such selfless admonitions?" Nazariah swung a wing around and cut Sam through the chest. Again Sam landed on his back across the mounded snow. The Fallen bent over him. "You make me feel pity, brother."

Sam chuckled and spit aside blood. "It is good you can feel such a selfless emotion before dying, brother."

Sam swung the halo and jammed it into Nazariah's chest. It cut deep through muscle and bone and he pushed it all the way in. The angel shrieked in the unnatural myriad of tongues that sliced like knives in Cassandra's brain. It vibrated in her ears, threatening to crush the fragile bones. Her mouth went dry, and she tried to scream, but the noise in her skull took away the ability to vocalize. Falling to her hands and knees, she gritted her teeth.

Silence swept over the park as if the angel's cry had been sucked into a vortex. The Fallen one's entire human form shattered, dispersing into a hail of glittering crystals. Dark wings dropped in a pile of anthracite ash.

Sound rushed back to Cassandra with a buzz in her veins and eardrums. The cold brushed her face as she pushed up from the snow.

Sam had slain one of his own. He stood over the carnage, head bowed and muscles flexing across his back, then dropped to his knees and fell to the side.

Cassandra ran toward Sam and plunged to her knees beside his body. Blue blood stained the snow. He still gripped the halo in a hand coated with more unnaturally colored blood.

"Sam?" The angel didn't move. His chest did not rise and fall, but she suspected it never had. Angel hearts did not beat. "Sam! Oh, you can't be dead. You'd be ash if you were—"

What could she do? Wasn't like she could call for an ambulance and have a team of doctors inspect him for life.

Her breath clouded before her face. Cassandra's lower lip wobbled. "Sam?"

He cracked open an eyelid and smiled at her. "Were you worried about me, bunny?"

"Yes. No." Bunny? He was joking when she'd thought him dead. But at times like this, humor felt necessary. "What happened to cupcake?"

"You look like a bunny wearing that fur hat."

A relieved smile swept over her entire body, relaxing her tense muscles. Surprised at her reaction to nearly losing him, instead of crying, she chuckled.

The moment had taken away her breath. Made her feel as though she'd lost something important to her. Coco was the only family she had. She'd let her down. She didn't want to lose this connection before it had even grown solid.

They looked over the pile of glittering angel ash.

"You killed him. Nazariah," Cassandra whispered, feeling strange awe. A divine being had been slain while she had watched. It hadn't felt right, blasphemous almost. Yet why such terrific dread befell her now, and not earlier for the Sinistari, made little sense to her.

"Had to be done. He was my brother, as are all the Fallen. His intentions were not so pure as mine toward the muses."

"He would have sought his muse, and—" Attempted to have sex with her, with or without her permission. Or he may have even come after her. "He called you outlaw?"

Sam stood and helped her up by the elbow. He shuffled off blue snow from his legs and replaced the halo at his hip. A slap to his pecs, revealed by the slashed shirt, dusted off more snow and alerted Cassandra just how sexy a half-naked man standing in a blue snow pile could be.

"Yes, I am the outlaw Fallen that all the others despise."

"I don't understand."

He dusted off his shoulders, then studied the angel ash. When he drew up and looked at Cassandra, she wanted to wipe the trickle of blue from his lip. But something about him felt rigid and closed. He'd killed one he called brother. That couldn't have been easy.

"I Fell with my brethren," he said, "because we were under the seductive spell of mortal women. We wanted to make love with them and have sex with them, and indulge in all the pleasures their bodies could give us. And we knew only the muses could give us the pleasure we craved. It was a selfish means for Falling, but we did it because that's what children do, they rebel."

Most, anyway. Cassandra thought of all the times she'd wanted to walk away from the cause, to stop studying angels and how to kill them or get away from them, and just be…normal. But normal always led to death. She hadn't been prepared to give up so easily.

Rebellion would have to wait.

"After I Fell, my mind did a one-eighty," he continued. "I looked upon the mortal women, so gorgeous and seductive. They were real, living, thinking beings who had not asked to be hunted by the Fallen. I wanted them. I wanted to feel them, to taste them, to become a part of their softness. But to really look at a woman, to peer into her eyes and feel her heart beat and soul pulse? I saw that they were real human beings. Not mere objects to be used for selfish pleasure. I admired them for their beauty, but wanted to know them for their thoughts, their dreams, their desires and aspirations."

Cassandra knew she gaped at him, but couldn't stir herself to speak. He talked a good game, but his actions would show his real truths.

He smirked, and those sexy lips teased dangerously. "My brethren did not care to have me preach the mortal woman's beauty. They wanted to have sex with them, not admire them. So I became the outlaw. The Fallen who would not band with his brothers, and in fact, the one who would slay any Fallen who thought to harm or physically attempt a mortal woman. Then the flood came and swept us all away."

The outlaw angel. Sounded sexy.

"And now I've been summoned to earth again, I have little desire to harm you, or any female."

"You just want to go home," she confirmed.

"When the time is right. I want to help the muses, Cassandra, to keep them from the Fallen ones' hands."

"You—" Cassandra could wrap her mind around what he'd just said, but it was astonishing all the same "—*don't* want to have sex with me?"

"Oh, I do. I am a man on this earth, and like all others. And your kisses…" He whistled appreciatively. "Don't get me wrong, Cassandra, you are all things to me. Desire, beauty, humility, peace, life and sensuality. But I won't take from you what I want. You deserve better than that.

Besides, I can recognize a want and know it's not a need or compulsion."

"There's nothing wrong with wanting."

"Is that so?" He tilted a playful smile on her.

If she'd had this conversation with a man in a nightclub they'd both understand that she had just given him permission to indulge his wants. And the angel did get it. That twinkle in his eyes was classic.

"I will slay any Fallen who thinks he can take a muse for his wicked pleasure," Sam added.

Wicked pleasure sounded appealing.

Cassandra lifted her chin and chased away that thought. *Bad, Caz. Don't start wanting him.*

"You're in control," he offered shyly. "I will follow your lead. Should you kiss me, I will kiss you back. Should you touch me, I will linger on the softness of your skin. Should you—"

She pressed her fingers to his mouth. "So you're saying I can trust you?"

"What I'm saying is, we are meant for one another through some greater means." He lifted his sodden shirt to reveal the sigil on the back of his hip.

Cassandra stroked her wrist through the jacket. Though she couldn't see it, her sigil glowed warmly.

"Just because our sigils match doesn't give me a license to attempt you without first getting to know you. I want to know you, Cassandra."

"And then you'll have your way with me."

"And then *you* will have your way with me. Or so I can hope."

She got caught in his sexy smile and managed one herself. If he was speaking the truth, then she could get behind his crusade against the other Fallen. But trust him? That was still up for debate.

"Your hope will win you a kiss." She stood on tiptoe to kiss him. "For my champion. Selfless in the face of danger."

"Ahem. Don't mind me."

Startled, Cassandra, wobbling against Sam's chest for support, turned to the man who stood over the angel ash. Dark, and dressed all in black, he held a palm high over the ash—and something amazing happened. A swirl of twinkling lights rose from the ash pile, twirling, floating as if by magic, and affixed to the stranger's hand.

"The soul bringer," Sam whispered reverently. "Just doing his job. The Fallen keep the souls of mortals in their hearts."

"I know."

The Fallen had taught mortals all crafts. Samandiriel had taught mortals silversmithing. Yet in Biblical times, those crafts had been deemed immoral and sinful, so when those craftsmen died, their souls did not go Above or Beneath, but instead were trapped within the Fallen's glass heart.

It sounded romantic, but when she thought about it, Cassandra was saddened the mortal souls had been kept in stasis for centuries. "Do you have souls in your heart?"

"Some. I can feel them flutter on occasion, as when I look over your silver work. I am not proud of keeping innocent souls imprisoned, and will gladly relinquish them upon my death."

And just like that, the soul bringer shifted into a dark blur and disappeared. In his wake, a wind stirred the snow into a blizzard and gushed the Fallen angel ash into the air toward the heavens.

"No, we can use that!" she shouted. "That stuff is not mortal souls, but angel…ash."

The ash was carried away. Gone.

Slapping a hand over her heart, Cassandra whispered a prayer for her sister and that she and her boyfriend could locate Ophelia before it was too late.

"There will be more." Sam nodded at the imprint the ash had left on the snow. "The Fallen are apparently being summoned to Berlin."

"Do you think the vampires know I've had the muse brought here? That I planned to bring others here?"

"I feel sure they do. You've brought other muses here?"

"It was supposed to be a means to organize and teach one another. I hadn't expected all this to happen now. They're on their way here as we speak. I've got to send them away. Berlin is too dangerous."

"Indeed. Nazariah will not be the last. The

vampires will summon as many Fallen as they've names and sigils for. The Fallen will come and they will not relent."

Cassandra gasped. What had she done? Lured all the muses into a trap? She glanced to the ground where not a trace of angel ash remained. "I've no weapon against the Fallen."

"What am I?" He patted his hip and the halo glowed briefly. "You've already named me your champion, Cassandra. Come, all ye Fallen! Bring your mightiest, your fiercest. As long as I am capable, I will let no Fallen bring harm to a muse."

His declaration brought a tear to her eye and Cassandra plunged forward to hug him. That startled him, and he didn't immediately embrace her in return. But when he did, she thought she felt his warmth, the flow of his blood and the beat of his heart segue with hers.

It wasn't possible. Not without his earthbound soul. Something he didn't want to claim, yet wore at his hip as a weapon.

She could trust he would stand alongside her in this battle, even stake out the vanguard to protect her. That gave her confidence. "You say you have no purpose here on earth? What about rescuing all the muses from their destined fate?"

"I will do what I can. But you imply our destiny is not favorable."

"No, I—" Yes, their destiny did seem that way. If one believed in destiny. "I will accept your offer to champion me."

"And what will you grant me in reward?"

"Uh, what do you want?"

He nuzzled his nose beside her ear and whispered, "Only that you will hold my hand when I ask."

Hold the guy's hand? That sounded simple enough. She could do him one better. "I think I owe you a kiss."

"You had mentioned something of the sort earlier."

"If you want it," she said, allowing her inner tease careful reign, "take one from me."

"Ah?"

Sam bent to meet her mouth with his. And Cassandra melted against his body, wanting and willing to surrender to his protective embrace, and knowing it was not so wrong as she'd once believed.

Her angel had finally come for her.

Chapter 6

"Are you hungry?" Sam asked Cassandra. "Want me to run down the street and pick us up some schnitzel? I haven't tried it, but it sounds like an interesting meal."

"I am hungry." They had rented a room at the Radisson Blu across the river Spree and close to the bustle of the city. Cassandra could eat an entire produce department, but she wasn't keen on meat. "We could order room service."

"If you want." He opened the door. "I'm still going out, bunny."

She tugged off her fur hat and tossed it onto the bed. "What for?"

Sam shrugged. "Angel stuff."

Narrowing her gaze at him, Cassandra said, "I think you just lied to me."

His smile wasn't practiced enough to hide the truth. He closed the door behind him, leaving her clinging to wonder. She hadn't thought angels could lie.

What was he up to? She should follow him but she was tired, and right now the easy chair felt like a big ol' hug.

She tugged out her cell phone from the backpack near her feet. Time to check in with Coco. The phone rang and rang, and when Cassandra expected it to switch over to message, a male voice answered.

"Cassandra?"

"Uh, Zane?" She'd never spoken to the boyfriend. He had a nice, deep tone. British, too, but with a Welsh brogue. "Where's Coco?"

"She's…occupied at the moment. How are you, love? You see the snow swirling out your window? It's storming something fierce here in Hamburg."

"Zane, where's Coco? Is something wrong? Did you guys find the muse?"

"What's that? Oh, the muse. Right."

Cassandra did not like that Coco hadn't answered the phone. She always carried her cell phone in a pocket or a hip holster, so she must be in the vicinity. Zane was not telling her something.

What was with the evasive men in her life lately?

"Zane, tell me exactly what is happening right

now. And do not lie to me. I will find you and kick the shit out of you if I sense you are lying."

"Don't get your britches in a bundle, love. Coco said you were a tough one."

"You're stalling, Zane."

"Right then. Uh, Coco is…how shall I put this?"

"Put it exactly as it is. What is going on?"

A heavy sigh preceded a rapid flow of words. "Your sister is cleaning evidence from the room."

Shooting upright from the chair, Cassandra paced before the bed, phone clutched fiercely. "What sort of evidence? What room?"

"We found Ophelia in a motel along the Twenty-four. Dead."

Cassandra slapped a palm to her forehead. "How?"

Zane's heavy sigh rippled through her tense muscles. She understood this was difficult for him, but out with it already.

"It appears she's given birth. I suspect the birth is what killed her. She's been dead about three hours."

"Mercy. Where's the baby?"

"Yeah, that's the disturbing part. Coco, love."

Cassandra heard her sister's sniffles in the background and Zane told her who he was talking to on the line. "Put Coco on, Zane, please."

Leaning over the bed, Cassandra pressed her elbows on it and bowed her forehead to the counterpane. This could not be happening. Why had Ophelia taken off on her own?

I'm not handling anything well. I should have been there to accompany the muse. And she'd abandoned Coco for Berlin two years earlier. *Way to keep the family together, Cassandra.* Granny would be so disappointed.

"I'm sorry, Caz. We were too late." Coco sucked in a long sniffle. She sounded as if she'd been crying and her nose was running. "I think she ran off because she knew it was coming. She kept saying she didn't want to burden us with her problem. I don't think she understood we only wanted to help her. Oh, it's so awful."

"It's not your fault, Coco." She summoned strength by inhaling through her nose and closing her eyes. Time to stop kicking herself for what she couldn't affect, and summon courage. Coco would need her to be strong. "You did the best you could. There are forces greater than you and I at work here."

Hell, she wished she could be there to hug Coco and to kick Zane's arse for allowing the muse to disappear in the first place. But really, no one was to blame. Angels and vampires? No mortal could ever prepare for that.

"Make sure she gets a proper burial."

"We will. Zane's got that under control. But, Caz..."

"It's okay, Coco. You don't need to say any

more. We'll figure things out. As long as you're safe."

"Zane is here. I am always safe with him. Oh, Caz…" New sniffles echoed on the connection. "In the bathroom, where I think she gave birth… there are tiny, bloody footprints."

"Footprints?"

"From the baby nephilim. It…it walked away."

Cassandra slapped a palm over her mouth. Heavy, gasping breaths kept her silent save for the pound of her heartbeat in her ears.

The nephilim was supposed to grow to maturity over seventy-two hours. It was too hideous to imagine, and she'd never quite believed that part when Granny had taught them the lore.

The newborn had walked away after the birth?

"Where are you, Coco?"

"We're at a cheesy little motel on the east side of Hamburg."

A good three-hour drive from where Cassandra and Sam stayed.

"We're going to try to track the…the…you know. I'll call you in a few hours."

"Yes, do that. Do not forget to call. I'm at the Radisson Blu with Sam."

"Sam?"

"Yeah, er, he's this guy I met. Not sure how long we'll be here, but let's make this our base. Room three twenty-one, all right?"

"Got it. Three twenty-one."

"I'll leave a key card for you at the reception desk. Check in every hour, Coco. Or I'll worry."

"Will do. I love you, Caz, but please, be careful. If you could see this. Oh…"

"She'll be keen in a few," Zane's voice said, claiming the phone from his sobbing lover. "We'll stay in touch. But we've got to see if we can pick up the monster's trail. I hope it's headed away from the city."

Monster hit her brain like a swift strike from a tire iron. She unkinked her clenched fingers. A monster walked the earth. What Sam had hoped to prevent, what she had wanted to prevent, had become a reality.

"Thank you, Zane. Take care of my sister. And the muse."

"Will do."

Cassandra tossed the phone onto the bed and ran into the bathroom to splash her face with cold water. Tears mixed with the water and she sobbed loudly.

Sam stalked across the midnight snow, marveling at the sight of streetlamps glistening on the surface of white. Tucked within utter violence and strife, the world possessed indescribable beauty. One could not exist without the other. Such a delicate balance.

Even Above balanced in such a manner. It made sense. How could one recognize and label beauty if they had not known ugly, as well? Same with love and hate, good and evil. Desire and disgust. Truth and lies.

He hadn't lied to Cassandra about his intentions when leaving the hotel room; he'd only avoided giving her all the details.

He shrugged up the sleeves of the blue sweater she had purchased for him in the hotel gift shop. She kept insisting he wear a coat outside, but he could not feel the cold. Perhaps he should, so as not to raise curiosity.

Nah. He did not care what others thought when they looked upon him. Though he understood that as people matured they did develop a self-conscious habit of concern for other's opinions. He was a newborn on this earth, and glad for it. The only opinion that mattered was Cassandra Stevens's.

He found a clearing amongst the spruce trees, just behind a park bench. Bowing his head, he bent to one knee on the snow. Spreading out his arms, he opened his palms upward and briefly wondered what the chill air would feel like against his skin. It would bring him too close to mortality for comfort.

And yet, Cassandra's innate warmth felt great upon his skin. That part of the mortal condition he enjoyed.

But he wasn't here on earth for holiday.

Reciting a few words to conjure the one he wished to speak with, he then waited, unsure how, exactly, the archangel would arrive.

Raphael was not the archangel who oversaw the Fallen. Their leader, Samyaza, either currently walked the earth or was still trapped in the Ninth Void—or had been slain. Actually, the Fallen were more freelance than an organized crew. Once their feet had touched earth, they'd dispersed.

Raphael oversaw the Sinistari, which should make little sense, until a person realized the Sinistari were forged from the Fallen. And where the Fallen did not possess divinity because their feet had touched the earth, the Sinistari had been taken before touching earth and forged into demon and sent Beneath, where they waited for a summons to track Fallen.

Summoned by Raphael, or so Sam suspected.

Someone cleared his throat behind Sam. He swung a look over his shoulder. A thin, well-dressed man in striped trousers sat on the park bench, one ankle propped over a knee. He had forgone winter wear as well, and tilted his head in question at Sam.

"You going to ignore me all day, Outlaw?" Raphael inquired in a British accent.

Sam stood and slapped a hand to his chest. It always startled him to meet a fellow angel on earth. When Above, they did not resemble the human shape, but rather took the form of a feeling. It amused him to see the mortal form each angel assumed. Apparently, Raphael wasn't into machismo and might, but rather wielded a sly sense of fashion.

"Raphael, thank you for coming."

"Get on with it. You obviously want something. Everybody does. Mortals, demons, even the rebellious Fallen. Walking the earth again, I see. And to no good end. I cannot and will not pull rein on my Sinistari, so do not ask."

"I wouldn't dream of it. I can handle the Sinistari."

"Do you still have the last one's blade?"

"I do."

"Hand it over."

Sam slid a hand over the halo at his hip. The blade he'd tucked in his boot. If he were to step up to the vanguard properly armed... "I'd prefer not to."

Raphael gestured with his fingers and the blade slid out of Sam's boot and slapped into the archangel's grip. A blue glow surrounded the weapon and it dispersed to nothing but a shimmer.

"You are aware the mix of Fallen and Sinistari have been joined by vampires," Sam stated. "And we're not all fighting on the same side."

"The Fallen started it all."

So the archangel would accuse? Interesting. "I suspect it will matter little to you I've reversed my decision regarding Falling."

"You suspect correctly. But I do adore that your brethren name you Outlaw. Strangely ironic."

"Will slaying my fellow Fallen, those bent on

tampering with mortal females, restore me in The Most High's good graces?"

Raphael crossed his arms and harrumphed. It was a good ol' British gesture that Sam noted with curiosity. "I sense you want to return Above?"

Sam nodded. "I made a mistake Falling."

"You Fell with purpose!"

Head bowed, Sam accepted the truth. "But I have seen the world through compassionate eyes. And now I wish to redeem myself in His eyes and return to a job that gives me satisfaction."

"He has no say, one way or another, who goes and who returns."

"I cannot believe that."

"The Arcs keep a tight rein on the gates now. But look, you lot Fell on your own, so what makes you think He has any control?"

He'd never thought about it that way. The angels did not take direct commands from The Most High, yet their reverence for Him went beyond all imagining.

"Much has changed since your Fall, Samandiriel the Outlaw."

He winced at the Arc's apparent delight in using that title.

"You and your brethren forced us to create the Sinistari race to police our own. It was quite a slap in the face, if you ask me."

"I don't wish to see the day nephilim walk this earth."

"You should have thought of that before you

Fell with lust in your eyes. Lust breeds nasty nephilim." The Arc shuddered. "There's one walking the earth right now. I can feel it."

"Then slay it!"

"So simple as that? You, who used to smite upon command, are too quick to your guns. It is not my judgment call."

"But the creature is your miss. Had your Sinistari slain the responsible Fallen…" Sam let the condemnation hang.

He should not be so bold. He revered Raphael. And indeed, his way of taking care of a problem involved a proper smiting, which certainly had no place on earth—unless the smitee was a vicious vampire or one of the Fallen.

"Whatever calamity this child of dark divinity visits upon the earth is now for the mortals to suffer," Raphael said sharply. "I am surprised you are not pleased. It is what will occur when you mate with your little muse. Bunny, isn't that what you named her?"

That was an endearment only he could use for Cassandra. It gave him a sense of closeness to her, and she seemed to take to it. And anything she took to pleased Sam, as well.

Sam noted he did not care for Raphael so much now. "As I said, since walking amongst the mortals, I've had a change of heart."

"Your glass heart does not understand the ways of change. It does not evolve—it only exists in the time in which you land. You take on the morals and motions of the world around you, but you don't truly understand them, do you?"

Giving him no time to respond, Raphael continued, "And since when does an angel care about mortals? They are but creatures put here to live and die. They believe God Himself controls their destinies, that they live and die because of his hand. It is ridiculous! Yes, he gave them life. But he does not predetermine their deaths, nor does he reach down to force an untimely death. Yet always he is blamed for taking the young ones, the frail and disabled ones. A mockery, I tell you."

"It is their manner to seek answers for the ineffable. They are evolving, learning, gaining knowledge. It is a slow process that will last for millennia. We should not make judgments."

"Then why not remain on this evolving earth you wax over? Why must you be away from these helpless mortals you deem unfit for your judgment?"

Sam shrugged. Yes, why ask for removal from a world in which Cassandra Stevens existed? When he stood near her, everything felt right. Wondrous.

He shouldn't think about her. *He mustn't.* "It is my desire," Sam said. "I was wrong. I admit it."

"You've haven't taken your muse?"

"I desire her. And I respect her."

Raphael shook his head sorrowfully, perhaps even disgusted at his moral reply.

Sam swung an angry sneer at the archangel

and clenched a fist before him. "That is the problem with the Fallen, even the Arcs. They believe they've the right to take as they please. We have no such right. While here on earth, we become a part of this realm. We must live by their rules. I would not think to harm Cassandra."

"If you believe sex harmful you've been fed some bad information, Outlaw."

"It is harmful if attempted against the woman's will."

"Ah. Yes, well, there is that. Don't get me wrong, I am on board with the whole respect-the-muse thing. You surprise me." The archangel tilted his hat to reveal his eyes, brilliant with violet and azure. Sam could not look upon him for more than a second or the divine burn would eat into his mortal skin. "I suppose I can see to granting your return to Above…in favor of your changed mind."

"Really?"

"Of course. I am not so rigid I cannot accommodate a true champion."

"I am no champion." Although, if Cassandra would have him as her champion, he would walk the world for her, and smite every last vampire.

"You've taken out a few vampires," Raphael said. "The Sinistari I will miss, but you can continue to kill your brothers. That'll give my Sinistari ranks a helping hand."

"Trust me, if a Fallen lands within my senses,

he will be dead. Thank you for your generous gift, Raphael."

"But you'll need to do something for me."

Of course. There was always a "but." Who said the angels did not quickly learn the ways of humanity? "Anything."

"Bring me the book the muse possesses."

"The one with the names and sigils? But she destroyed—"

"She did not. And she has no clue what the book really is."

"What is it?"

Raphael harrumphed and adjusted his position on the bench, crossing an elbow over the back of it. "It contains the code for the Final Days."

"The one that will make all the angels…?"

The archangel nodded dourly. "Cassandra Stevens's book, a collection of names and sigils that when ordered correctly, holds an ancient coded word that when spoken, will send all angels plummeting to earth to smother mankind with their multitudes. Their wings will burn human flesh, young and old. The earth will become an ashy cemetery of both mortal and the divine."

Sam swallowed. "I think the vampires may be after the book."

Raphael did not reply and, instead, shimmered away. The empty park bench bore no sign anyone had sat there, the snow that lay on it undisturbed.

"Cassandra's book," he muttered. To consider the Final Days gave even him a shudder. It would bring death to all, human, divine and those in between such as the Fallen. "She has a copy of it on the computer, but I wonder…"

She must still have it in actual book form. She had protected it for years from falling into the wrong hands; she would not have disposed of it even after putting it in digital form. Yet if he explained Raphael's hands were the best to place the book into, she wouldn't go for it. She was not keen on angels.

"I'll have to convince her to change her mind. She likes to kiss. That could work."

Chapter 7

Cassandra had gotten it together and remembered to order room service before Sam returned looking kissed by winter, red spots on his cheeks.

"I didn't think you felt the cold," she said, gesturing to his cheeks.

He touched his face and shrugged. "I don't. Are they rosy?"

"A little. It makes you look…"

"Mortal?"

"You've already mastered that. Supper's here."

He lifted the stainless steel lids to inspect the food. The rich, spicy scent of sausage filled the room. After talking to Coco, Cassandra's hunger had waned.

"Kraut and sausage? Mmm, and potatoes with vinegar and garlic. Smells delicious. What's wrong, Cassandra? Did you contact your sister while I was gone?"

"I did, and they found the muse."

"That's excellent."

"It's horrible. They found Ophelia's dead body, and tiny baby prints walking away from the scene."

Sam swiped a hand over his face and pushed the food cart aside. "That is unfathomable."

His reaction struck her as very human. It made her feel as though he wasn't so different from her, after all.

"They're tracking it right now," she said, "the nephilim. It couldn't have gone far from the hotel. Could it? Sam, it walked away after the birth."

He winced.

"I told Coco we'd focus on the vampires."

Cassandra had drawn a hard sheen over her demeanor. Easier that way. No one ever saved the world while sobbing manically.

Keep telling yourself that. Chin up, Caz.

She plopped onto the bed in front of the room service cart and tugged it closer. "So we'd best eat up, fortify our strength for the big fight, eh?"

"Are you okay about this?" He flexed the fingers of one hand near his thigh, but remained still. Struggling inwardly? "I'm not big on emotion, but I can see you're trying to put up a front. Cassandra?"

Apparently the angel wasn't so hard, after all. Glory Hallelujah. "Yes, I am okay with it. Or at least, as okay as one can possibly be about the situation. I've been bawling like a madwoman for the last fifteen minutes. Kinda glad you weren't here."

"I should have been here for you."

He sat on the bed beside her. Hands on his lap, he didn't try to hug her or console her with a kiss or a touch. And that was a good thing, because she wasn't sure if a simple touch might annihilate her makeshift battlements and spring open the floodgates again.

For a man who confessed little insight to emotion, he was doing fine by simply sitting near her, offering his presence.

"I ordered wine and beer," she said, tendering her tone to one much lighter than she felt. "Wasn't sure which you'd prefer."

"Whichever you don't want. I've tried wine but not beer."

She handed him the mug and he tilted back a healthy swallow. "This is very good."

"You'll become an honorary German in no time, buddy. They do love their beer."

She leaned forward to flick on the television to a news station, and tuned the volume to low. The added distraction helped her mind to distance itself from the phone call.

Her silver rings tinged sweetly on the goblet rim as she tipped back a sip of wine.

"Tell me what brought you to the craft of silver-smithing?" Sam asked around a bite of sausage.

"It's so weird my angel—er, *you* are the silver guy."

"I am the original master of silver, yes."

"Yes, the master of silver." She rubbed the underside of one of her rings. That Samandiriel, the angel, had introduced the craft of manipulating and forming silver *to the world* blew her mind. She would not be practicing the craft today had he not taught people thousands of years ago how to do it. "Wow."

"What?"

"I just thought about it," she said.

"Ah." He nodded, grinning. "Good to know the craft survived the centuries. It is not so much handy as decorative, though. Yet I sense the decorative arts still hold great value to adorn and with which to invest."

"It wasn't something I felt inclined to do all my life," she explained. "Not like a compulsion. Though I would expect it knowing what I now know about you and me. Anyway, it was a short chapter in our industrial arts class on metalworking. I took to it immediately, and felt like silver was something that spoke to me, as weird as that sounds. The metal does what I want it to do, and yet, all I'm doing is finding the shape it wants to be."

"I like that. Finding the shape it wants to be."

"I still need to master the art of planishing. I can do it, but even a speck of dust will leave be-

hind an impression when hammering. It's a subtle
art form."

"I can show you. Once mastered, you can create spectacular reliefs on the silver."

"I sculpted an angel and finished it only days
ago. It's…"

"Me?"

"I think so." She turned a wondrous grin to
him. "As I was creating the sculpture, I knew it
would be you. I mean, I've never known what you
would look like, only that the sculpture was you."

She'd wished for Sam all her life. To either end
it all, or make it right.

"I understand muses often paint, draw or create
facsimiles of the Fallen without realizing what
they are doing and, when finished, are not always
aware what the end results mean to them."

"I knew what it meant when I looked over the
finished piece. I put the sculpture on the dresser
overlooking my bed. He watches me sleep."

She looked aside, ashamed she'd admitted
something so personal to him. Something *about*
him. About the two of them.

Was it still just a silly dream, or was there really a *them*? Granny had taught her how to *kill*
this man. Yet here she sat, drinking wine and eating a meal with him.

"Did you make those rings on your fingers?"

"Yes." She offered her hand, and he inspected
the three silver rings before she realized that one
would surprise him.

"This is our sigil," he said, tapping the ring on her thumb. Urgency tightened his jaw. "Why would you put this sacred symbol onto a piece of jewelry?"

"Because it is sacred. And…because I was feeling rebellious last year. I made a small collection featuring half a dozen angel sigils and sold them."

Sam pushed up her sleeve to reveal the sigil on her wrist. His pulsing jaw implied the annoyance Cassandra sensed.

"I only sold about a hundred pieces. Nothing ever came of it."

"What did you expect to come of it?"

"That maybe I'd kick-start the bloody apocalypse." She leaned back on the bed, feeling her ire rise for her inability to help Ophelia when she had needed it most. "I've carried this burden all my life, Sam. I was in a dark place, wanting it to all be over. I know you can't understand. But like I said, nothing came of it. A few people bought my pieces at an art fair. That's about it."

"Yet the vampires knew exactly where to look to find you."

She had never thought of it that way. Had a vampire purchased one of her pieces and guessed she was a muse? The encounter with the two vampires in the alley had been coincidence. They'd been surprised to learn she was a muse.

"If you're implying one of my customers was a vampire, it's a long shot," she said.

"We must consider the vampires have more

resources than imaginable. And that their operation is precise and organized."

"Yeah? Bring on the bloodsuckers. I am prepared."

Cassandra dragged her backpack onto the bed. She unzipped it and pulled out the long, narrow box perfectly sized for a stack of rulers.

"What's that?"

Finished with the meal, Sam pushed the cart near the door, then moved a chair out from the desk and sat. He stretched his arms back behind his head, and for a moment Cassandra got lost in the pull of his soft blue sweater over his chest. Tight muscles flexed beneath. How much did she want to be that shirt, hugging his skin?

"What? Do I have food on me somewhere?"

She shook her head and tore off the packing tape from the box. "No, I was just…"

Admiring a very fine form. And wondering why the man she wanted most was the one man in the world she should avoid. Kill, even. How unfair was that?

It was imperative she redirect her dire thoughts. And this little prize was just the thing.

"This is something I ordered on eBay. You know what eBay is?"

"Something to do with the internet, yes? It's amazing the technological advances the world has experienced. Do you know, when I last walked the earth, if we wanted to talk to someone fifty leagues away, we'd have to hop on the back of a donkey and travel there?"

"Remind me to get you a cell phone after the apocalypse."

"I wouldn't have anyone to call."

"You could call me."

A smile curved his lips, as if it jumped upon him and, once there, he liked it so much it spread further, barely able to contain his glee.

Again, Cassandra tilted her head down, but this time it was to hide a rosy blush.

She carefully extracted the metal device from the box and pulled away the Bubble Wrap. It had been advertised as a titanium punch, but thanks to her basic research on vampires, she'd known exactly what it was when she'd seen the circular crest emblazoned on the side of the cylindrical object.

Mortals not in the know wouldn't have a clue, which was why she'd been able to nab this handy-dandy thingamabobbie for fifty euros.

She studied the crest imprinted on the titanium column. A circle with the points of four stakes meeting in the center was surrounded by the name of the organization that used this weapon.

"The Order of the Stake," she read.

"I haven't heard of them," Sam said, leaning forward to look over what she held.

"They are an ancient order, rumored to be formed by King Henry III of France at the end of the sixteenth century. Or maybe Charles IX.

History is a little shady which Valois king it was, if indeed it was a king." The cylinder fit her grip nicely, and she wielded it as if to stab. "The order is made up of knighted mortals who hunt vampires, and this is their weapon of choice."

In demonstration, she smacked her free palm against the weapon's base. "Plant this against a vampire's chest, and..."

She took her hand away and with her other hand compressed the spring-action clamps in the grip with a squeeze. A titanium spike pinioned out from the cylinder, eight inches long and sharpened to a deadly point. The force of the action bobbed her hand.

"That'll leave a mark," Sam said.

She spun the stake as if a majorette's baton. "What it'll leave is a pile of ash."

"Let me see that thing, bunny."

He studied it from end to end, figuring out the return mechanism, a button on the end, which snapped the stake back into the cylinder. Experimentally, he stabbed the air with it. "As we'd say in the ranks, this will smite nicely."

Cassandra took it back. "It's mine. You've your halo and a demon blade to do your smiting."

"Fair enough." He patted the halo at his hip, but Cassandra didn't notice the blade was missing. "I wager you'll do some damage with that thing."

"Oh, yeah." She stabbed it in the air a couple times.

For a woman of her petite size and limited

strength this was exactly what she needed to force the stake through flesh, muscle, bone and, finally, heart.

According to her research, most young vampires could be extinguished with a stake through the heart. A few older, tough ones also required decapitation. She wasn't into hacking off heads, so she hoped if she did come face-to-face with a vampire again, it was less than a century old.

Sliding off the bed, she poked the stake at an invisible vampire. Performing a high roundhouse, she swiped her arm around, aiming at the bloodsucker. She dodged and swung underhanded with the stake to its heart. Score! If she would have had this in the alleyway, those thug vampires wouldn't have stood a chance.

She spun around to find Sam grinning bemusedly at her. Shrugging and looking aside to hide her blush, she returned the stake to the cylinder.

Sam thumbed his lower lip and followed her movements as she sorted through the backpack. She could feel his gaze on her skin as if gently stroking fingers, but a breath away from a real touch.

"What's wrong?" she asked without looking at him, still trying to look busy.

"Can we kiss again?" he asked.

Oh, yeah? Cassandra straightened.

Times like this a girl should stake out on the roof and wait for the big bads to approach. The world was falling apart and darkness threatened now that a nephilim walked the land. But it was cold on the roof. And they'd pulled vampire duty, which wasn't possible until the sun went down. Which should happen any minute now, but the curtains were drawn, so she couldn't be held responsible for knowing the exact moment darkness fell.

That was all the argument she could summon.

Cassandra tossed the stake on the bed and straddled Sam on the chair. His surprise at her easy compliance made her want to giggle, but she was too focused on the gorgeous lines of his square jaw. Cut solid and straight, as if from stone or silver, yet so real.

But not a mortal man. *Don't forget that.* And not a man who wanted to stick around after the glory was gained. *Double don't forget that, Caz.*

She leaned in and kissed his mouth, a mouth that accepted without directing, received without demanding. He was still new to intimacy, and his inexperience emboldened her. Hard to believe she had ever worried about him attacking her.

But it was possible; that had already been proved.

Disregarding niggling intuition, Cassandra followed her decadent heart into a dangerous place, where she felt most comfortable.

Sam spread his hand up her spine and pulled her tightly against him. The warmth of him was real. The sinuous glide of his muscles beneath her palms heightened her desire. Everything about him seduced her to drop her guard.

Tracing the fresh stubble darkening his jaw with a fingertip, she then brushed her lips over the sexy scruff. The rough sensation stimulated her nerve endings, and she dashed her tongue along his jaw where perhaps God himself had carved this man from an ineffable substance. Too incredible to fathom, and yet had she not also been created by Him?

Kissing along his jaw, she took his measure, finding the crease where his ear met his head a particularly enticing spot to tuck her tongue. His deep, longing moan signaled approval.

Down his neck she placed a kiss against the vein that did not pulse, and there, up under his chin, and then to the hard Adam's apple, before licking the cool flesh at the base of his neck.

"Cassandra," he murmured. "Cass…"

Had she rendered him speechless? Ha! Score one for the muse and hand her the control. She needed to feel that right now. If she could manage one aspect of her crazy life, she could then, hopefully, control many more.

Lifting the sweater emblazoned over the breast with the AquaDom logo over his head, she tugged it off and tossed it aside. Bowing over him, she explored hard pectorals too solid to be anything but sculpture, yet his skin begged for her to press her palms flat to take in as much of him as possible. His nipple grew harder when she dashed her tongue over it.

Sam gasped and thrust back his head. His fingers slid into her hair, gently claiming her and keeping her upon him. The ribbons within her hair slipped over his chest and arms. She teased her tongue to the other nipple and he gripped the nape of her neck, wanting to pull her hard against him but somehow resisting that dominant move.

The muscles in his arms tensed against her rib cage, and his thighs flexed under hers. She was giving him a new experience, and it was a hell of a lot of fun. But how far dare she take it?

She wasn't ready to go all the way. Would she ever be ready for that? It was foolish to think she could enjoy the fun of sex without the very real consequences of—no, she wasn't going to think of that peril right now.

Why not? You love danger. Angel boy, here, offers it in spades.

Pressing an ear to his chest, she listened, but it only confirmed what Granny Stevens had told her. "Your heart doesn't beat."

"My heart is solid glass. It cannot beat."

"Not without a soul." Her hand strayed to flick a nail across the halo at his hip. The key to his soul.

"Does that trouble you?" he asked.

She studied his eyes of azure, gold and violet, freckled with emerald. She had been given the facts. She wasn't a skeptic. "It's just different."

He touched her bottom lip with his forefinger. "Our one difference."

Cassandra licked his fingertip and noticed it was smooth. Really smooth. She studied his finger, searching for the whorls. "You've no fingerprints."

"Without a soul, I've not the unique prints that make you mortals what you are."

Pressing his finger aside her cheek, she held him there, fascinated and a little freaked.

Danger, Cassandra. Don't stop now. You don't have much time left before the world falls down around you.

"Right," she whispered, and then sat back and pulled her sweater off over her head.

Sam's eyes widened. He couldn't repress that sexy innocence-chasing-charming smirk. So she wasn't much for bras. Her 32Bs liked the freedom.

"Those are so…wow." His hand on her hip flexed. "Can I…can I touch them?"

She took his hand and placed it over her heart. "Touch me. Feel my heart beat."

He exhaled and conformed his printless fingers over her heart, which covered her entire bare breast. "It's pounding."

"It's excited about something," she offered with a surprising flush of heat to her neck. That heat moved through her being, warming her everywhere and moistening her between her legs.

This was no tease. She knew exactly what she wanted from this man.

Sam flattened his hand upon her chest and his fingers paralleled her hard nipple. "They're so round. They fit perfectly in my hands. Now I understand why men like them so much." He cupped her other breast. "Does it feel as good for you as when you licked mine?"

"Give it a try," she dared on a husky voice. Intimacy always brought out her inner harlot. And when in the presence of a Biblical being? Well, then…

Arching her spine, she met his mouth with her breast as he bent to taste her flesh. A moan hummed in her throat. A tilt of her head swept her beribboned hair across her bare back.

In answer to her desirous moan, Sam closed his mouth around her nipple. He didn't lick at it with his tongue, but she didn't need that. The intense connection radiated through her being, tendering every inch of flesh with a giddy tingle.

As he moved to kiss her other nipple, Cassandra squeezed her thighs against his, wanting to capture the warm hum coiling in her groin, but also toying with the untouchable sensation's fleeting tease.

When the world was falling apart around her, she needed a reminder of the sweetness reality could offer, the utter, breathtaking intensity that formed when two beings touched and learned one another.

Sam pressed an ear to her chest and listened,

chuckling softly. "That's you, breathing, living, being. It's remarkable."

Not so remarkable as touching an angel. This man was her enemy? The one who would threaten the world's safety by merely having sex with her? It didn't seem possible. It couldn't be.

Well, she knew the Fallen was only capable of procreating while in half form. He had to shift and his wings must be unfurled for her to become pregnant. So in this complete human form, could they get busy without worry of her becoming a nephilim baby mama?

Don't even consider it!

She wore birth control implants in her upper arm. She couldn't get pregnant—not by a mortal man. But she wasn't stupid, and would not believe such precautions made her safe in this situation.

A pinch to her nipple stirred a chirp of delight. "You think so?"

"I want more," he said, and kissed his way down her chest to her stomach. "All of you."

Cassandra raked her fingers through his hair and tilted his head back to study his eyes. Emerald, violet and a sparkle of gold. She need fear him only if they glowed blue.

"What?" he asked.

"Just checking. I, uh…I don't want to take chances, Sam." *Oh, really, Danger Girl?*

"Chance is one of life's great joys. You open yourself to opportunity and experience. Look at me. I love chance!"

"I mean with you going all evil angel on me. Can we…" She sucked in her lower lip, not wanting to have this discussion, but not so stupid she would avoid it. "Can we do this? Without you… you know?"

"If a chance of my harming you existed, I would not have allowed this to happen. I can control the shift to half form. You're safe with me, Cassandra."

"I want to believe that. But Granny told me the Fallen have this compulsion. A compulsion means something you can't resist. And you've even talked about it. So why can you resist right now?"

"I'm not resisting. I want to touch you everywhere, taste every inch of your skin and feel your softness. Mmm…" He kissed her breast. "Suck on you until you moan."

She pressed fingers to his mouth. "If we had sex would you turn all nasty-winged Fallen on me? How do you know the compulsion won't come upon you when you're…in the throes?"

"Ah." He winced and trailed his fingers over her bare stomach. "I don't know. I've…never gone that far with a woman so I'm not sure how far I can take this before the compulsion strikes."

"That's not good."

"What we're doing right now is good."

She kissed him and pressed her forehead to his. "It is, but I don't want to have to stake you should you suddenly decide to make a nephilim with me."

"Stakes aren't effective against me."

"Sam, you don't understand."

"Yes, I do. You don't want to take the risk of what our intimacy could lead to."

"Oh, I'm all about the risk. I just don't want this to go so far I…" Allow emotion to enter the picture, like love and want and need. Because those things threatened far more than becoming a baby mama.

Was she retreating so quickly? She had engaged them in this intimate dance.

"I guess I do have the repellant spell. If you go evil angel on me, it'll give me a minute to escape."

"I hate that we need a precaution like that, sweetie bunny mine."

That one was over-the-top, but it still made her smile. "You do. You…really do care about me?"

He nodded.

"But I'm the only woman you've gotten a chance to know. Who's to say once you've spent some time on earth, chatted up a few more ladies, you won't feel the same attraction to them? There's nothing special about me. And don't bring up the sigil and our destinies."

"Then I've no argument. All I know is right now I want you, Cassandra. Just like this. Our skin brushing against one another. Our mouths giving and taking breath. Beyond that, it's all new to me."

A statement in no need of further argument. Cassandra bent and opened his mouth with a deep kiss and wrapped her legs about him and the chair.

"Mmm," he murmured. "You smell so good."

They kissed and Sam stroked her breasts until she began to feel the beginnings of orgasm humming in her core. And while her body was ready to fly and take the angel along with her, some insistently prudish part of her demanded she take it slower. Resist the release, because it wasn't right yet. They were yet so new to each other.

Tilting back her head, Cassandra bit her lip as a pinch to her nipple twisted the coil in her belly to a tightness too good to resist. Then she heard the public safety alarm beep on the television that jabbered quietly behind them.

"What's wrong, bunny? Am I doing this wrong?"

Her attention averted to the television, Cassandra's libido dropped off the scale. Pushing away from the best kisses she had ever received, she went to the bed and stood before the TV, arms crossed over her sensitive breasts.

She narrowed her gaze to study the brief, grainy video being looped over and over on the screen. The newscaster stated a strange being had been sighted in Berlin. Bystanders described it as tall and deformed, but most definitely human. It growled and stomped about on club feet, and had knocked down a streetlight and damaged three cars. It was considered dangerous, and people should run if they saw it.

Cassandra stepped backward, right onto Sam's foot. She wobbled, and he caught her shoulders, supporting her. "Do you think that is the...?"

"I've never seen one before. The image is very poor. It could be anything."

"I've got to call Coco." She scrambled for her cell phone and found it under the backpack.

Sam angled his head to study the blurred image of what was obviously a bald, distorted head. The mouth was wide and opened in a roar. Beyond that, there was no evidence to show that it was anything more than a man with a multitude of exterior defects. But he knew. Something inside his hard glass heart pulsed. And it wasn't a pulse of desire or happiness.

He did not fear, such as did mortal men. But what he saw on the television injected horror into his being. A nephilim walked the earth.

Chapter 8

Sam tossed Cassandra her backpack, which was loaded with the necessary weapons. "We need to take action. If there's a nephilim stalking the streets of Berlin, we have to find it."

"I agree. But Coco and Zane are on its trail. And I trust they've got a handle on that situation." She slid on her coat and then the backpack. He hadn't liked it when she'd put on her shirt, covering those gorgeous breasts. But he couldn't think about the sensual things he wanted to do to her body right now.

"Although," she said, "it's only been an hour since I talked to Coco, and she was still in Hamburg. It's a three-hour drive from there to Berlin. They couldn't possibly have kept up with it."

Sam grabbed her arm, stopping her from leaving the room. Apparently she did not gauge the seriousness of the situation. "I will not endanger another being by getting them involved in our troubles. Most especially not a relative of yours. We can do this alone. We must."

"I don't think so, buddy." She tugged from his grasp.

"My name is not buddy. And you will respect me for the skills I bring to the table. I have experience with this sort of thing."

She opened the hotel room door and swung a doubting look at him. "Really? How many nephilim have you tracked and slain?"

Stating the obvious was not going to win his favor. But that cute, defying stare she cast him was. "That's not the point. What's important is that the creature is of my ilk—"

"Sam, listen," she said as she followed his hasty strides down the hallway. "I agree I don't want Coco involved. But her boyfriend has once already slain an angel."

"Mortals are not capable of such a feat."

"Yes, I know. But he did it, so I think I want to put my trust in that he may have some crazy skills should they actually find the nephilim. And do you even know what is the one thing that can kill a nephilim?"

"Certainly a Sinistari blade, and I've the halo."

"Wrong. You don't know?" She jumped before him, stopping them at the door that opened to the snowy parking lot.

Actually, he didn't have that knowledge, but he didn't want to say so. He'd developed a sense of pride since arriving on earth and didn't want to reveal his lack of knowledge. What *could* kill a creature born of the divine and earthbound?

"I'll enlighten you," Cassandra said. "Granny taught me there's only one thing can kill a nephilim. And that one thing? Coco has it."

He opened his mouth to argue, but realized she wasn't a stupid woman. She knew things. And much as he did know it all after walking the world, the precise method to slay a nephilim wasn't coming to him at this moment. And the vampiress had not that knowledge when he'd scanned her mind. "What is it?"

Cassandra leaned the back of her head against the door, which was frosted with snow flowers, and gave him the most serious brown eyes. "Angel ash."

Those words darted an icy chill up his spine, and he didn't normally feel things like that. There was only one way such an item could be obtained. "From a dead angel?"

She nodded.

Sam swallowed that information awkwardly. That made *him* key to slaying the nephilim—in a way that did not sit well with him.

"So that's why you were upset when the wind took away Nazariah's ash. How'd your sister get her hands on something like that?"

"I told you. She and her boyfriend killed a Fallen a few months ago."

"That's too incredible to believe that mortals—"

"It was Zane who did the slaying. But Coco was the one smart enough to gather up the remains. She is bringing the angel ash with her, but the two can't possibly be in Berlin yet."

"Exactly. I think it wise we pick up the task your sister began and stop the monster before it starts killing innocent people. You saw the news report. It's creating chaos. It won't be long before it gets hungry and—"

"All right. I get it." Her brown eyes flashed at him. She'd heard something she hadn't wanted to hear, and it twinged deep inside Sam's chest to know he'd caused that aggravation.

He shouldn't be feeling things like regret or sympathy. Or desire. He sure as hell should not have been kissing his muse. Because he wasn't positive he could resist the compulsion should their kisses stoke those dark desires that he knew lived within him. He felt a desire to take her, his newly developed morals be damned.

Was it so wrong to want what He had given man? A woman, a lover, a friend and companion. Someone to hold his hand.

Sam looked at his hand, not daring to clasp it within Cassandra's gloved hand. He wanted someone to hold it and mean it, not as a simple gesture.

Was this the struggle mortal men experienced

when attempting to accomplish something important while in the company of a beautiful woman?

He had not expected to be distracted by the muse. But there it was, or rather, there she was. Distracting him with every syllable, every move, every soft sigh. Hell, even watching her swing a stake at invisible vampires had turned him on.

"Sam? What's going on in that brain of yours?"

"Huh?"

"You're giving me the glad eye."

He rubbed his eye, wondering exactly what that meant and hoping it wasn't something he'd got stuck in there. Then he looked at his hand again. Would she ever hold it?

Why do you care? You want to go home!

"I thought we were discussing monsters and methods to annihilate them. What's up with your hand?"

"Hmm? Oh." He tucked his hand into the pocket of his leather pants. "I was thinking about mortal men," he said.

Her forehead quirked, and he laughed, realizing what he'd just said could be construed incorrectly. "Women are such a treat. It's no wonder men will walk worlds for them, do crazy things to impress them, perhaps even die for them."

"That only happens in fiction," she said bluntly. He sensed a distinct lack of belief in her. Had she never been with a man who would walk the world for her? "This is real life, buddy."

"Is it? Real life with monsters?"

She sighed. "You got it. Like a horror movie come to life. Are we going to stalk nephilim, or what?"

He pulled her in for a hug, because it felt right and good to hold her close. And it felt as though he gained strength from her, a reason to continue, to jump forward into the fray and slash away at the enemy even though he was going against his brethren and their progeny.

And if she chose not to hold his hand, then he would find a way to earn that respect and trust from her. He would champion her.

"Nephilim it is. Let's do this."

They stomped through the park where Cassandra guessed the nephilim may have passed. The news video clip had not shown street signs, but she felt sure she'd seen the Berlin Cathedral in the background. Of course, if the nephilim had walked from Hamburg to Berlin in such a short time, there was no telling where it was now.

She wished they had a car, but it seemed Sam was not aware of creature comforts that made her life a little easier. She wasn't going to pout like a girl. So it was cold. She had a warm jacket, gloves and boots.

The night was still, bright with city lights and a sprinkling of snow. Ahead, a vast parking lot fronted the river Spree. Cars covered in a foot of snow sat here and there. Nothing else could be heard except for the hum of an overhead streetlight and the distant thump of subwoofers in a cruising SUV.

Racing up to parallel Sam, she nudged his arm with an elbow. He slowed to allow her to keep pace.

That's right, angel boy, I'm still here.

A week ago she would have answered *hell, no* had anyone asked if she'd ever join with the enemy to fight the cause. Sam wasn't the enemy.

Yes, he was.

Truth? On the list of her enemies, Sam landed fourth after vampires, other Fallen and the nephilim. She'd term him a friendly hostile.

Glory hallelujah, Cassandra, you are certifiable.

Whatever. She would probably require a padded room after all this was done.

A black van rounded the corner and entered the lot behind them. It was moving too purposefully for a random drive through a quiet lot this late at night.

Cassandra tensed, ready for anything.

The van skidded to park and the driver hopped out, leaving the vehicle still running. Dressed in jean jacket and gray army-issue camo fatigues, he banged out a bowlegged race toward them. No gloves, no hat.

Not mortal, Cassandra guessed.

"Vampire," Sam growled and pushed her behind him.

Cassandra didn't stay there. She stepped to

Sam's side and, before he could protest, the vampire charged him. The two went down, Sam kicking high and the vampire somersaulting over him to land on his feet.

"Nice to meet the two of you," the vampire said in thick Russian, bouncing on his feet and punching his fists in the air like a prizefighter. "Name's Rovonsky. My boss wants a word with you both."

"Let me guess," Sam said. "Antonio del Gado? The Anakim tribe leader."

"Oh, you're good," Rovonsky said. He winked at Cassandra. "But not so pretty as the muse."

A great thump shook the ground, and Cassandra spun to spy a hulking black creature approaching with arms pumping and armor glinting.

"Sinistari," she whispered.

Not as if she hadn't expected another one to be summoned. But seriously? Didn't they have enough trouble already?

Dropping her backpack, she unzipped it and rummaged about inside. "You take the Sinistari," she yelled to Sam. "I've got the vamp!"

"I'm on it!"

Without pause, Sam charged past her, leaving the vampire with fists raised for a fight he wouldn't get. Metal and muscle clashed as the Fallen and the Sinistari met in the parking lot beside the black van.

"I guess I get to play with you," the Russian bloodsucker teased.

Cassandra swung toward the leering vampire with the spring-action stake—and missed.

The vampire kicked her in the calf, knocking her sideways and she went down. The titanium cylinder rolled across the snow-and-ice-packed tarmac, away from her grasp.

The key hazard fighting a vampire was blood loss. If she could keep away from its fangs, she could survive this tussle.

Her hips crushed to the cold ground as the vampire landed on them with his knees and grabbed her neck. "I can't kill you, but the boss didn't say anything about not biting you. You are going to taste sweet."

Fangs grew over his lower lip and he lunged toward her neck. Cassandra blocked the move with a forearm. Fangs gnashed through the Gore-Tex sleeve and she felt the cut at her elbow. So much for avoiding the teeth.

She would not become a vampire cocktail tonight.

Ramming up her knee, she managed to place it below the bastard's rib cage. He grunted and spit blood. Must have bit his own lip. Heh.

Pulling her leather glove off with her teeth, she threw it aside. Clawing her hand, she slashed it toward the lunging vampire's face. Two fine red lines appeared on his cheek. He snarled and slapped at her, but missed when she slithered out from under him.

The slippery ground worked to her advantage,

and one push of her boot toe slid her on her stomach to the stake. Slapping a hand on it, the cool titanium shaft fit against her palm.

Air huffed from her lungs as the vampire landed on her back and lifted her by the neck. Without so much as a grunt of exertion, he brought her to her feet. Then her feet went airborne as he swung her about and slammed her onto the boot of a car.

A thick blanket of snow softened her landing. Stake hand flung high, it sank into the fluffy snow above her head, disguising her weapon from the vicious vampire who climbed upon her.

Swinging the stake forward, she aimed. The vampire chuckled when he saw it. "Looks like your pointy thing lost its pointy part."

She shoved it against his chest. He smirked to reveal his fangs.

"We'll see about that." Squeezing the trigger released the stake. The jolt of connection thumped against her palm, but she held firm as the stake pierced bone and heart muscle in one easy glide.

The vampire opened his mouth. Blood dripped out and splattered against her cheek. He winced, looked ready to cry, then ashed.

A gray cloud formed in the shape of a man over her, and then dropped like a heavy blanket onto Cassandra's body. She scrambled off the boot to shake the nasty ash first from her arms and then, with a few jumps, the rest of her body.

"Take that, bloodsucker," she said, and clicked

the stake into the titanium receptacle. "One vampire down, one..."

She'd forgotten about the demon and the angel. Where were they?

Growls rose from the other side of an RV. Cassandra walked a wide arc around the Silver Bullet camper, stake held at the ready. On the other side, Sam held the Sinistari pinned against the dented metal wall.

The demon slashed its deadly blade, missing Sam's face by a whisper. The blade was supposed to be dipped in qeres, an Egyptian poison effective only against angels. One slice from that blade and Sam was a goner.

If the demon won, it would walk away and leave Cassandra untouched. Its only goal was to slay the Fallen. And that had once been her goal: to make sure the Fallen didn't get anywhere near her, and if at all possible to slay it to prevent it from harming other muses.

But Sam was the outlaw the other angels despised. He was on her side. She needed him more than the Sinistari needed another feather in its cap.

But most of all, she had to admit she wanted Sam around because she liked him as a man. Behind the warrior lived a new, curious man who marveled over everything and who had a sexy sense of tease, which attracted her like no man ever had before.

She entertained the idea of them having a relationship. Of getting as close as two people could. Of not having to do it all on her own. Because… he was hers. They were destined for one another. Just because destiny ruled she should carry his monster child didn't mean she couldn't change that destiny.

"Sam," she gasped as the demon threw his opponent through the air.

The angel landed on the icy tarmac and slid against the wheel of a sports car. The impact moved the car and the rear of it crashed into the next car and the next in a domino effect.

Sam leaped up and whipped the halo toward his aggressor. The demon ducked, laughing at the ease with which it avoided the danger. The halo boomeranged back to Sam's grasp.

She needed to do something. To save her destiny.

No. He was capable. *Have faith, Cassandra.*

Faith? She'd lost her faith the moment Granny had filled her brain with her horrible destiny. Faith was for the lost, the desperate. Faith was a sham.

Sam stabbed the halo up into the demon's heart, stepped back, then ran and kicked the creature in the chest. The demon soared backward, hung over the river momentarily, then dropped into the Spree's murky, cold waters.

Cassandra ran to Sam's side. "You did it! But your halo? You'll need it!"

"That's what I was thinking. Bad move. Wait here. I'll get it back."

Running toward the river, the angel, fearless when he should be otherwise, leaped.

"No!" Cassandra raced to the railing. "Don't do it, Sam! Angels can't swim!"

Chapter 9

Hands clasped to her chest and clutching so tightly she might snap a finger, Cassandra peered over the still surface of the river Spree. Chunks of white ice dotted the brown water. He'd jumped in a minute ago.

A full minute.

"Where is he? He's drowned. Angels can't swim. That's the whole reason for the flood. God sent the flood to sweep the Fallen from the earth. Oh, hell, why did he do that? He's…"

She couldn't say the word *dead*. Didn't want to think or put it out there with her voice. He was not. But who could stay underwater so long?

Probably an angel. But not an angel who couldn't swim.

She mounted the railing, prepared to swing

over it and climb down the riverbank but knew that would prove foolish. She could swim, but it was December, and the water would take away her breath and give her hypothermia in less than thirty seconds. She was not suicidal.

Another minute passed.

Pacing before the railing, Cassandra rattled her fists near her thighs. Snow fell silently, melting on the water's surface, unaware of the frantic crash of emotions colliding inside her.

She was angry Sam had done such a stupid thing. Fearful he could be dead. Torn, because now she'd been left to fend off the Fallen, the demons and the vampires by herself. How could he do that to her? Leave her like this?

Then she was proud because Sam had defeated one Fallen and two Sinistari. And it wasn't as though he'd jumped in after the halo because the earthbound soul it contained held value to him. He'd wanted to retrieve the weapon that could ensure further success. Sam did not think of himself, only of innocent mortals.

Why?

How could he have developed such compassion toward mortals in so short a time? She was the only one he'd related to since arriving on earth. She couldn't have had such a powerful effect on the guy.

No, it had happened thousands of years ago. After his Fall. He'd looked upon mortal women and decided they were real, feeling beings not to be used for selfish pleasure. That was when compassion had won over her Fallen angel.

Would it now prove his death?

Your Fallen angel? Oh, Cassandra, you fool. He doesn't belong to you.

Nor could he claim possession over her. They were not an item. She didn't get to have relationships. Only other women, who didn't have the apocalypse hanging over their heads, could enjoy that.

Yes, yes, cry an entire river, Cassandra. Stop feeling sorry for yourself, right now.

Another minute—hell, possibly five minutes had passed!

Cassandra searched the calm river surface, not seeing air bubbles or a waver on the brown sheen. He was gone. Sam had sacrificed himself without a second thought.

She fell to her knees before the railing and pressed her head against the cold iron bar. Tears slipped down her cheeks, burning trails to her jaw. Granny Stevens could have never anticipated a muse getting along with her Fallen counterpart.

Sam was not like the other Fallen. He had looked into her eyes and she had seen the respect in his. He was here on earth to save her from himself.

"Oh." A lump caught in her throat and she gasped out sobs. "Please come back. Your bunny needs you, Sam. I can't do this without you."

Turning her back to the railing, she put her head against her knees and sobbed.

Water splashed. Cassandra jerked her body up for a look down the bank. A head emerged from the river, followed by broad shoulders, and the dripping wet clothing that clung to her outlaw angel.

"Sam!"

He spit out cold river water, the most disagreeable substance he'd ever tasted. Water soaked his clothing, dragging him down, wanting to repossess him to the depths. A dense lethargy stretched his calf and thigh muscles painfully.

Sam fell to his knees upon the snowy bank, the halo clutched firmly in hand. He'd retrieved his only chance of succeeding against the enemy.

A saving grace embraced him. Cassandra slid into a kneeling hug and, sobs accompanying her repeated prayer of his name, she clasped her arms about him and clung to his sodden body.

Over and over she whispered his name. Claiming him. Making him her own.

It felt so good, he didn't say he suspected the cold water would harm her more than him as it soaked through her coat and hair. Instead, he buried his face in her wet, beribboned hair and closed his eyes. So this was comfort? The clinging warmth of someone who cared for him? He never wanted it to end.

Or was it something more?

Why did she cry? He hadn't been under so long, had he? She knew he was immortal.

"You could have drowned!"

Ah. Yes, the whole "angels not being able to swim" thing. True, yet drowning was out of the question.

"I was walking along the riverbed," he said. "I cannot drown, only I don't know how to swim and cannot float to stay above water. I had to find the bank and climb up it. Think about it, Cassandra. The Great Flood swept us all away, but did not kill us."

She nodded and sniffled, sorting that information through her brain. Then she punched his shoulder. "You scared the crap out of me!"

"Sorry." Despite the weakness his mortal muscles felt, he stood, lifting her in his arms. Already her body shook minutely. "You need to get warm."

"The hotel is up the street," she said on a shiver. "I—I can walk. Hell, this water is freezing on my sk-skin."

"No time."

He eyed the black van the vampire Rovonsky had driven. It was still running, spewing out exhaust in a thick cloud. It would provide Cassandra warmth, and it might offer a few clues to the vampires' location.

Inside the back of the van was empty. No blankets or even a tarp; nothing to aid getting Cassandra warm. Sam reluctantly set her down on the corrugated steel floor, and she chattered softly, "T-turn up the heat."

He moved into the driver's seat and scanned the controls, but they displayed tiny embossed symbols instead of words. This was the second time he'd been responsible for her nearly freezing. He certainly had no clue how to actually care for a mortal woman.

What made him believe he could ever earn her trust?

"The one with the wavy lines, like heat waves," she said, then dropped to her side and curled her legs to her chest.

Sam turned the heat to high and adjusted the circular vents so they blew toward the back, then climbed beside her. "I'd snuggle against you, but I'm wet and not warm at all."

"Take your clothes off, and we'll see about that."

"How will that…?" He tugged off the wet shirt and tossed it aside. His body did not register the cold air against his skin. "I guess I do warm when I touch your skin. You're sure?"

"Sam, stop talking and just do it. I'm freezing!"

"Very well. Slip from the coat and take off your clothes, then I'll put the coat back on and nestle you close." He shuffled out of his leather pants while she slipped from her clothing. They worked quickly, unconcerned for the other's appearance, and when she was bare, Sam curled next to her, pulling her back against his chest. The back of her wasn't wet, but she was very naked now.

Sam chided himself for noticing how hard her nipples were, tucked against his wrists, and when she pressed her bottom to his groin, he sucked in a breath at the utter pleasure of connection.

He held a naked woman against his skin. She felt fragile and smelled sweet. Vanilla and mint. *Mmm*... He inhaled.

"Jacket," she chattered.

As she turned her body to face him, Sam pulled the jacket over her shoulders and arms and coved her between the fabric and his body.

Cold, thin fingers pressed to the base of his neck. The tip of her icy nose nudged his chest. "Thank you. Shouldn't take long. To warm up."

His erection stiffened, making him uncomfortably aware of how desire worked. "I'm not doing that on purpose," he offered.

She chuckled softly. "I know. And were I warmer I might enjoy it, but right now..."

He rubbed her arms through the coat. "I'm sorry."

"You've nothing to be sorry for."

"I'm sorry. I don't understand as much about the human condition as I think I do. You may be strong on the outside, but you're delicate. So complex, yet easily felled. I should practice care around you."

"I'm a big girl. For the most part, I can take

care of myself. Just don't splash me with icy river water ever again."

"I will not. This weather is not conducive to survival. Why do you live here?"

She chuckled. "I've been asking myself that a lot lately. Not that London is much warmer, mind you. I miss my sister. I think I'm moving back next spring."

"Why not right now, to get away from the cold?"

"You forget the vampires are in Berlin. Probably I should stick around until we solve that little problem."

That she could make light of their situation further enamored him. He admired her inner strength. "It's not your responsibility to save the world, Cassandra. Even a small portion of it."

"Someone has to do it."

That made him smile. This delicate mortal was hard as steel inside. "You warming?"

"Yes, and so are you. This feels good, Sam. Your skin against mine. Sacred."

He flinched at that word. It suggested worship of something divine, or being devoted to something greater than oneself. Could she possibly feel a connection to him? The notion was too grand to consider.

Nor should it be considered. Cassandra needed protection—not his desire.

She murmured a soft, satisfied noise and nestled closer to him, her hip nudging his erection, which ached for something he could not name but he knew would require a more intimate invitation.

It consumed his thoughts. Erection. Soft skin. So close. Must touch. Must…

No, he wouldn't force anything on her. Any intimacy must be directed by her.

Sam bent his head to Cassandra's and breathed in winter's flavor. It mingled with her scent in a cool minty tease. And she slanted her head to kiss his neck, there, where he swallowed. He tensed. The touch seemed to burn into his flesh and mark him.

"Cassandra, I have to warn you—"

"I know." She pulled back and met his eyes. "This is awkward in an 'I want to get closer but I don't think it's right' kind of way, yes?"

"It is right. It feels right. I don't know anymore." Meeting her eyes, he wished he'd the ability to do a soul gaze like the witches could perform. He could scan her thoughts by placing his palm over her forehead, but he would not. It felt wrong. Intrusive. "You've pushed me beyond my understanding. I don't want to do anything wrong by you."

"You won't. I trust you." She kissed his chest, sparking a blossom of fire that he knew would remain long after they ceased to touch.

Cassandra shuffled to sit, clasping her arms across her bare breasts. The loss of her warmth against his skin was palpable, and for the first time Sam gauged the difference between the cold and the heat. And he hated it. He actually hated something.

"We should get our wet clothes on and head to the hotel," she suggested. "I'll drive."

"Good idea. And I'll search for clues back here." He touched a chain hung overhead from a steel hook. "Looks like they had plans to contain something."

Cassandra shuffled into her clothes and he followed suit, finding it not so easy to put on wet clothing as it was to take it off. Muttering about a wet wedgie, she climbed into the driver's seat and shifted the van into gear.

Pulling open a compartment on the inner van wall, Sam found a tranquilizer gun, rope and more chain. "I think they planned to hunt the nephilim, but I suspect this gun would do little but irritate the thing."

"Keep it. We can use it," she called back.

He liked the way her brain worked. Actually, he liked everything about Cassandra Stevens. Her brain, her beauty, her skin, her naked breasts, her kick-ass skills and her easy acceptance of him.

It would be tough to say goodbye to her after he won his return Above.

Chapter 10

Cassandra and Sam snuck into the Radisson Blu through a back door because their wet attire left much to be desired. They took the elevator to the third floor, which overlooked the quarter-million-gallon AquaDom, a massive fish tank in the center of the circular hotel that boasted an elevator through its center.

Coco opened the door and the two of them slapped into a tight hug. "You're here!"

It had been months since Cassandra had been in London to visit. She felt like the same Coco, and smelled like her, too. She always wore cherry perfume.

"Oh, sweetie, it's so good to hold you. You're wet?"

"We had a little run-in with the Spree. Can I

borrow some of your clothes? I didn't pack beyond a few weapons."

"Yes, take whatever from my suitcase and change right away or you'll catch a chill."

"Too late for that. Already beyond chilled." But what a way to get warm, with a naked man. "Did you track the nephilim here?"

"No, but we heard the radio reports of a creature stalking Berlin and Zane floored it to get us here."

Her sister tugged Cassandra into the small room sporting a king-size bed, television and two chairs. "I'm so sorry, Caz, I lost track of the muse. One minute she was there, the next—oh."

Coco peered around Cassandra's shoulder. She drew her tongue along her upper lip, eyes fixed on the man who filled the doorway. Coco was anything but discreet.

"Coco, this is Sam." He stepped forward to offer her sister his hand. Which she took, and stepped up to study him blatantly from head to toe.

"Sam. Nice to meet you. He's wet, too," she whispered back to her sister. Cassandra did not miss the curiously desirous tone in her sister's voice. "Where did you find this one?" Coco cooed.

Should she reveal he was a Fallen one? Probably not the best time to do so. She and her sister had never lied to each other, but a little omission of details never hurt now and then.

"Right here in Berlin," Sam offered. "I tracked your sister through the sigil."

"What?"

Cassandra winced and flashed Sam the evil eye before putting an arm around Coco, who had visibly shrunk back from Sam.

"Your sigil?"

Coco's shoulders shook, and Cassandra hated that her sister had been thrust into this nightmare when it was only she who was the muse. Coco got all the residual fallout on account she needed someone to share this with.

"That means he's a… Is he? Stand back, angel!" Infused with a sudden rush of bravado, Coco thrust up her palm, which was painted with a henna angel ward.

Sam looked away from the symbol, but wasn't thrust against a wall and didn't start to burn or even sizzle.

Coco looked at her palm. Back at the unshaken angel. "Huh. That's supposed to work a lot better than that. Oh, Cassandra! He's really…?"

"He's a Fallen one," she said, hugging her sister about the shoulders. "And put down your terrible ward. He's harmless."

Sam cleared his throat.

"Well, not harmless," she corrected with a smirk at the annoyed angel.

"To her I am harmless," he interrupted. "I am your sister's Fallen, and she is my muse. See." He twisted and tugged up the wet sweater to reveal the sigil on his hip. There upon the tanned muscle the spiral sigil sat like a beacon.

Coco's body slumped in Cassandra's arms in a dead faint. "So much for keeping secrets," she muttered.

Sam helped Cassandra lay her sister's limp body on the bed. Coco Stevens had spoken in a pale blue voice, which was weird to him that he even noticed. Normally only the muse caused the synesthetic reactions to her voice that enhanced sound by superimposing it with color. Maybe it was because the two were sisters.

Cassandra was concerned her sister had fainted; she'd never done that before, but he reassured her because he knew Cassandra needed a guarantee that her sister would be fine.

Digging through Coco's duffel, Cassandra snagged a pair of black leggings and a soft blue chenille sweater and left the room to put them on.

When the light flicked on in the bathroom, Sam heard, "Oh, look at this hair!"

He smirked. He loved her hair. It was long, dark, betwisted with curious ribbons, and it blew over her shoulders in waves. He wanted to crush it all against his face and lose himself within the luxurious depths.

He eyed the sister. Her hair was short, but as dark as Cassandra's. They had matching tiny noses, pert lips and the same soft cacao skin color. But no sigil on her thin wrist. Good for her.

Cassandra wandered back into the room, tugging down the sweater that emphasized her breasts and curvy hips.

"You two look similar," he commented.

"Good thing."

"What's your makeup?"

"My what?"

"Your features and your dark skin. You both are exotic."

"French, British and African-American. Daddy was a merchant marine, so he traveled a lot. He met my mother on an expedition to Jamaica."

"He and your mother are no longer alive?"

"Car crash sixteen years ago. On the day of their divorce."

That made Sam curious, but he sensed questions would not be appropriate.

Cassandra rubbed a palm up her opposite arm. "The last few years of their marriage were volatile. Coco and I spent a lot of time with Granny." She shrugged. "Love is dangerous."

"It shouldn't be," Sam offered. "I'm sorry for your loss." He leaned over her shoulder, sniffing.

"It's my sister's perfume."

"Smells like fruit. I like it."

"I'm not sure what we'll do for a change of clothes for you," she said.

"The leather pants are already dry." He tugged out the sodden sweater from his abdomen.

"Let's use the blow dryer."

She directed him toward the bathroom. The

main door opened and in marched a man with short, spiked blond hair, a coffee cup in hand and sporting a nasty scar from forehead, through his eye and down his cheek.

"Coco, I—oh."

Sam immediately sensed the intruder's nature and grabbed him by the throat and slammed him against the bathroom door. Coffee spattered his arms but he didn't feel the burn. His fingers crushed about the man's neck.

"Sam! Stop it!"

"He's a vampire, Cassandra."

"A what? No, I—I think he's Coco's boyfriend."

The vampire garbled nonsense words.

"Let him talk," Cassandra demanded. "Who are you?"

His jaw tensed. Sam did not like taking orders from a woman when he was trying to protect her. The man was a vampire; he smelled the subtle remnants of blood.

"Zane!" The sister flew off the bed and tugged at Sam's arm, but it was as if a gnat going after a hawk. "Let him go, you big bully! He's my boyfriend!"

The vampire dropped, wobbled and caught himself against the wall. Coffee dripped down the walls. Coco snuggled into his embrace.

Cassandra and Sam shared stunned looks. He was glad she appeared as surprised as he because, if not, the world truly had tilted on its axis.

"Coco?" Cassandra stepped beside Sam and moved his arm around her waist. She needed his support. He liked feeling needed, and drew her closer. "What's going on? Is he really a vampire?"

The vampire stretched his neck and lifted his chin defiantly, but he let Coco do the talking.

"He is." Coco gave a little lift of her tiny shoulders. "Surprised?"

Cassandra's eyebrow quirked.

"Guess we both have surprises, eh?" The sister angled a defiant stare at Cassandra.

Zane offered his hand to Cassandra. "Nice to meet you. Coco has told me a lot about you."

Cassandra shook, but Sam felt her resistance and spread a hand across her back to reassure her he was there. "Coco hasn't told me enough about you."

"It's not like you told me about your angel," Coco defended.

"*My* angel? We just met the other night. And he's not mine."

Ouch.

"The sigils don't lie," Coco argued.

"And you are avoiding the fact you've been dating a vampire for months and you didn't think it was important to tell me?"

The woman who'd been caught in a lie lifted her shoulders and gave her sister the big sad-eyes treatment. Sam suspected it wouldn't work on Cassandra. She was a tough one.

What he wanted to do was get the vampire

alone for a few moments to find out what he was up to, but he'd stand at the ready for now. Interesting, the bloodsucker had a scar. Their kind normally didn't scar.

"He killed the Fallen we tracked," Coco said. "And we're in love. So! We've better things to do than judge one another's choice in men." She angled an intense glare at Sam. Effective. He tangibly felt her forced yet curious scorn.

"I agree." Cassandra squeezed Sam about the waist, which went a way in obliterating the "he's not mine" statement. "We have to act, and fast. The nephilim is running rampant. You bring the ash?"

Zane flipped open the lid of a hard-shell suitcase and drew out a large, clear bag.

"It's in a Ziploc bag?" Cassandra accepted the bag and held it up before the window to examine it.

Controlling an outright gasp, Sam reached to touch, but retracted as if the plastic and its contents might burn him. "Is that really…?"

"Angel ash," Coco confirmed gleefully. "Zane took out a Fallen in London a few months ago, and this was left behind. But I'm sure you know all about what happens when an angel perishes on earth."

He did, but looking it straight on like this gave him a strange sense of mortality. And in a flimsy plastic bag? Sacrilege.

"I saved the feather that was left in the ash," Coco said proudly. "It was black iron."

"How does a vampire take out a Fallen one?" Sam asked the smirking vamp. "He should have made mincemeat of you."

"To be honest," Zane said, straightening and drawing on a serious demeanor, "I attribute most of it to luck. But I do have this." He lifted a chain, coiled at his hip, to display a three-pronged blade curved like a scimitar.

"That's a Sinistari blade," Sam said, utterly at a loss for further words.

Vampires were much less powerful than the slayer demons. When it came to angels and demons, vampires crept along the bottom of the food chain. They were nasty things that fed on mortals to survive. Sam felt the urge to wipe the bottom of his boot on the rug right now. Which was strange in itself.

When had he become so judgmental? First it was Raphael, and now the vampire. Was this mortal realm sinking into his psyche so quickly?

"Yeah, he wasn't using it," Zane said. "We made a deal, actually. The blade for a serious stack of chips at the blackjack table. Those demons do like to gamble. And sin. A lot."

Clever. The only way a vampire could compete with a Sinistari—lure it to sin.

"Well then, we're properly armed," Cassandra said. "We've two demon blades. Sam has one, as well."

"Not anymore." Sam wasn't going to reveal the truth in front of the vampire. "I used it on a demon, but left it in his heart."

"I thought you took it?" Cassandra asked.

"No," he hurriedly provided. No sense in admitting Raphael had taken it away from him as if a favorite toy being removed from a naughty child. And yet the lie served another plunge into mortal depravity. "But I do have this." He tapped his hip.

"Yes, he's got a halo."

"So do we!" Coco tugged out a halo from the suitcase.

The weaponry and knowledge this group had of Fallen and Sinistari blew Sam away. But then he should expect nothing less from Cassandra's sister. The entire Stevens clan, actually. That Granny Stevens—he sure would have liked to meet her.

The sister offered him the halo to inspect but he politely refused. He didn't want to touch another Fallen's halo. "The weapon is ineffective in a mortal's hands."

"She's discovered that," Zane said, with a secretive wink to Coco. "Doesn't do the boomerang return to a mortal."

"But it does give hope!" Coco enthusiastically chimed. "I love holding it." She clasped the halo to her chest. The pixie's brown eyes gleamed with adventure untold.

"So let's get to it," Cassandra said.

"She's not coming," Sam said. He caught Coco's frown and it didn't feel right in his chest. What was with these women and their ability to make his glass heart ache?

"I agree." Cassandra snatched the halo from her sister's hand. "It's too dangerous, Coco. You know you're not trained for this."

The sister was about to protest, but she sighed, stuck out her bottom lip for an effective pout and conceded with a nod. "Of course, you should hold the halo. Seeing that you do have a Fallen angel who wants to do you serious harm standing right next to you."

"I do not—"

"I'm holding the halo so you don't feel you can come along with us," Cassandra countered over Sam's reply.

"Fine. But Zane can go."

"We don't need fang boy to stumble over," Sam said.

"Fang boy?" the vampire said incredulously.

"Cassandra and I know what we're doing. We'll take the ash—"

"But he's a ninja!" Coco protested.

Sam tilted his head at the vampire, who offered a sheepish shrug. "He doesn't look Japanese."

"I've the skills and the know-how to track both the Fallen and vampires," Zane said.

"Why would you help us track vampires?"

"I don't like what the Anakim are up to. Harming muses? That's not my bloody scene. I want to stop what's happening as much as Coco and Cassandra do."

"You two should discuss this." Cassandra pushed Sam toward the door. "I need to talk to Coco alone."

"You want me to leave with the vampire?" Sam cast the vamp a glare. Where was the stake Cassandra owned?

"Please." Her fingers to his chin softened Sam's stoic need to remain in charge and dismissive of the vamp. "Just go down to the bar. It's right below the AquaDom. You two can share a pint and stare at the fishes. I'll be right there."

Sam kissed Cassandra's fingers and did not miss her sister's gasp of surprise. Her let go of her hand with reluctance.

He had wanted a few minutes alone with the bloodsucker. "Fine. Come on, vampire, I'll buy you a drink."

"As long as it's mortal," Zane said.

Sam gaped. As did Cassandra.

"Just kidding. A vampire joke, eh?" The vampire straightened his smirk. "You have cash? One thing I know about you Fallen sorts, you don't have two pence to your name. I'll buy. See you in a bit, Coco. Nice to meet you, Cassandra. Gotta go make some face time with the winged one."

Sam rolled his eyes. This one was going to try his every mortal nerve.

"Oh, Coco. A vampire?" Cassandra searched Coco's dark brown eyes, twins to her own, but couldn't find a reason to admonish. Though she'd like to punch her in the arm, not hard, but to show her disapproval. "Why didn't you tell me?"

Her sister plopped onto the bed and leaned back on her palms. "I figured the last thing you needed right now was to hear I'm in love with a vampire."

"Love? Oh, my God." She sat next to Coco, clasping for the rosary under her sweater.

Where had she gone wrong? All these years of training and taking her sister along for the ride... had she neglected to teach her what a real relationship was all about?

Like you know, Cassandra.

Coco said, "I adore him. He adores me. He spoils me, Caz. Always doing things for me, and we spend entire weekends making love."

"Sounds blissful." And creepy. "What's with the scar? I thought vampires healed instantly?"

"Oh, not instantly, but pretty fast. It's from the demon blade. He didn't give the demon chips in Las Vegas. That's just his story. In truth, he fought him for the blade."

"Doesn't sound smart."

"Zane is incredibly smart. He used to be a spy for the SRS before a vampire bit him."

"Poor guy. So he hasn't always been a vampire."

"Nope. And he wouldn't have asked for it if offered."

"But I just met him so I don't know if he is

trustworthy. Does he bite you? Oh, no, did he change you?"

"Don't be silly. The last thing Zane wants is to make me a vampire. I love him for that." She teased the collar of her turtleneck with a forefinger. "And he only bites me about once a week, and never takes too much. It's so incredible, Caz. You would never imagine it could be so good."

Hell. Her sister was a vampire's blood bitch.

"I think I'll stick with not putting that image into my brain, if you don't mind. As long as he treats you right. And you trust him? You're sure he's not on the vampires' side?"

"Positive. He's former tribe Anakim—"

"What? But they're the ones we're after!"

"Don't worry. He genuinely hates that they are capturing muses and trying to mate them with Fallen. Zane is kind and he wants to make it stop. He's a good man to have on our side."

"Don't you mean a good vampire?"

"Don't judge, Caz. It's not as if I woke one morning and said to myself, 'Hey, I think I'm going to find myself a vampire lover today.' I met him the night I went looking for the halo, *for you,* if you recall. He rescued me from the big bad angel."

"And now you feel you owe him?"

"Don't be absurd. Just because you've never been in love doesn't mean it can't possibly happen to me. You're jealous."

Cassandra gaped, but shut her mouth abruptly.

Was she jealous? Neither of the sisters had ever been lucky in love. Coco had a quirky personality that most men read incorrectly as eccentric. Cassandra had always been too focused on her work. They'd ignored the prom to go to martial arts class, and dates had been few and far between ever since.

"I'm sorry, Coco. If you trust him, then I do. And if you love him, then I'm happy for you."

They hugged and Coco squeezed her extra hard, which felt great. Come spring, she was definitely moving back to London. She could create her jewelry anywhere, and yet, be happier back at home near her sister.

"So tell me about your angel. I can't believe it. After all Granny taught us…"

Cassandra lay back on the bed, and her sister joined her. The two stared up at the ceiling, hands clasped. It had been too long since they'd taken the time to be next to each other and share their lives and secrets.

Way to start the convo with the big secret, she thought of her sister. But then, she had her own.

"Sam is an outlaw Fallen."

"An outlaw? Oh, that sounds sexy. He's got a halo strapped at his hip like some kind of gunslinger, and he hunts Fallen angels. That's so freakin' romantic."

"When did you become a romantic?"

"I've always been one. You were too focused on kicking butt for romance. Too bad, too. My sister finally gets some lovin' and now she has the apocalypse to deal with."

"It's not the apocalypse, just a small crisis."

They both laughed because if they shared one thing in common regarding men, it was a self-destructive desire for the bad boy. "Sam abhors the Fallen who believe they've a right to abuse their muses any way they see fit."

"Like raping them because that's why they Fell?"

"Yes. He would never harm me, Coco."

"I believe you. You may not have had a lot of boyfriends, but you have a keen instinct about people. That's why I usually vet my boyfriends through you before the second date."

"You have dated some real tossers."

"But, thanks to you, not for long. So, what's sex with an angel like?"

"Coco!"

"Like we've never compared notes before." She rolled onto her side and caught her head against her fist. "Dish, and I'll tell you about vampire sex."

She wasn't at all interested in sex with fangs. "We haven't had sex."

"Why not? Can't he? Is it true about angels having no sexual parts?"

"No, that's not true." And she had the proof thanks to their snuggle in the van. Very nice parts.

"Oh, right. Only when he's in half form? But

then, wouldn't he feel the compulsion Granny told
us about? Oh, Caz, I'm worried about you getting too close to this Fallen. He's the one. Your
destined Fallen."

She grabbed the halo from the end of the bed
and put it around Cassandra's wrist. "You keep
this close. No matter how much you trust him."

"Don't worry, Coco. I trust Sam. To a degree."
She took the halo in both hands and flipped it
around before her. "He can have sex in the human
form he is in now. We've kissed and cuddled, and,
to tell the truth, I want him. I really want him."

"Who wouldn't? The dude is ripped and handsome like a movie star."

"You don't need to point that out to me. And
he wants me, too, but it hasn't felt right yet. I'm
learning to trust a man I've been taught wants to
get me pregnant with a monster. You know?"

"I can't imagine how it must feel to have him
be kind to you instead of mean. Poor Ophelia. Her
Fallen was not kind to her. And now she's dead. I
can't get the image of those tiny, bloody footprints
from my brain."

Cassandra curled against her sister's body and
hugged her. "We'll stop it all," she said, not feeling the truth in those words.

Because really? Who could stop something so
innate and powerful as an angel wanting to mate
with its intended muse? And the only way to stop
the nephilim from being born would be to kill

the muse before she had given birth. A cruelty of which Cassandra could not conceive.

There were yet too many angels who could be summoned to earth. And if the vampires had names and sigils, they could bring them, one after another, to this land.

Of course, they couldn't have names and sigils because she still had the book. Maybe. Why hadn't she checked the bathroom when she'd had a chance? It was where she'd hidden the original book.

"Let me go with Zane," Coco said. "He's trying to get hold of a Council member, another vampire, who lives in Berlin. The more people we have tracking the vampires, the better. I've got the same martial skills as you do."

"What is the Council?"

"It's a group of vampires, witches, werewolves, faeries and so on that kind of oversee the paranormals on earth."

"Whew! You've surpassed my knowledge on all things not of this realm."

"I don't know much beyond that. Zane gave me the fast and dirty version. He doesn't want me to get too enmeshed in the paranormal. I love him for that. Anyway, this guy—Ivan, I think is his name—might have connections to other vamps in the area, and maybe even the Anakim."

"Then I'll leave that to Zane. Sam and I have to find the nephilim."

"Please can I come along, Caz? Zane will protect me."

"Protecting you will distract him from the task."

"But the halo. I know how to use it."

"I thought you wanted me to hold it? Besides, it's only an effective weapon in the hands of an angel. If you slashed with it, it would merely cut, never cause death."

"I know. I forget these ooky-spooky things have weird rules that don't always apply to mortals."

"Ooky-spooky? Would your boyfriend fall under that category?"

"Sometimes. But don't tell him that."

"I won't."

"His scar is so sexy."

Cassandra smiled at her sister's admiring tone. She really was head over heels. What an awesome place to be. She wanted to talk about a man in that same way.

She already thought about Sam that way. *Hmm...*

"Do you have a laptop?"

"Yes, why?"

"You can be our command central. Can you set up a city map and keep us all in contact through cell phones?"

"I should be able to." She sighed. "I'll give my phone to Zane. But you know I'll be worrying a hole through the rug about you."

"You wouldn't be Rococo Stevens if you weren't worried about something, sweetie. Do you think they're getting along, our boys?"

"Doubt it. Zane has an arrogant streak a mile thick."

"Yeah? Well, Sam wears a divine attitude so cocky it'll knock your man's streak down to size."

"Good thing we brought them together in a public venue."

"Oh, yeah."

Chapter 11

Sam had accepted the pint the vampire bought for him, and was already on his second. It was much stronger than the beer he'd consumed earlier with Cassandra. He liked this stuff. It went down smooth, and it warmed his chest and gut. And for a guy who didn't normally feel cold and heat (unless it was Cassandra's skin) he enjoyed the experience.

The vampire tilted his beer to Sam. "Just so you know, instinctively, I want to slay you instead of share a drink with you."

"Vampire, I could break your neck before you notice me flinch." Sam burped, which was so new to him that he chuckled and did it again.

"True that." Zane sucked down the entire beer.

"But a broken neck won't kill me. Just piss me off and make me want to kill you all the more."

"Then I'll be sure to use the fancy spring-action stake Cassandra owns."

"She has one of those? Brilliant! Those things are hard to come by. I thought the Order of the Stake kept a tight grip on them."

"And I once thought the Sinistari would never give up their blade, come death."

Zane stroked the thick scar on his cheek. "It's a long story. Suffice, the deal was mutual."

"Mutual, my arse." Another burp. Sam smirked. "Heh. This beer is awesome."

"And you are getting wasted on your second pint. Slow down, bloke, we've business to hand. Although...those fish are bloody fabulous." The vampire gazed up at the massive aquarium, which served as the centerpiece of the hotel. The bar curved around the base of the tank. "You ever see a blue one like that before?"

"Yes, I've seen all animals across the world." Sam ignored the fish in favor of watching the condensation trickling down the side of his glass mug. He blinked. His vision blurred. Odd. "So, business. Like following the pretty little muse all over this snowy wonderland as she traipses after the bad guys. What is it with that woman? How do mortal men do it?"

"I was once mortal. And I am a man."

Sam grunted. "That's stretching things. You're a bloodsucking longtooth. Heh." He liked the oath, and while normally he wouldn't use slang, the beer was working a number on his inhibitions. "I mean, how do men handle women? They're all tough and sexy and walk around in those tight shirts that show off their bouncing breasts."

He squeezed the air before him, imagining Cassandra's soft pair in hand.

"She's so soft. I want to touch her. All the time! But how to do that without being lewd? And what's with calling me buddy all the time? My name is Samandiriel. Though she shortens it to Sam. I like that. It's like I'm hers. And she's mine."

"Oh, bloke, you got it bad."

"Got what? Have I picked up some mortal disease? Because let me tell you, my head is spinning and all I can see is Cassandra, Cassandra, Cassandra. And all that hair. Why are there ribbons in it? They are pretty, but I don't know how they can stay in there. Hey, I haven't seen that orange one before. Nice."

The vampire chuckled. "Fish. Who'da thought?"

Sam lifted his mug and viewed the tank through the bottom of the thick glass. "My head is moving, but my body isn't. Is that normal?"

"Your head is bloody spinning because you can't hold your liquor, angel."

"No, it's because of Cassandra. Cassandra. Cassandra. Cassandra."

"You can't stop thinking about the pretty bird because you're in love."

"Love?" Sam slapped the counter and gestured the bartender refill his mug. "That's ridiculous. Angels don't know how to love."

"Wait a minute." The vampire turned to face him, and Sam did not like the close proximity, but when he tried to move away, he only swayed and a silly grin clapped onto his face. "I thought you blokes were all about the love. Demons can't love and angels can't hate. What's up with that?"

"Oh, we exude love and all that crap. But to feel it?" Sam scoffed and reached for the fresh pint. "Bunch of bollocks. We wouldn't know love if it hit us smack in the face."

"I wager Cassandra hasn't hit you in the face yet, but I do know you've received the blow to your heart. You are silly over that girl."

"Men don't do silly. I am a man. We do macho and all that alpha stuff."

"Right, and that works for show, but when you're alone with your woman and she's snuggled in your arms, the best thing in the world is to breathe her in and hold her tight."

"So true." Sam stared at the massive aquarium. An elevator ran through the middle. He could see people in the glass elevator pointing at the sea life. "I'd need a soul to be able to love, though. Don't have one of those. Too costly."

"How much are souls going for these days?"

"Sacrifice," he slurred. "It would require staying here on earth. I want to go home."

"Ah. I imagine Above is a might nicer place than here on earth. That is, if you're into pearly gates and heavenly choruses."

"There's an entire tier of angels that only sing His praises," Sam said. "They sing all colors of creation. You know Cassandra's voice is violet and pink? And your Coco's is blue."

"Is that so? I think you'd better stop with that pint, mate. You're not a Sinistari. They're the ones who like to indulge."

"You know it. I am an angel. Hear me roar."

"Yeah, bloke, don't do that angel roary thing in here."

Sam stopped before emitting his cry of myriad tongues. "Why not?"

"We paranormal sorts gotta remain inconspicuous, right?"

"Gotcha."

They stared at the fish tank again. The dizzy wave in Sam's head began to lessen, and images of the colored fish grew sharper. One was the exact color of Cassandra's voice. Nice.

"So, does love make your chest warm and tingly?"

The vampire clapped a hand across Sam's shoulders, which he didn't mind so much now. "It does. It also makes you think about the girl all the time."

"And what I want to do with her?"

"You bet."

"Like touch her," Sam said in a dreamy tone.

"Oh, yes, women are soft and curvy, and I like when they squirm if you touch them just so."

"Right. Like when you touch her below the ear."

"Or glide your tongue behind her knees."

Sam nodded. "That sounds awesome. The knee, eh?"

The vampire agreed. "Try it sometime. Drives them silly."

"Yeah, but I've the angelkiss. Can't lick my girl or I'll make her itch."

"Oh, right. Forgot about that. But you can kiss her?"

"Those kisses." Sam sighed. "They make my glass heart pulse."

"Seriously?"

"No, but it feels that way. Like a phantom pulse."

"Cool."

They paused to observe the fish. Around them, morticians from the conference were chattering in a various languages.

"So look at us, chatting over a pint," Zane said. "Getting to know more about each other than I care to stomach. Who'da thought angels could get drunk?"

"I'm not drunk."

"Right." The vamp shook a dismissive hand at the bartender and Sam inspected the bottom of his empty mug. "Tell me, Sam, why should I believe you want to kill the vampires to stop something you Fell to do?"

"Because I said so." Straightening, Sam thrust back his shoulders. He'd assimilated the alcohol and his system was beginning to come out of the intoxicating effects. He didn't like having to explain himself to the longtooth. And he would not. "What about you? You're Anakim. The very tribe we're after."

"Former Anakim, and brimming with secrets from the fold."

"If you know so much, where are they?"

"They'll be underground because that is Antonio del Gado's MO. Close to the center of the city because it's easier to dispatch drones from a central location and the mortal energy at the center is strongest. He needs the energy to summon the Fallen."

"He summoned me."

"And he won't stop until he's summoned as many as he's names for."

"I dispatched Nazariah already. Does he have many names?"

"No. Probably less than three or four. So there's you, the dead angel, and I know of one other that he summoned to London, because I slew that wanker. But I've been told there is a book of sigils they've obtained from a muse in Paris."

"But if they've no names, the sigils are useless."

"There's also a book of names that matches them to the sigils. Cassandra owns it. You aware of that?"

Now clear and alert, Sam eyed the vampire warily.

"You do know about it. Is it in a safe place?"

"She's got it on her computer. I had her erase all the files."

"But she's still got the original book. She'd never dispose of that. Coco says it's like her bible, along with a grimoire her grandmother gave her."

"Is that so?"

Where had she hidden it? Must be in her home somewhere. If she was smart, she'd have stashed it in a security box at a bank.

Cassandra was incredibly smart. But would she part with an item she blasphemously considered her bible?

He should return to her house and tear it apart. Because he needed the book to return Above, but also because the vampires likely had the same plan. "You think del Gado will go after the book?"

"If he's not already got it in hand? Definitely."

A cell phone rang and the vampire answered. "Ivan, yes? Good to hear from you." He put up a finger for Sam to wait, and that aggravated him. Mortals had no sense of politeness regarding their technological devices. They had been having a conversation.

"You've a bead on where Anakim may be hiding?"

On the other hand, this sounded interesting.

"How many vampires in Berlin do you think will help us?…Yes, I can meet you, but this is rather urgent. You know there's a nephilim terrorizing the city?…Yes, you're right. Are you close to the Radisson Blu?…Fine, I'll wait here for you."

He snapped the phone shut. "That was Ivan Drake. He's a big shot in the vampire community and serves on the Council, which oversees all the paranormals in this mortal realm. He may have helpful information regarding tribe Anakim."

"You go, vampire." Sam clapped him across the shoulders as the vampire had previously done to him. A weird male bonding thing, but it seemed to offer some reassurance. "I have something I need to do."

He stood and patted his pockets, but it was just a gesture—he didn't have money. "You said you were buying? Hold off on sending out the troops after Anakim until I return. We need to orchestrate our every move."

"If that is true, why the hell are you taking off on your own? Are you listening to me? Bollocks!"

Sam smiled at the outburst. He did favor the Brit's tendency to spout colorful oaths.

"He had something to do?" Cassandra paced the floor before the bed in the hotel room. The vampire shrugged. "What were you two talking about before he left?"

"Er, you don't need to know all of it."

"What? Are you hiding something from me?" She tugged out the titanium stake from her backpack and smacked it in her palm.

"Caz!"

The sisters exchanged admonishing glares.

"Fine." Cassandra tucked the stake behind her back. "But he's holding out on me."

"Not at all, love. It was just guy talk. We put back a few pints and watched the fishies. Oh, and we chatted about how the vampires have been summoning the Fallen."

"And that made him leave?"

Zane shrugged. "Said he'd be right back. It'll give Coco time to plot out our moves on the map." He leaned in to kiss Coco on the forehead. "Right, love?"

"I've entered the coordinates for the nephilim sighting, as well as all the places Caz said they've seen Fallen," Coco said, clicking away at her laptop. "When's the other vampire going to arrive?"

"Ivan should be here any minute now."

"I'm going down to get a drink," Cassandra said. Then she added, because she didn't want them to suspect, "Can I bring something up for you, Coco?"

"Wine. White." She focused on the computer screen. "A bottle!"

Cassandra closed the door, wishing she could

have taken her coat, but she hadn't wanted them to suspect. She took the elevator to the lobby, used the phone in the bar and called a cab.

She suspected where Sam had gone, and he had a whole lot of explaining to do.

Chapter 12

Sam hastened up the stairs, and when he sensed the malevolent presence in the vicinity of Cassandra's loft, he leaped, taking an entire run of stairs in a bound.

Her door hung twisted from the top hinge, and amidst the catastrophe of her scattered furniture and personal items, six vampires snooped, tossed and destroyed. At sight of him, the living room window shattered and one of them escaped.

Vacillating on whether to go after the one who'd alighted or take on the others, Sam decided the scared one could go. He liked a challenge.

The next vampire sighted him just as Sam reached to shove his fingers into its chest. The heart pulsed once in his hand. He tore it out and flung it away. The vamp dropped silently.

Two vampires charged him. Another aimed a pistol Sam figured he'd found in Cassandra's arsenal, and fired.

The bullet skimmed his skull, and cool blood drooled over his eyelid. He blinked at it, and lost focus on the brigade that pummeled him backward to the floor. Two vamps went at him, punching ribs and kicking his all-feeling kidneys. He did not like the pain that accompanied this mortal form.

With a gesture, Sam flung off his attackers from his body. One vamp collided with the wall skull-first, and stuck there in the hole formed by his head, the other vampire smashed into the one who'd shot him.

The vampire missing a heart turned over and went on all fours. He searched the pooled blood for his heart. With enemies who weren't much for death, this battle was going to prove a challenge.

The vampire, tossed carelessly toward her while she stood in the doorway, gaped at the sight of her, then flashed a fangy grin as his body collided with hers. She pushed him off, yet he wasn't in the mood for dancing. Growling, he lunged for her.

Cassandra had not come unprepared. She had just enough time to position the stake, and with a squeeze, the vamp's lascivious smirk disappeared into a cloud of dark ash.

Sputtering out the nasty ash, Cassandra assessed the situation before rushing into chaos. One pile of vamp ash in the kitchen. One in the doorway behind her. The living room window was smashed, likely where they'd entered. But that didn't explain the busted door.

Currently, three vampires were attached to Sam. One bared his fangs and bit into Sam's arm.

"Stupid bloodsucker," she muttered and walked in, yet she did not feel the need to go all kick-ass. Sam obviously had the situation under control.

The vamp who'd taken a bite looked up at her, blue blood drooling over his lips, which began to bubble. He slapped a hand to his mouth and jumped off Sam, leaving only two vampires attached to the angel. His whole body began to jitter, skin bubbling and veins expanding.

Cassandra stepped back and turned her head away to avoid what she expected to be—

The vampire burst into not ash but fleshy bits.

—a big freakin' explosion. Angel blood was never safe for vampire consumption.

"I will never get this mess cleaned up," she said, looking over the gray velvet couch, stained with vampire bits and blood. "You need any help, Sam?"

A vampire flew and landed on the couch on his spine, arching backward in a painful crunch that would have broken a mortal's back.

Sam swung the halo across a vampire's throat, reducing his opponent to ash. "Oh, hey, Cassandra. Just making some new friends."

"I can see that."

"I've got everything under control."

"So I should have saved the one you tossed at me for you?"

"Did I toss a vampire at you? That was rude."

He jumped up, and the couch vampire made a lunge for him. Swinging out the halo, without even looking, Sam managed to catch the blood-sucker across the chest, cutting deep. Cassandra ducked to avoid the spatter.

"Sorry," he said. "I'll make sure the place is cleaned up."

"By who? Crime-scene cleaners? This is a nightmare."

"But all the vamps are dead."

"And the reason they were here is also dead with them."

"Actually, I think they were looking for your book."

"The book?"

"The one with the sigils and names."

She gaped at him. "I told you it was all on the computer."

"You wouldn't have destroyed the original," he said, confident of his knowledge.

Granny Stevens had written down everything inside that journal and Cassandra had drawn the sigils she'd dreamed with the correlating names. It was irreplaceable. And she didn't have it all scanned onto the hard drive. Of course, she hadn't destroyed it.

"You're welcome," Sam offered. The angel looked over the destruction and offered her a wince. "I'm sorry about the mess."

"How did you know they'd be here? You were just in the bar with Zane. He said you had too much to drink. I don't understand?"

"Call it a hunch."

A tangible fizzle occurred and, as expected, all blood in the room ashed, except the blue puddles, which were not vampire.

It freaked Cassandra so much she wanted to scream at the insanity of her life. But with a few deep breaths, she managed to keep it together. Now was no time to fall apart. The enemies were dead; that should give her some comfort.

"I suspect Antonio sent his minions after the book so he could summon more Fallen," Sam said. "Zane said he'd only a few names matched to sigils. Seems like they've summoned all they can without your book."

She nodded, scanning the floor, not at all relieved the crime scene had now turned into an ash convention.

"Are you okay?" He reached to touch her face, but she flinched and walked into the kitchen to get a glass of water.

She downed a glass then leaned over the sink. For just a moment, she wanted the world to stop. *Hey, Cassandra, it's all a fairy tale your grandmother once told you. Angels aren't real, nor are vampires.*

But it was real. And she was not one to tuck her head down and hide.

"What aren't you telling me, Sam?"

"Zane mentioned the book, and I wanted to get my hands on it."

"For what purpose?"

"Suffice, it will be safer in my hands than the vampires'."

She avoided looking down the hallway toward the bathroom. "It's not in your hands, and it's not going to be, either."

He nodded, accepting but, she sensed, not forgetting. He wanted the book. For what reason? The sigils and names could only call forth more Fallen. Did he want to bring them here himself to then slay them? It didn't make sense, because if he did not summon them, they remained imprisoned in the Ninth Void—the best place for the Fallen.

Just when she'd decided trusting Sam was a good thing, now he changed the rules of the game.

"The vampires had to have come in a vehicle," Sam said.

"There was a black van out front when I arrived," she said. "Let's check it out."

The black van pulled out of Cassandra's parking lot, but skidded on ice. Sam gripped her hand and began to run, and they were able to keep up for about a block. Apparently the vampire who had jumped through the window had been waiting around to see if his buddies returned.

"We need a car!" she called.

Sam stopped abruptly, and she slipped trying to stop. He turned and caught her as she slid into his embrace, her breath huffing out in clouds. "Caught ya."

Oh, yes, he had. Caught against his hard muscles, sheltered by his overwhelming presence. And not minding at all. She could lay her head against his shoulder and cry after all she'd been through, but she resisted the urge to fall apart.

Sam had wanted the book as much as the vampires had. She should have checked to be sure it was still safe.

"We can't do this on foot," he said.

"The van is long gone," she said. "But if you do your superspeedy run thing, you should be able to track him."

He nodded and took off, but stopped and turned to her. "I'll be right back. I won't leave you alone."

She snapped him a salute and told him to get going. It tugged at her heart to watch him run away. Taking all that awesomeness of man away from her. He was her only protection from the dark forces messing up her life.

"What are you thinking?" Shaking her head and slapping her arms across her chest, Cassandra turned and stalked toward her building. "He's better off without me."

But she knew now she was not better off without him. She needed the supernaturally talented

Fallen angel. He was fighting on her side. And with crazy vampires running rampant, and a freakin' nephilim stalking the city, she had to admit she didn't feel so confident anymore.

Had she grown into a false sense of confidence over the years? Training, learning, preparing for some cataclysmic event. Never actually having to put those skills to use against real danger. Had she ever truly believed it would come true?

A part of her had always hoped it would not manifest in reality, that Granny had been a little off her rocker. Because monsters weren't real and belonged underneath the bed, not on top of the bed trying to get into a girl's business. Those were the worst kind of monsters. The ones who would harm women for their own pleasure.

Stopping before the building, Cassandra scanned over her third-floor window. Dark, it did not reveal the havoc inside. Dead vampires everywhere, which were now only dark ash, but she wasn't sure about the blue blood spattering the white walls.

She winced, not wanting to go up but feeling a nudge inside her to man up, be a big girl and fight the good fight.

Problem was, the good fight was tough. It hurt. And it scared her.

But she had to stay strong for Coco. And for all the muses in the world who weren't aware what the funny little brown mark on their arms meant.

For Ophelia, who had discovered too late what her sigil meant.

"For yourself," she whispered, stroking the sigil that did not flash blue right now because Sam was too far away. "You're not going to let them defeat you. You're twenty-seven freakin' years old. You haven't even begun to live."

If taking out a few monsters who stood in the way of her enjoying life was required, then so be it.

Confidence giddied through her veins. Marching up the snowy front steps, Cassandra ran through the foyer and up the stairs. The iron railing hugging the last flight was bent, and she couldn't force it back into shape. The landlord would never believe the truth—that a demon had landed on it while battling with an angel.

"Wonder why none of my neighbors heard the fight? Does no one notice when vampires break in and loot someone's place?"

It was early evening. Most on her floor were still at work or just driving into rush-hour traffic now.

As she stepped around the hanging door into the loft, her cell phone rang. "Coco? You and Zane have any luck?"

"We did. Ivan Drake had information about a new influx of vampires within the last few days. We're going to look for them later, but in the mean time I just got a call from Lucinda, the muse from Ireland."

"Hell, I forgot about the others. They were all flying here together."

"Yep, and their flight just landed. Zane and I are headed to the airport to put them back on flights."

"Good thinking. Send them anywhere but here, Coco."

"Will do. While we're at it, Ivan said the Anakim may be found south of the Waldfriedhof."

"That's a cemetery."

"It is? That makes no sense. Zane said vamps aren't about the gruesome and coffins and things."

"Yeah, but maybe those vampires are stuck in the dark like tribe Anakim are. We'll check it out. You get those muses safe. Talk soon. Bye."

She swept a look over the havoc in her flat. Holes were punched in the wall, and how had those ceiling tiles gotten smashed out? "I'll definitely lose my deposit for this."

Deciding she could not return to this tattered remnant of her life until after the vampires had been stopped, Cassandra made quick reconnaissance, gathering a change of clothes, the Taser, her bank info and the flash drive with all her important financial records. Granny's grimoire and...

Cassandra's heart dropped. The book of sigils and names was not behind the tiles beside the toilet tank, because that wall had been smashed open, likely by a vampire. That was not good on too many levels to imagine.

Hooking her backpack over a shoulder, she walked into the bedroom to see if she might have missed anything. Her eyes swept over the silver angel.

The wings were cool under her fingers, yet the sculpture warmed the more she maintained contact with the silver. "Just like Sam."

Maybe that was the key? She needed to stay close to him, keep their connection strong, to maintain his humanity and keep him grounded in this mortal realm.

Maybe then he'd give up the idea of returning Above.

Because you want him to stay. "Worth a try."

She sped down the stairs and met Sam at the front door.

"I've found them," he said.

"Waldfriedhof?"

"I didn't get the address, but there is a graveyard nearby."

"That's the place Coco verified with the vampire Council member."

"I can lead you there."

"They have the book, Sam. I'd hidden the book in the bathroom...."

"We'll get it back. It's imperative. Come on."

Chapter 13

The cemetery Coco had directed them to was surrounded by a dense urban forest. They decided to park a ways off so as not to draw attention to their arrival. And Sam wanted to reconnoiter for guards along the way. He said he could home in on the vampires' vibrations.

Cassandra plunged through the slushy snow after him. "How does that work? You homing in on vampires. You got super vampire senses? I thought vampires couldn't tell if they were standing next to another vampire unless they actually touched?"

"I can sense them, as I sensed your sister's boyfriend. It's like their shimmer when touching."

"Okay, but don't call Zane that, please. I'm

having a little trouble wrapping my head around Coco dating a man who bites her."

"He bites her?"

She winced. "Yes."

"Kinky."

"And you know about kink, Mr. I've Only Been on Earth A Few Days?"

"I spent an hour in Las Vegas. I learned a lot there."

She caught his smile, laced with sly memory. "A whole hour? And you must have spent a night walking the world, so that's about six to eight hours."

"Six, exactly."

And he'd spent a sixth of that time in Vegas? Wow. "Learn any gambling tricks?"

"No, but do you know the showgirls walk around without anything to cover their breasts?"

"It is common knowledge. Did you enjoy that? Wait. Stupid question. Let's move along, shall we? And you keep your showgirl fantasies to yourself."

"Yes, let's hurry. And I promise to keep my fetish for rhinestone-studded panties a secret. Oops."

Shaking her head and laughing at his coy flirtations, Cassandra tracked close behind Sam.

He paused as they gained the train tracks hugging the urban forest that surrounded the cemetery. Heeling the track with his heavy boot, Sam closed his eyes and she thought he might be feeling for vibrations. She wasn't sure what his angel powers were, beyond strength, but she had seen him move a vampire without touching him, so he had some kind of telepathic judo going on.

Tugging her hand, Sam led her down the tracks.

"We should have split up the angel ash," she said, "in case we get separated and they run into the nephilim before we do." Coco had commandeered the Ziploc bag with the ash. "I sure hope she brought it along."

"If not, her vampire will protect her."

"Yes, but they both seemed to have forgotten Coco was supposed to stay out of this."

Sam stopped center of the tracks and pulled her into a surprising embrace. "Zane does love her."

"How do you know? Did he tell you when you two were down at the bar? Because vampires lie."

"Everyone lies, Cassandra. And it wasn't that he told me, but I heard it in his voice. He adores your sister. And much as I'd prefer to stake him for the sake of taking out a vampire, I know he's a good man."

"But he's from the very tribe who are attempting to capture the nephilim."

"Which has its advantages. Trust me, I know your sister is in good hands."

He kissed her then, and his lips quickly warmed against hers, and when she wanted to slip her hands under his shirt and melt against him, he nudged her onward.

Sighing, Cassandra wished her life would have tossed her this eligible bachelor before the world decided to end. And in human form, pretty please, one with a soul.

Antonio del Gado closed the red leather-bound journal and patted it reverently. He'd summoned another Fallen, and had plans to summon yet another after confirmation was received on the location of this one. He couldn't go about willy-nilly bringing Fallen to earth unless his scout marked their landing. Otherwise the summons would be worthless.

Such a coup Westing had found this book. He deserved a promotion, and the man would have it. But what could he give a vampire who could already walk in the sun?

Perhaps a delicious blood slave. Or a witch. Yes! A witch from whom he could drain her magic and gain power. He'd see to locating one as Westing's reward.

And when finally Antonio could walk in the light, he would take a witch for himself and gain earth, air and water magic. After centuries of shrinking from his enemies as the sun slashed the horizon, he would never again cower.

"There's movement in the north, boss." Bruce opened the laptop. "I think it's the Fallen you just summoned. One of my men was able to tag him with the GPS gun Rovonsky made. Look at it move."

The map on the screen showed a green dot moving from Germany to France, and toward Spain. That quickly.

"He's walking the world," Bruce confirmed. "We'll nab him when he circles back to Berlin."

"How do you know it'll circle back?"

"I don't, but there are a bunch of muses on their way here. He'll find them sooner or later."

"Good work, Westing. Now go out and see if you can tag Samandiriel. Or the muse. One or the other, and then we'll be able to use them both."

"I'm on it, boss."

Even through her coat, Cassandra felt Sam's hand on her shoulder as they walked side by side. He was always initially cold, but took on her heat quickly. She liked to think they made their own heat, and that one needed the other to flame such a fire.

Silly romantic stuff.

Coco had been right. Finally a handsome, interesting man lands—literally—in her life and she has to worry about saving the world instead of batting her lashes at him.

"I like you, Cassandra."

Startled by the strange, breathy confession, she did a double take on the angel's expression. Face forward, his eyes briefly darted to hers, and a boyish grin captured his sexy mouth.

"Is that okay to say?"

And here she'd been denying all the romantic

silliness jiggling about in her brain. Very well, who said a girl couldn't fight some monsters and have a little fun at the same time?

"Yes, it is," she offered decidedly. "Do you know what like is?"

"Is it me wanting to be with you all the time, and when we're not speaking, always wondering what you've got going on in your mind? And me unable to see any other woman when you are near me because your beauty distracts me?"

Wow. "Uh, sure. That sounds like like."

"Do you like me, Cassandra?"

"What, no bunny?" The wind swept up snow-flakes in a glitter before them. "I do. I wonder what goes on inside your head and want to know more about you. And I dreamed you before you came to me, so what's that all about? I've never believed in destiny, but maybe there's something to it. And you are incredible to look at."

"I also admire your smart mouth."

"Do you now?"

"It's sexy. Better than a Las Vegas showgirl's rhinestone-encrusted—"

"All right, buddy. Just know I don't do rhine-stones, so that's a fantasy you're going to have to keep close to the vest."

"You outshine the cheap paste jewel. You could outshine silver."

"I'm not sure about that."

"I am. I like the ribbons in your hair, too. How do they stay in there?"

"They're woven in. You really like them? They're something that sets me apart from other women, but some guys assume I'm too edgy."

"I like edgy. That means you know how to kick a vampire's arse, right?"

She chuckled. "Oh, yeah. But my skills tend to threaten men who want a frilly little woman who looks sexy all the time and wouldn't dream of showing them up in a fistfight."

"I can relate to those men."

"You can?" Here she'd thought Sam different than the others. "You're starting to take on the ways of the world, I guess." And her idea that staying close to him, always connecting, may just be helping.

"I said I can relate, but that doesn't mean I prefer a weak woman. You're perfect for me, bunny."

She tugged the tie strings of her hat and beamed up at him.

"So what comes after like?"

"I'm not sure." Oh, yes, she was. Love came next. Or was that infatuation? Worship? Tenderness? "A mix of things probably."

"Such as? More than kissing?"

She ducked her head to hide a shy smile. The man did like to kiss. And how much did she like kissing him? Enough to stop the world and steal another kiss before the world stopped them?

Cassandra stepped out in front of Sam and threaded her arms about his neck when he walked into her embrace. "If you're so curious as to what comes next, you should start exploring. You might find something you like."

"I'm already at like, I want to go beyond." His colorful eyes smiled wider than his mouth. Such a sexy, roguish smile. "Will you let me go beyond?"

"Yes." She went on tiptoe and kissed him, wishing he weren't so tall and she so short, because she couldn't get a good connection. Then he lifted her and placed her on the rail track so she met his height.

Pausing amidst the chaos, they kissed sweetly at first, testing one another with glances and dotting their mouths together quickly, then slower, then quick again. The playful connection chased away her anxiety.

Cassandra surrendered to her desires, and with her guidance, Sam's motions became more amorous and needy. The squeeze of his hand along her ribs claimed her. And for a moment she wanted to be one of those frilly women who looked to their man for protection.

She'd never had a man to protect her before and had always scoffed at the idea. She could take care of herself. Mostly. In a way, they were equals, both focused on a mission, yet Sam allowed her to wear her strength as the badge she'd earned. She'd never had that from previous lovers.

He pulled away from the kiss, his eyes darting back and forth between hers, and whispered wistfully, "Vampires."

"Right." She kissed his chin and his jaw, and lower to his neck. "We should go after them."

"Uh-huh." His fingers traced her jaw as they kissed on the mouth again, deepening the kiss with their tongues and tasting each other as if starved for something they could only get from the other. "Should go."

His cool hand slid under the neck of her sweater and a finger almost managed to flick her nipple, but the tight neckline wouldn't allow it.

Frustrated, Cassandra stepped back. "Right. Save the world, and all that rubbish. Rain check?"

"Rain? In the winter?"

"That means, can we put a bookmark in this embrace and save it for later?"

"Ah. Rain check. Yes, I can do that, so long as we don't have to literally wait for the rain."

"Come on, angel boy." She clasped his hand and tugged him along the tracks.

"You're holding my hand."

"I'm leading you," she corrected.

"So, it's not like an official hand hold?"

"Uh…" She shrugged. "Why?"

"Just…nothing at all. Lead on, bunny."

An oncoming train sounded its horn, and Sam lifted her and spun her away from the tracks to walk alongside the swiftly moving freight cars. Cassandra's laughter was muted by the noise.

If Granny Stevens could see her now, she would clap, and up would bubble her infectious laughter celebrating Cassandra's happiness.

Then she would rap Cassandra across the back of her hand for even speaking to a Fallen one, let alone kissing one.

A metallic thump sounded close by. Sam shoved her roughly. "Get away."

"What?"

She *felt* the sweep of wing before she saw it. As she stumbled across the snow, she touched her cheek where it burned. Blood splattered on the dirty snow. Red blood. The wing had cut her.

Behind her, a Fallen angel leaped from the top of a freight car and collided with Sam, forcing them both to ground in a grapple of fists, legs and wings.

Wings of green glass?

"Jade," she murmured, and shuffled farther away across the snow. The vampires had succeeded in summoning yet another Fallen. And it obviously recognized Sam as the outlaw.

The jade angel stretched out his arms and roared in that awful sound that had Cassandra scrambling to plug her ears. But before she did, she noticed the glowing blue sigil on the side of its neck.

"Hurry, Coco, this one is close to his muse."

The Berlin airport was unusually crowded for the midnight hour. Coco clutched Zane's hand as they scanned the arrival gates for the muses. "I don't know what any of them looks like."

Zane kissed her cheek. The scar that cut

through his left eye and rendered it white didn't disturb her at all. It never had. "Relax, love. Don't panic."

"I'm not panicking."

"Oh, yes, you are. You've got that open-mouthed, wide-eyed, I'm-freaked look going on right now. We'll find them. Have I ever let you down?"

"No, you're always there for me. When angels come after me, you slay them. When the neighborhood dog chased me down the street, you barked at it. Heh. That poor dog hasn't barked or chased me since."

He kissed her deeply, and Coco abandoned her panic. Just like that. Zane's kisses always did that to her. "Whew! And when you kiss me, you make the world right."

Another kiss and a squeeze of her hand. "Maybe just a small portion of it. Someone's crying?"

He tugged her toward a sitting area where the crowd had backed away because a huddle of women stood around a loudly crying woman.

When they got close enough and she could see between two of the women standing before her, Coco saw the glowing blue sigil on the wrist of the one who cried.

"The Fallen is close," she said.

"Then we'd better not waste any time."

Zane approached the group of women cautiously and introduced himself and Coco. They were relieved to see them, but the crying one babbled in Swiss, which was a language neither Zane nor Coco understood.

"Tell her we're going to put her on a plane," Zane said to a petite red-haired muse.

"We just got off a plane," she argued around a yawn.

"And now you're getting back on. It's the safest. The Fallen are stalking Berlin."

With that announcement all the women began babbling and another started to cry. Zane cast a helpless look to Coco.

"Let me handle this," she said, and stepped in to embrace the circle of frantic women.

Sam had defeated the Fallen with the circle sigil. It had glowed so Cassandra had known the muses were in Berlin. She hoped Coco had gotten them out of the city.

Now Sam, with wings unfurled, stood with his back to her, looking over the destruction. Green ash from the angel's wings glittered amongst the crystal ash from the body. A single jade feather fluttered away on the wind, but she didn't chase after it. That was a trophy she had no desire to keep.

But as for the angel ash…

Sam's wings captured the pale winter moonlight and dazzled her eyes. She wanted to touch them, to discover if they were as solid as silver, or soft and flexible as they appeared. Her sculpture could never have captured the individual filaments in actual angel feathers. They fluttered softly in the breeze, as if they were eiderdown.

Taking a step toward him, she extended her hand to touch.

Sam twisted at the waist, his wings drawing close to his back and thighs. His eyes glowed blue. The sigil glowed on his back; he'd pulled the shirt away during the fight. Blue blood trickled from his hairline.

He tilted his head at her, wonderingly.

As if he'd never seen her before.

Chapter 14

In the moment their gazes connected, Cassandra's gut clenched. Her mouth went dry. Heartbeats paused. Her breath hushed out in a cloud.

That was not a look of admiration or respect on Sam's face. Dark eyes arrowed onto her like a rifle sight. The Fallen had sighted his muse.

"Oh, hell, no."

Her boots slipping on the icy snow, she turned to run. Everything Granny Stevens had taught her screamed through her brain. Always keep a weapon on hand. Never approach the Fallen, even if in human form. You are not stronger; you must be smarter.

Regrets that she had ignored intuition and followed something so inane as her heart stabbed relentlessly.

She'd let Granny down.

Flapping wings stirred the air and spun snow-flakes about her head. He pursued closely. Too close. No mortal could outrun an angel.

"No, Sam, this is not you!"

What was she saying? His current form was the real angel, or as close as an earthbound angel could get to being whole again. And that angel had only one goal on this earth—having sex with her. Which should be appealing, but Sam was not in his right mind now; he was being controlled by the compulsion.

A silver wing tip snapped around her waist, stopping her retreat as if a theatrical hook to pull an actor off the stage. Cassandra clutched the wing. It was cold, yet soft like feathers, which seemed impossible were she not touching it. Her boots scrabbled for hold, but she couldn't find purchase on the slick ice.

Another wing curled around her shoulder and brushed her neck. Too malleable, and pulsing with movement, as if another limb strapped with muscle. Also, too alluring for the danger she could not avoid. The wing caressed, warming and entreating her to relax, to succumb. An ethereal scent overwhelmed her senses. So sweet and delicious…

"No," she cried as she went down, palms slapping the ice. "Not you, it's not you."

Her body flipped, skidding on the ice. Wings pinned down her shoulders. Sam's face appeared above hers. His grin touched an evil Cassandra had not before seen from him, even when he'd shifted earlier on the rooftop. His intense stare crept over her face, down her lips and chin, leaving a frosty shiver in its wake.

"Please, Sam." Could she appeal to his inner goodness? Was it possible to touch the man he usually was and bypass the angel's vicious compulsion to own and master her? "Look at me, Sam. Listen to me."

Hell, she needed…something. No weapon would suffice.

Faith. She needed it now. But was it right to call upon faith out of the blue? She'd denied it up until now. Could it be hers for the asking?

You know it can be.

Her heart racing, Cassandra said whatever came to mind. "You're too kind for this."

A wing slipped around her shoulders and lifted her, cradling her head in a nest of silver feathers.

"You don't want this," she warbled, hating when her voice betrayed her fear.

"Yes, I do," he growled. Not Sam. His eyes darkened, making it difficult to see different colors; they were growing black. "My precious muse."

"I'm not Sam's muse," she said. "I'm his… I'm his bunny! The girl he likes to hold hands with. I'm not yours. You're a monster."

She cringed. This man was not a monster. A

monster was the nephilim. Sam was...struggling against his inner darkness. He had to be.

Please let him see beyond the compulsion.

A single silver feather pulled away the sweater from her neck and she felt the stroke as if a soft sweep. He smelled like nothing she could name, but like everything she desired. Her lids fluttered.

"Not here, Sam. Think. The Sinistari could arrive any moment."

Staying focused was becoming more difficult. In his appearance he remained the same, sexy, buff man she desired like no other. She did want him, but... But what?

"Must have you." He bent and laved his tongue under her neck and jaw. The angelkiss burned, but he pulled away abruptly, eyes widening.

Releasing her, he shuffled away. The rosary tugged about her neck, forcing Cassandra to swallow. *That* had given him a fright?

No time to wonder over it. She grasped the halo at his hip and slashed her arm across her chest, hoping she'd cut some part of him.

Cold angel blood spattered her face. Wings released her.

Cassandra dragged herself up, and slipping and sliding on the bloody ice, she raced toward the warehouse just ahead. Swiping a hand over her face, she wiped off the blue blood.

Behind her, Sam yowled. She'd left the halo embedded in his shoulder...or neck—she hadn't looked where she'd landed it.

Likely, the shallow wound would only give him pause, but that was all she needed. And hell, if she'd known the rosary would have detoured him, she would have wielded that a lot sooner. But how had it worked against him?

Skidding into the open warehouse doorway, she gave a hoot upon seeing there was an actual door to close. Slamming it shut, she pulled the rusted iron bolt into lock position. The door frame was steel, yet the walls were corrugated tin.

"That will never keep back an angel."

Searching the darkness, her eyes adjusted to the haze. Gray shadows revealed shapes of stacked pallets and cardboard boxes. Empty wood spools as high as her shoulders may have once wound wire or plastic tubing. Nothing she could drag in front of the door without great effort.

Which meant she had better hide.

Something thumped the door as Cassandra rounded a stack of pallets. He cried her name, and it had never before sounded so mournful. Had he changed back to mortal form? She couldn't take the chance of finding out.

The door flew inside, and she scrambled to get away, but tripped over a wood pallet and sprawled on the floor.

The angel appeared, silhouetted in the doorway—wingless.

Or were his wings stretched out behind him? She couldn't see. The shadows hid his complete form. So she wouldn't take a chance.

Remembering she did have a weapon, Cassandra thrust out her hand and shouted, *"Agothé!"*

Dragging herself upright along the slatted wood, she didn't look to see where he had landed. Running outside and along the warehouse wall, she cursed the thick ice coating the ground beneath the soffit, and slapped a hand to the corrugated tin as she went down, scrabbling for purchase, and finally buffeted into a snowbank.

Something landed in the snow above and before her, sifting down flakes that sparkled like diamonds and kissed sharply over her face.

Sam bent and extended his hand. "I'm sorry, Cassandra."

"Sorry?" She stabbed her fingers into the snow and used it to lever herself up. He was a man now, no wings. *But not really a man. And never can be one without a soul.* "You weren't going to touch me tenderly and shower me with kisses just now."

"I know, I… It's the compulsion."

"No bloody shit!" She backed away from him, brushing the snow from her arms and knees. "You should have seen the look in your eyes. It was as if you wanted to eat me. And they got so dark, almost black."

"Sorry."

She gaped at his simple apology. It wasn't enough. It could never be enough.

"The fight with the Fallen…it angered me and brought up my wings. I…was out of my mind and thinking only as a Fallen. I'm thankful you were able to get away from me." He touched the cut on his neck that dashed a blue line through his skin—her handiwork. "Forgive me?"

"Forgive you? You think you know so much about me? You know nothing!"

"I am trying to learn. Teach me, Cassandra. Make me understand you."

She slapped her shaky arms across her chest and gave him her back. The angel seemed to sense her utter hatred for him at the moment.

But to be truthful with herself, it wasn't hatred. And it wasn't fear. It was her inability to just walk away from the guy. Because she liked him. How crazy was that? Despite the fact he had his moments of unthinking focus that compelled him to want to have sex with her, whether or not she approved, she liked the hunk of angel.

She admired him for his truth and honesty. He would never try to gloss over the compulsion and expect her to accept that part of him. He abhorred that side of him.

She adored his accidental innocence. Sure, he knew about showgirls and their skimpy attire, but inside he was still learning the world and wondering at everything he encountered. How awesome was that?

But what she liked most about him was his willingness to help mortals who were unlike him. A Fallen should have no concern for feeble humans. And yet, Sam walked amongst them as if he belonged, and could think of nothing beyond ensuring their safety.

And hers.

"I can forgive you," she started slowly, still unsure if she were saying the right thing or just acting from her heart, "if you'll do one thing for me."

"Anything."

If his heart was in the right place, he would allow her this test. This breather. He knew so little about her, and yet, she wanted him to know more, to know it all. But how to do so when walking toward chaos?

Just take some time. You need it.

Her heart stuttered and wondered if this was the right thing, yet she ignored that tremble and said, "Let me walk away from here alone. Don't follow. I have to get away from you."

"Please—"

"You can't do that for me?"

He bowed his head and nodded. "I will do whatever you ask. But you may be in danger."

"No more than the danger I just escaped. Stay away from me, Sam. At least…" She swallowed the tears she didn't want him to see. "Until I come to you. Promise me."

He nodded. "I promise."

He had followed.

Cassandra looked out the window from her third-story loft. Below in the park, the snow swirled, creating an undulating blanket of lush dunes. An angel sat on one of three rope swings, his bare back to her building.

A wingless back. *Thank, God.* Yet he wore no shirt because his wings had torn it away. Someone would surely get suspicious. And though she knew the cold affected him not at all, the urge to toss him a shirt made her fingers flinch.

She pressed her palm against the cold glass and winced when the image of his glass heart formed in her mind. An angel's heart was cold red glass. It did not beat. It could not know love.

Could it?

Granny Stevens had told her if a demon loved it was deemed a sin, and if an angel hated, that was their greatest sin. But could they know love? Angels were supposed to embody love, but were the Fallen included in that bunch? They'd rebelled. Surely, love would not come so easily to those lusty angels who sought sex.

She and Sam were so different. Though they wore the same sigil—had been destined for one another—they could never be the same. They looked the same, most of the time. But when he was shifted to half-angel form his differences were too apparent. He could not control his compulsive need to mate with her in that form. Yet she understood he struggled with it.

There could never be a "them." Not unless he became completely mortal. And it would be easy.

He simply needed to place the halo holstered at his hip above his head to receive his earthly soul.

Would he do that for her? Did she want him to?

"Yes," she whispered.

Yet he'd told her he wanted to return Above. The outlaw angel had a mission here on earth. When all the Fallen, vampires and nephilim were slain, he would leave.

He'd leave her.

And she wasn't sure how she felt about that.

Okay, so she did know. It hurt that he could walk away from her. And it troubled her that she'd already developed an attachment to him. The very man Granny had warned her against for over a decade!

"You're not thinking straight." She was allowing her heart to influence her logical thoughts.

"Love doesn't happen this easy. I'm just…infatuated. I want him like I want any other sexy man when I'm jonesing for some intimacy. Get a grip, Caz, this is not love."

It was only like. And like was a long way from love.

Outside, Sam formed a snowball and tossed it to a boy bundled in a black snowsuit with a hood lined in fur, which only revealed his eyes. The scene was too normal except that the man wore no shirt.

She turned and clasped her arms about her stomach. "I wish you were still alive, Granny. I need you now."

She needed someone to talk to. And Coco was too wrapped up in love with her man to focus and be clear about Caz's life, to give her insight to what it really felt like to be in love. Cassandra had plainly recognized the look on her sister's face. Her eyes were bright and she never stopped smiling when Zane was in the room.

Walking into her bedroom, she glanced in the vanity mirror. Her eyes didn't look different than usual. She tried a smile, but it quickly wilted.

In the mirror's reflection, the silver angel called to her. She turned and ran her fingers along the line of one wing. Proud, bold and ethereal was the look she'd been going for as she'd sculpted this piece. She hadn't thought much about the design before diving in and following the swing of her ball-peen hammer as she had pounded life into the silver.

She'd created Sam. She had known at the time he was her angel and had romanticized meeting him one day. He would look at her and fall in love and forget the reason he Fell. They would embrace and live happily ever after.

Cassandra tucked her head against her elbow and began to cry.

The boy was about eight, Sam figured. He caught the snowball Sam tossed him against his chest and crushed it with his too-big red mitten. He chuckled deeply. His cheeks were rosy and he oozed a kind of glee Sam had not known until now. It lifted his spirits.

Children truly were closest to Him in their innocence and wonder. Sam possessed the same curiosity for the world, and felt sorry for the humans who had grown away from or had deliberately abandoned their wondrous innocence.

The world was meant to be seen through the eyes of wonder.

He'd followed Cassandra to ensure she safely made it wherever she'd planned to go. He wished she hadn't returned to her home. The Sinistari knew where it was, though she should be safe from the demons. But if they were aligning themselves with the vampires now, he trusted no one.

The vampires knew where she lived, as well. The place must be a mess with the remnants of the vampires they'd slain earlier. How could she stand to be in there?

"That lady is watching you," the boy said in thick German.

"The one in the window?" He didn't turn around. He'd broken his promise to let her be alone.

"She's pretty."

"How do you know she's watching me, eh?" He shaped another snowball in his bare palms and tossed it to the boy, who again caught it, smashed it and let out a gleeful chuckle.

"She's looking right at you!"

"Maybe she's watching you?"

"Ouff, no! How come you don't wear a coat and gloves? My mommy would yell at me if I went out without them."

"I forgot them."

"I suppose it's because you're an angel."

Sam gaped, but then realized he was being seen by a child. And there was nothing wrong with that. "What about you? Your cheeks are turning red."

"I am the a-bob-i-dable snowman!" he declared proudly.

Sam felt inclined to raise his arms in triumph to match the boy's gesture. "You are!"

The boy squatted to pack together some snow. He wasn't so successful in forming a ball with the heavy wool mittens, but he managed a chunk that dispersed before it made it to Sam.

"Try again," he said. "Is she still watching?"

"*Ja.* Does she love you?"

"Why would you ask that?"

He shrugged.

"Do you know what love is...?" He mined for the boy's name. "Peter?"

"Sure, it's when Mommy and Daddy get all kissy face."

Sam laughed this time. That was an essential part of the human relationship, but kissing didn't necessarily imply love. Or did it? When Cassandra kissed him did she feel love? He felt something, but how to know if it was love or merely his innate lust?

"The lady is gone now." Peter formed another snowball.

Sam twisted to sight the window on the third floor. Then he remembered he wasn't going to do that, and quickly shifted his shoulder. He hadn't a chance to see her.

He admired Cassandra's beauty, strength and determination. She was an amazing woman who could take care of herself. She had family, and had been taught by a doting grandmother how to protect herself and survive in the world. She didn't need protection, but he liked protecting her.

And she was an amazing artist who had seen him before she'd known him. When he'd touched the sculpture, formed by her hands, Sam had felt the emotion imbued within the silver. It veined in deeply, as if blood, and possessed a pulse, which, he guessed, must match her pulse.

Had that creation been love? When he worked with silver it was the embodiment of love. His means to the emotion. It was remarkable Cassandra had taken up the craft, but he sensed her destiny had been marked since birth.

Was his admiration for her love? He wanted love, but he needed a soul for that to happen.

A figure appeared in the window and made a gesture that looked as though she wanted him to come inside.

"Go!" the boy said.

"You think so?"

"She wants you to go to her, don't you see?"

"Thanks, buddy."

"See if she will give you a shirt. But don't bend your wings when you put it on!"

Putting a finger to his lips to signal the boy keep that bit of information silent, Sam nodded. "Our secret, yes?"

"My mommy would never believe me anyway." Smiling with new confidence, Sam strode inside and up to Cassandra's broken door.

Chapter 15

Sam knocked on the door frame and stepped inside to fit the door back into place. It was cracked down the edge, and she needed a new one, but he was able to fit a hinge into the iron rings and turn the knob to secure the door.

He stepped back to admire his makeshift handiwork. One push and the whole thing would go down. They certainly didn't make them as sturdy as they did in the time when he first Fell. Although, now he thought on it, doors hadn't been popular back then.

Then he realized he'd invited himself inside, and turned abruptly to the woman standing right behind him.

A genuine smile curled beneath sparkling brown eyes. That was a good sign. He hoped.

The faint shimmery trail slipping over her cheek indicated she'd been crying.

"Forgive me," he said, not daring to touch her for he'd barged in as if it were his right. "I cannot apologize for the compulsion when in half form. But I can apologize for frightening you. I swore I would not harm you, Cassandra. I will take my own life, should you ever stand threatened by me again."

"Don't be so dramatic. Sam, please, come in. You need a shirt."

Head bowed, he entered her flat. The lights were out and twilight burnished the high-gloss cement floors glamorously. He saw no signs of vampire ash or blood.

He stepped to a very specific place and sought Cassandra's eyes, but she strode into the living room, not noticing. Her hair fell freely down her back, the white ribbons standing out while the red ones were tucked. If he could twine himself amongst her hair like those ribbons, he would be endlessly happy.

The silence felt like a gift, an exquisite offering she allowed him to experience. He fancied he could hear her heartbeat, and perhaps he did. He wondered if his own could beat, if it would sound like hers.

Sliding a hand over the halo at his hip, he gave a moment's thought to how easy it would be to claim his earthbound soul. Easy, but he'd sacrifice Above to do so. No angel could do that. Not for long.

"I did some cleaning," she said. "It wasn't difficult sucking up the ash, but my vacuum cleaner is groaning for it. You know what I suspect about the broken door? It was faked."

"I don't understand."

"Well, vampires need permission to enter, right?"

He nodded.

"So I suspect they had a mortal break in—because they certainly could not. Mortal enters my apartment, turns and offers an invite inside, and vampires can enter. Maybe? Can someone who doesn't own the home offer the invite?"

"Seems the only possible way they could have entered. Clever deduction."

"Yeah, well, too bad it's possible. I could raid the laundry room for a shirt again. Or you could pull on one of my old T-shirts. I have a big one that might fit."

"I'm fine."

Her eyes strolled up his abdomen and to his face. "Yes, you are." She strode toward the long gray velvet couch. Glancing at him, she asked, "You'll join me?"

He spread his arms. "I thought to give you opportunity to capture me in your angel trap. I stand in the right spot, yes?"

Blinking, her sightline then flashed to each of the three positions where the trap must originate.

"Yes." She leaned forward, thinking. Or considering? "You're not trapped unless I speak the spell."

"Go ahead. I am worthy of such punishment for ignoring your request to stay away."

"You are, but it doesn't make for easy conversation with you standing trapped way over there. Come over here."

Released from the self-imposed prison, Sam exhaled and joined her on the sofa. He didn't sit close enough to touch her, though his bare skin screamed for connection, for a contact he hadn't known he needed until desire coursed through his being. This was not like the compulsion he felt in half form. It was subtle, softer, yet insistent.

"Did you contact your sister?" he asked. "How does she fare?"

"The muses have been sent home on separate flights. They haven't sighted the nephilim yet. And I've had the news on until you came up. The local stations have dropped the story about the monster sighting, dismissing it as a costumed prank."

"If only."

"I forgive you, Sam." She stroked her hand aside his cheek, forcing him to look at her. He breathed in the fresh winter scent still dusting her skin and the underlying musk of woman. "You scared the crap out of me after you slew the jade angel, but I know what I've gotten into. I am a smart, rational woman. And I fully intend to take the good with the bad."

"You can't mean that." He palmed her hand, still cupping his cheek. "Mortals will, time and again, choose goodness and safety over what may be wrong or harmful. It isn't in their nature—"

"I'm not like every other mortal, Sam. I'm attracted to danger."

"Danger is—"

The kiss was a surprise, and Sam could but accept that she wanted to give it to him. Even after he'd gone after her so viciously? He could have— No, he would not think it. It was over. Truly, she was not like other mortal women. Cassandra was strong. Fierce.

His.

Dropping his apprehensions, he slid closer to her, deepening the kiss to taste her want, and give her a taste of his. Doubts and worries would not distract him. She was worth his full attention.

The kiss stirred his body and ignited a flame that coiled deep in his loins. Desire and passion rose to the surface. She was the key to his pleasure. His only means to pleasure, if truth be told. The Fallen could have a mortal woman, any mortal woman, but to truly know pleasure, they must seek it from their muse.

Didn't mean he had to whip out the wings to enjoy that pleasure. And he thanked his creator for that. Now, if the compulsion would hold off he'd be golden.

Gliding his palm down her neck, he savored the

smooth texture of her, and noticed a subtle rise in temperature as his skin brushed hers.

"It doesn't itch anymore," she noted.

"Itch?" Hell, he recalled licking up her neck when he'd been in half form. The angelkiss was not one of his finer habits. "Sorry."

"It's okay. Just don't do it again."

No, he mustn't purposefully lick her, even if out of desire. Though he'd mouthed her nipple in the hotel room, so obviously that was okay. Maybe he had to be in half form for the angelkiss to be effective? He stroked his fingertips along her neck, a little tentatively. "How does my touch feel to you?"

Tilting her head, her hair swished over her shoulders. She clasped his hand at her throat and drew it along her jaw and bowed forward, cupping his fingers over her cheek.

"Like being touched by something unimaginable. It's a hard, yet soft touch, if you can understand that. Your skin is initially cold—like a silver sculpture—but as soon as we connect, we melt together."

"Like silver melting into a new form under the careful flame."

"Yes. But I don't want to be careful anymore." She bent to his mouth and kissed it, gently tugging his bottom lip with her teeth. "Together we become something unique. I want to take it as far as the silver will allow us to go, Sam. I want to sculpt something new with you. Kiss me. Touch me. Take me against your body and learn love with me."

"Teach me everything, Cassandra. How to please you, how to become a part of you. I want the act of sex to be real love between us. Do you trust me?"

"That you won't shift?" She nodded. "I do. I know it only comes on you when you're angry or in the heat of battle."

So far as he knew. "I promise not to lick you, either. Though, it will be difficult. Your skin was made to be tasted."

"It's weird how your kisses, when our tongues touch, don't make me itch."

"The angelkiss is made with intent."

"So maybe if your intention is to please instead of harm, a few licks won't hurt?"

He shook his head, unsure of the answer.

"We'll take things slowly." Standing, she extended a hand to him. "Will you take it?"

He stared at the offering, and his heart warmed until he thought he felt it pulse. She offered her hand to him. A simple offering steeped with immense meaning. That was all he had wanted after his initial Fall, someone to hold his hand.

He placed his palm against hers, holding it, measuring the body heat that seemed to liquefy between the two of them.

"Sam?"

"Yes," he whispered, giddy with the rush of

having his desire fulfilled. "I will follow you any-where."

She led him into the bedroom where pale moonlight dashed across the purple fabrics covering the bed. Decorative pillows in deeper shades of violet and red glinted with sequins but resembled jewels, and a sheer purple canopy hung over the entire bed. It looked like a lush respite in a maharaja's kingdom. It even smelled of cin-namon and vanilla in here, exotic spices to rouse his senses.

Sam walked around to study the angel sculp-ture. He stroked his fingers along the wing and sucked in a breath. He could read her thoughts, the thoughts she'd been thinking at the moment she'd created this object.

He will come for me someday. I want him to come to me. He is mine.

She had wanted him all along? Sam glanced to the bed.

Cassandra slid onto the bed and, with a kink of her finger, gestured he approach.

Stripped of a shirt, the moonlight jealously playing across his abs, the angel stalked toward her, his eyes shaded and predatory, yet curiosity lightened them. He was a man who wanted to learn, to experience all the world could offer him.

Cassandra intended to offer it all.

Pushing aside the purple chiffon curtain, he crawled onto the bed, moving slowly over her, up

from her feet, where he stroked his thumb along
the arch, and to her knees, where he kissed each
one, and to her hips. He stopped over her breasts
and the smile he flashed up at her spoke more
than words.

Cassandra tugged off her shirt. Her bare
breasts tightened with goose bumps and her nipples were ruched.

Moonlight flashed on the line of beads snak-
ing around her neck. Sam studied the rosary but
didn't touch it.

"They're certainly no Vegas showgirl's rhine-
stones." She pulled it off and held it upon her
palm. The peridot beads twinkled as if green ice.
"I didn't think a cross would mean anything to
you. It's a mortal creation."

"It doesn't, but I respect it as a symbol of your
faith. Obviously it has power, enough to startle
me out of the compulsion."

"Then maybe I'll keep it close." She set it on
the nightstand but an arm's reach away.

A symbol of her faith? Yes, she was beginning
to realize perhaps her faith wasn't so absent after
all. Thanks to Sam.

His breath hushed over her breasts. Her nipples
tightened. Tenderly, he touched them, feeling their
shape and texture. The experimental touches shivered through her being, and she sucked in her
breath.

"Taste them," she murmured. Sam let out a
moan as his lips circled her nipple and his hot

breath huffed over it. He didn't dash his tongue across it, and she ached to feel that pleasure, but his breath was equally tantalizing as it stroked indelibly, lazing over her skin with his heat.

He took his time, trying it this way, and then another way. A breath here, a long smoldering trail that circled her breast there. The sensation roared over her flesh, blazing fire across her chest and stomach to her loins.

She slid her fingers through his hair, liking that he was never room temperature, always cool, a refreshing elixir to her heated skin. He kissed her palm and wrist over the sigil, which glowed softly beneath his mouth. It declared her his, and she didn't mind that at all.

His torso hugged hers, making her very aware of his erection, which strained for release. Cassandra slipped her fingers inside the waistband of his pants and tugged.

"You want them off?" he asked, nuzzling his closed lips over her nipple. "Take them off."

"I thought I was teaching you?"

"You are. I'm learning that I like it when you undress me."

She caught a finger behind the metal button on his borrowed jeans and popped it loose. The zipper she slid cautiously, and he shoved a hand down to help her do it carefully. No boxers, briefs or anything else between him and his pants. Mercy.

Gliding her hands over his muscular buttocks,

she gave them a firm squeeze before shoving down the pants. Sam worked them to his ankles, and had to stop and twist onto a hip to kick off his boots.

Cassandra sat up on her elbows and caught a glimpse of his erection, springing heavily with his movement. He was uncut, yet the head of his penis emerged as if a ruby fruit that begged suckling. "Well, well."

He turned and noticed her interest. "You like this?"

Tracing her tongue along her lip, she nodded enthusiastically.

Grasping her hand, he kissed the mound of her palm, then moved it to his penis, which she took firmly. He growled as she squeezed. "That feels better than anything I've felt here on earth."

"I could say the same. So hard, and thick. Mmm…"

When she moved her fingers up and down, shrugging his skin along the rigid shaft, he groaned deeply. "Cassandra, you are making me even harder. Do you know what your touch does to me?"

"I have an idea." She wrapped her legs about his hips and pulled him down, snuggling his penis against her stomach. Hers to command. "You make me so wet, angel boy. Feel. Touch me here."

She guided his fingers into her folds. His eyes, fixed to hers, spoke surprise and elation, and captivating curiosity.

"I do know how this is supposed to work," he said. "Yet I never imagined it would be quite so heady."

"You still feel…like yourself?" She had to ask. Instinct wouldn't allow her to plunge blindly into this encounter.

"Not going to shift, Cassandra." Yet their eyes both briefly glanced to the nightstand where the rosary lay. "Promise."

His fingers, still exploring her, thumbed the peak of her entrance.

"If only I could feel your tongue there," she murmured deeply. "That's the sweet spot."

"Let's try it this way." He sucked his forefinger, then placed it, wet and hot, against her swollen nub. He slicked it about, slowly, then firmly. "Doesn't itch?"

"No, that's, oh…"

"You like it when I go slow like this?"

"Mmm-hmm, you've just the right touch. Not too hard, not too soft. Oh, Sam."

"You're so hot and wet. I want you all over me, Cassandra."

Inside me, she wanted to say, but what he was doing right now was too good to make him stop. And the angel did need to learn, and how to gain experience without practice?

Closing her eyes, she stretched her arms above her head and under the pillow. Silk fabric kissed her skin. Hard, muscled flesh melted into her. Sam's masterful fingers found places on her she had never discovered herself. He owned her, this outlaw angel. Her body hummed at his direction. It danced and wanted to spin out of control, but she thought her reaction to his manipulations might freak him out.

And then she couldn't care because the orgasm attacked and Cassandra cried out, loud and long and moaning as her muscles contracted and she rode the delicious wave he'd created in her.

Kissing a path up her stomach and to her breasts, Sam gave a breathy "Wow."

She sighed and surrendered to soft laughter because her body was loose and relaxed and it felt right. "I come rather forcefully."

"That was amazing. Your body took off. Sort of spilled over. I did that?"

She giggled. "Oh, Sam, come here. Move up and put yourself inside me. I want you to fill me."

He kissed his way along her neck and over the sensitive skin on her collarbone to the edge of each shoulder in turn. When he finally reached her mouth she devoured his texture, the faint taste of salty sex and the sweep of his wanting tongue.

Gripping his erection, she guided him to her mons and the head of him, hot against her, felt like fire as he slid down and then inside. They both gasped at the intensity of heat their joining produced. It was as though he burned through her, yet it was a wanting, delicious burn.

He pistoned inside her, arms paralleling her and jaw tense as he got lost in the sensation. His eyes closed, he traveled to a new place, and she loved watching him over her, a student to sex and a master of her body.

He cried out. Clutched her behind the shoulder and drew her to him as he began to shudder and he stopped moving inside her. The angel fell deep inside the muse, trapping himself in freedom.

Chapter 16

Cassandra stretched like a cat on the slick satin sheets. Hair tumbled over her face, veiling her eyes from the hazy morning sunlight. Against her back the length of Sam's hard, muscled body warmed her spine. Somehow his body matched her temperature when they touched.

Smiling, she dropped her arm along the side of the bed and teased the rough seam of his jeans with a fingernail. The halo was still hooked at the waistband. She took the circlet between two fingers.

It was lighter than it looked, and it did resemble a kid's toy, as Coco had described after finding the halo a few months ago. It felt like tin, and wasn't shiny but dull. So weird. Shouldn't it be gold or silver and gleam with the intensity of a thousand suns and radiate divinity?

She smirked, and flipped the halo so it slipped over her hand to her wrist as if a loose bracelet. Rolling to her back, she held up her arm, wrist bent and halo crooked high at the base of her hand. Not exactly bling, but touching it meant more to her than any diamond ring ever could.

Touching it, and knowing its owner would not mind. And that he slept beside her, peaceful and exhausted after making love to her.

Making love!

They'd come together. And now she felt Sam could never harm her, even if in half form. The love they'd shared would touch his glass heart and keep his monster at bay.

Or was she dreaming? Making up happily-ever-afters because she knew happy endings were a crock?

Your mother and father were two very different people. They are not you.

Yet she and Sam were very different. He could become more like her, though. It might be possible to have a relationship if Sam were human. Yet she couldn't fathom being an angel—a divine being—and suddenly becoming human. Human must be so much less than an angel. He'd have memories of serving God, for goodness' sake!

Or would he? Beyond becoming completely mortal, she wasn't sure what happened when the Fallen claimed their earthbound soul. If he lost his memories of divinity, that might make transition to living on earth easier.

Wait. She did know. When Eden Campbell, a fellow muse, fell in love with a Sinistari demon and he had claimed his soul, he had lost all memory of Above. So Sam would, too.

But how to begin a new life as an already grown man? Suddenly planted on earth with no schooling or skills to find a job? Certainly Sam knew everything after walking the world, but did that translate to a job? As well, would he retain that knowledge if he lost his memory? She wasn't sure. He had nothing, no money or home. He'd have to find a sugar mama to support him.

Which she could entirely entertain doing. Taking care of him. Loving him. She could barely support herself selling jewelry, but who needed money when they had love?

Did they have love? It felt like love to her. Definitely something beyond like. But it was new love, so tender and untested. It could either develop into something strong and secure, or shatter like an angel's wings if they were not careful.

She took the halo off her wrist and twisted to look over Sam's sleeping body. Naked, he gleamed like a sun god. Beautifully tan, sculpted muscles defied the norm. She'd read stories that described a hero's abs as being rock hard, but his really were. Every part of him was solid, yet sinuous, begging for her touch. Again.

She moved the halo above his abs, paralleling his body as she drew it higher and held it there, over his face. Just a few more inches and it would be above the crown of his head. According to Granny, that was all a Fallen had to do to claim his soul—put the halo above his head.

Cassandra sucked in her lower lip. Should she do it? A flick of her wrist could change him forever. And he'd forget his origins, so it wasn't as though he could blame her for something he could not recall.

She wanted him human and normal and able to love her without the desire to return Above. It was selfish, though. She hadn't earned his love.

She lowered her arm and let the halo fall onto the floor.

"Why didn't you do it?" he murmured.

"Sam, I thought you were sleeping." Mercy, if he'd been aware of what she'd been doing. But apparently he had been. "I...couldn't. It's not my decision. Claiming your earthbound soul should be your choice."

"But you want me to claim it."

"I would never influence you."

He took her hand and kissed it. "I wish you would."

"To be honest, I wouldn't mind if you were completely human. I...well hell, I could see having a relationship with you."

"A permanent one?"

"Maybe. I've only known you a few days."

Which was another good reason for her to slow

down. If he became human and they didn't work out as a couple, he'd be left alone in a world not his own.

He rolled over and glided a palm across her stomach. Their skin communicated and heated in response. Her sigil glowed softly. Muse and angel, an impossible match. They'd defied possibilities.

"Raphael gave me an ultimatum," he said. "Before I can return Above, it must be accomplished."

"Which is?"

"I have to bring him your book of names and sigils."

"I see." That hurt.

Sam's face lingered inches from hers, so she would not look away and instead pressed the tip of her tongue against the roof of her mouth to stanch the burgeoning tears.

"I know you don't believe that the best place for that book is in the hands of an archangel."

"Oh, I believe it. Doesn't matter though. It's missing."

Sam sighed. "Right. There's a code within the names and sigils you've gathered. The code for the Final Days."

"What does that mean?"

"It means, should anyone ever recite the coded word—anyone with the knowledge and skilled determination to make it so—it will send the angels Above, all of them, plummeting to earth."

"That's…unimaginable. In my little book? But it's something Granny started, and I…" She didn't finish. She could believe it. She believed in angels and demons and vampires, why not the Final Days? "And you wanted it to give to Raphael?"

"Yes, for safekeeping. But…I didn't want it to be the currency to my return Above."

"Why not?"

"I will take my soul," he said. "I want it now."

"Really? But I thought you wanted to return Above? You said you felt worthless here on earth. That you served no purpose."

"I did after my initial summons to earth. I've had a change of mind." He leaned in to kiss her below her breast. His breath tickled and her nipple hardened. "I don't deserve to return Above. I realize now the arrogance of me to ask such a thing. I Fell with purpose, and that purpose was originally wicked. I chose this life upon earth. And now I suddenly want to go home? What kind of double standard is that?"

His thumb swept the undercurve of her breast and he moved to trace her tight, ruched nipple.

"But more so?" He kissed her, a combination of a suckle and a press of his mouth to her bottom lip. "All I ever wanted when I set out to Fall was someone to hold my hand."

The confession startled her. It was so simple, yet she completely understood the desire. She had held his hand and led him to bed last night. No wonder he'd acted so strange about it at the time. She'd given him his one real desire. And it hadn't been the sex.

"I don't want to leave you. I want to be with you, Cassandra. If you'll have me. Even if it's only for the short time you suspect we can have."

"Sam, that's a huge sacrifice."

"Abandoning Above? Yes." He moved onto his elbows, one to either side of her, his chest gently crushing hers. "But you are the reward."

"That explains why you went to my home that day. To search for the book instead of vampires. What do we do now that the vampires have the book of names and sigils?"

"I have to battle all the Fallen the vampires summon." He glanced out the window. Dawn had arrived. Exhaust from a parked car rose in billowy white plumes. "Much as I'd prefer to lay in bed with you all day, I think we'd better sharpen our stakes...."

Charging the vanguard could wait until after their shower. Cassandra insisted. It would only take five minutes.

Five minutes grew to twenty as the lovers slicked soapy fingers over skin and through hair and around hardened and sensitive body parts.

"Let me take down your hair," Sam murmured aside her cheek.

"Then we'll never get out of here. It takes forever to dry, lover. I thought we had a few vampires to stake?"

"First I'm going to stake you." He placed her hands over her head to grasp the towel bar and gripped it beside her fists. With a shift of his hips, he slid inside her, growling with pleasure as she enveloped him.

Angel boy had definitely learned sex.

An hour later they tromped through the un- marred snow in the cemetery. Coco had called and they'd planned a rendezvous. Tombstones were capped with four inches of snow and the pine tree bows hung heavily with more snow.

"Up ahead!" Cassandra took off in a run after seeing her sister wave.

Coco ran toward her, jacket open as usual. They collided in a hug, and Coco gave her a quick, cold kiss on the cheek. "Zane checked out the area. They're in the warehouse on the other side of the forest. We can gain access on the roof."

Sam arrived and said, "We'll meet you up there."

In seconds, Cassandra stood on the snow-cov- ered flat roof, wobbling to catch her equilibrium. She glanced over the treetops that separated the cemetery from the buildings. "I thought angels couldn't fly."

"That wasn't flight—that was a leap."

Zane landed next to them with Coco in his arms. The vampire nodded to them and set down his lover.

Cassandra was a little stymied at all the super- natural strength being flaunted yet, at the same time, fascinated. She and her sister dating an angel and a vampire? Who'da thought?

Not that she and Sam were dating. Yet. Maybe.

Hell, one day at a time, Cassandra. Don't pick out the wedding dress yet.

Sam held her with one arm, crushed against his hard-as-steel body. No jacket. No gloves or ear warmers. Their connection made him so warm. Cassandra wanted to unzip her jacket and press her skin to his, to bleed out some of that luscious Sam warmth. "Over here," Zane directed. He lifted an iron door, which opened to stairs. "They're at the opposite end of this building. The stairs are noisy so you have to move slowly."

"We'll go in and check it out." Cassandra started down the stairs. "Be right back," she whispered to Coco.

"We'll keep watch," the vampire confirmed.

She and Sam descended to a catwalk that lined the upper walls in the vast warehouse. They were able to stay out of view behind a low-hanging wide iron beam. Along the walls at the top, dusty multipaned windows let in little natural light. A glow of fluorescent lighting spilled over the farthest end of the warehouse.

It smelled faintly chemical inside, but she couldn't place the scent other than that it made her nose itch. This district had once been home to various manufacturing plants, so anything could have been processed here. And considering it was right next to a graveyard, that added a whole new assortment of smells and distractions.

Following Sam's silent gesture, Cassandra spied the conglomeration of figures at the opposite end of the building. The people were too small to make out, but one in particular did stand out—and above everyone by three or four heads. It was the monster, naked and yowling and fighting against restraints.

"They have the nephilim." She clutched the rosary beneath her sweater.

"Those chains won't hold long," Sam said. "Possibly a spell may be keeping it subdued."

"Subdued? The thing is yowling like a baby elephant and fighting against the chains."

Despite not having a clear view, she had to look away. The nephilim grew to full size in seventy-two hours? How had Ophelia died? Had the nephilim…? No, not while the size of an infant. The birth must have taxed her, and without proper medical care, she had bled out.

Had she seen her baby walk away from her? How horrible to witness a monstrous thing come from your own body. And she had been alone.

Cassandra clasped Sam's hand and studied the side of his intent face as he scanned the scene. What was he? Did he have nephilim inside of him? If that is what his child would look like, he had to— No. He was too perfect. The combination of divinity mating with humanity is what created the monster.

Yet what was she? Sitting here so calmly and accepting the man who could induce the horror of a nephilim upon her. And how? By having sex with her. Making love.

What if Granny had been wrong and it was possible to carry an angel's child without him being in half form at the moment of conception?

Sam looked at her. She gasped and pressed a hand over her mouth. He said he couldn't read her mind. But his multicolored eyes saw everything about her. Deep inside to her thoughts, her dreams, perhaps even her soul. How could he not? He was a freakin' angel.

"Promise you won't hurt me," she asked, her voice a mere whisper.

He moved in closer. Their breath mingled. "You have my word, Cassandra. You will not become the mother to my child. I swear it to you."

He kissed her, a seal to his promise.

She sucked in her lower lip, tasting his barely there flavor with her tongue. "Then I promise I won't hurt you," she returned. As if she could. Never had she felt smaller than right now, in the company of so much divinity.

He nodded, then said, "It's a good thing someone captured the nephilim. That means it's not out walking the streets, able to harm innocent mortals. It feeds on flesh and blood."

She nodded. "Go, vampires. Not."

A clatter below alerted them both. Cassandra

moved closer to the railing, the side of her body hugging Sam's torso.

"What are they doing? I can't see that far."

"There's a leader," he whispered. "Dark hair pulled in a queue behind his head. Looks Spanish descent."

"Sounds like the description I've been given for Antonio."

He squeezed her hand and lowered his voice. "The leader is injecting something in the nephilim's leg— No, he's...drawing blood."

"They're going to drink it," she said. "Can it be so easy as that? What happens when they've taken nephilim blood? They can walk in the daytime? What's so great about that? A lot of vampires already do that. Why do we need to fear the Anakim so much?"

"If it were so easy as taking blood I would suspect you've not much to fear from them. But..." He winced.

Below, shouts clattered. Cassandra saw what looked like crimson spattered all over the dais and the arms and faces of the vampires.

"They injected it into one of their own. Then... boom." Sam turned and settled to squat against the railing and the scene. "It's not going to be so easy. Which means they'll continue to hunt muses and Fallen in hopes of creating more nephilim. And meanwhile, they will torture the one they have in custody, if it stays captive for long. We've got to kill it before the vampires can figure how to use it to their advantage."

Cassandra swallowed. The idea of destroying a living thing did not sit well with her. But when the thing was a monster… "Its mother was human."

"You can't think of that, Cassandra. It is a monster, through and through. Wouldn't your grandmother want you to protect innocents?"

She nodded, but it was still hard to agree when she thought of Ophelia and her lost life.

"Your sister has the angel ash?" Sam flashed her a hopeful gaze.

"Yes, let's go back up," she said.

He directed her up the stairs. They emerged on the roof as another being landed on the cinder blocks edging the snowy surface. It spread out its wings of bone and growled at Sam.

"Everybody down!" Sam yelled, and charged the Fallen one.

Chapter 17

Cassandra pulled herself up from the snow. Her cheek had landed on ice when Sam had protectively shoved her down. She wiped away blood from her skin.

Two Fallen faced off at the corner opposite where she, her sister and Zane were. Sam, who remained in human form, was keeping the new Fallen away from them, she knew. But whenever he leaped from the roof, perhaps in an attempt to bring the Fallen along, the angel with wings of bone swept out a wing to grab Sam and whip him onto the roof.

"Zane!"

Cassandra grabbed her sister around the waist when she started after the vampire, who swung the demon blade on a long chain in an expert

move. "He's armed. You are not, so we're staying here."

"You're bleeding. Did Sam do that to you?"

"It's nothing, not his fault." Her sister's eyes
watered. "An accident, Coco." She hugged her
against her neck. "Worry about Zane. Just so long
as your lover doesn't stab the wrong angel with
that blade. I'd hate to protest your wedding because your new hubby killed the man I—"

Coco grasped the front of Cassandra's jacket
and her sadness burst into joy. "The man you...?
Love?"

She kept her mouth shut, which only drew her
sister's grin broader. She could imagine what she
wanted to hear, yet at this moment, Cassandra
wasn't sure how to answer.

Yes, you are.

Very well. She was sure.

He said he'd sacrifice Above for her. That was
all he had wanted, to return. And instead he'd
trade it all to simply hold her hand. How amazing
was that?

Zane slid across the roof, and landed at their
feet. The blond vampire shook the snow off his
head and smiled at Coco. "Got 'em right where I
want them."

"Don't you dare hurt Sam," Cassandra admon-
ished.

The vampire gave her a double take, then nodded, agreeing. "I think I should sit this one out.

Your Sam has things under control. You still have the bag of angel ash, love?"

Coco dug under her coat and drew out the Zip-loc full of crystal ash. "You take it. It'll be safer in your hands. You've got the big blade to protect—"

Zane stood, and immediately ducked as two angels soared over his head. The vampire's hand snatched at the air. The new Fallen had hooked the plastic bag with a wing tip.

Cassandra felt the sweep of a wing across her head and shoved Coco. "Let's move!"

"Watch it!" Zane lunged and flattened both Cassandra and Coco upon the snow. "Stay flat."

Blood dripped onto Cassandra's hand. It wasn't blue, which meant the vampire must have taken a hit. She sure hoped getting vamp blood on her skin wouldn't turn her into a bloodsucker.

"The bloody Fallen nabbed the bag," Zane said.

She managed to crane her neck in time to see the Fallen teetering, arms out and flapping, the bag of angel ash dangling from its broken wing tip. A thick blue line seeped across its neck.

Sam swung an arm before him, halo in hand, cutting another deep gash into his opponent's bare chest. The halo stuck and when he plunged it deep into the heart, Cassandra knew what would happen, and screamed.

Sam twisted, whipping the angel into the air to fling it away from them. A bone wing swept before him and he grabbed the plastic bag. The flimsy plastic tore away from the wing tip. Crystal ash spilled out, showering the sky, and the wind took it into a swirl.

"No!" Coco jumped, grasping at the ash in the air, but was unable to collect the minute flecks. A wing whisked over her head. Coco fainted.

The Fallen stumbled, knocking Sam over with its massive wing. He headed toward Cassandra and the others. Blue blood spurted from its chest where Sam's halo was embedded. Yet it roared and slashed forward a wing.

Zane dodged under the bone wing structure and shoved the demon blade up through the center of the halo and deep into the Fallen's heart. A spectacular explosion of angel ash filled the air around the vampire. Crystal flakes from the body glinted as if shards of glass.

The wind gusted again, taking the ash into the sky, along with the other remnants.

Sam dropped against the cinder blocks, head bowed and hand slapping the ooze of blue over his heart.

Cassandra ran over to Sam and saw the splinter of bone sticking out from his chest. Part of the Fallen's wing had lodged there. She grabbed it and yanked it out. Blue gushed from the wound.

It could not be a fatal wound. The bone would have had to pierce Sam's glass heart. Bone cannot go through glass. But she didn't know. Everything about the Fallen was ineffable, strong and strangely adamant.

Dropping the bone, she pressed her palms to

Sam's chest. "It can't be. Please! Tell me it didn't pierce your heart."

Sam grabbed her about the waist and pulled her to him. His breath hushed against her ear. "Don't worry, bunny. Just a little cut. My heart is intact."

"A little cut?"

He smoothed a finger over the cut on her cheek. "I'm sorry."

"For what? You're alive!"

"The ash."

Their only means of killing the nephilim trapped in the warehouse below had been dispersed and was now impossible to collect. As well, the newly slain Fallen's ashes had been whipped away by the wind.

"We'll think of something." She kissed Sam and pulled his head to her chest to hold him tightly.

It seemed around every corner they turned some new and deadly force was waiting to push them back the two steps they'd gained. It would be suicide to charge the vampire tribe right now. Not without an army of slayers—and angel ash.

"The wind took it all," Sam whispered. "It's as if we were not meant to be here at this moment. I don't understand it, Cassandra." He fisted his fingers. "It should have been so easy."

"Nothing worth accomplishing is ever easy."

"We need the ash to slay the nephilim."

"We'll get more somehow."

"Somehow? Right. I could…" He slapped his

wounded chest then studied the oddly colored blood that dripped off his fingers. A wince tightened his jaw, but he smoothed it away with a nod. "I have a plan."

"A plan?" Zane nodded, flipping the demon blade between his fingers. "We're listening." He bent over Coco and lifted her head as she came to from the faint. Smoothing his fingers over her brow, he offered a calm safety that Cassandra admired.

Sam studied his halo, tracing blue blood rimming the edges, and placed it against his chest, over his heart, the blade digging into the oozing wound.

Cassandra lunged for her lover. "No!"

She managed to shove him backward onto the snowy rooftop, which dislodged the halo from his chest. She grabbed the halo and tossed it to Coco, who caught it and tucked it behind her back.

Sam growled and wrestled her onto her back in the snow. He was gentle, but she couldn't have gotten free if she tried. He pinned down her wrists. "I have to do this!"

"You're not going to sacrifice yourself! The three of us cannot fight all the vampires and a bloody nephilim without your help."

Abruptly releasing her, Sam sat back on his heels. He looked to Coco, who fixed him with an impudent I-dare-you glare.

"You're not going anywhere, buddy," Cassandra said, gripping his bloody shirt. "Not until the nephilim is dead and we've got the book from the vampires. Got that?"

He nodded, silent in acquiescence. Yet at that moment he seemed lost, perhaps defeated.

"Then you can return Above," Cassandra added, "or wherever it is you want to go."

"I'll stay here with you. If you don't mind."

She lifted her chin, looking at him through her lashes. "That is what I want."

"We need to regroup," Zane suggested. "Coco and I need to recharge. She's been running on fumes for over twenty-four hours. And I'm a little worried for all the fainting you've been doing, love."

"Yeah, weird, eh?" Coco clasped her boyfriend's hand. Sam's halo dangled on her wrist. "Let's take a few hours and come up with a new plan of attack. We know where the vamps are now. We just need to figure how we can overtake them. Let's head to the hotel."

Sam held out his hand to receive, and Coco stared blankly at it.

"It's his halo," Cassandra said.

Her sister nodded and sheepishly handed over the weapon. "It makes me feel hope to hold it. Caz insists she doesn't feel it, maybe because she's a muse. We have the other one back at the hotel. But…it was nice to hold for a moment. Thanks."

Sam took the halo and studied it as the wind swept a cold breeze over the rooftop. He offered it back to Coco. "Hang on to it until we get to the hotel, will you?"

As if offered a great treasure, Coco accepted the halo and clutched it to her chest. Zane lifted her in his arms and stepped to the roof ledge. "Thank you." She winked at her sister. "See you back at the fort!"

Cassandra snuggled up to her wounded warrior, not caring her shirt was soaked in the blue blood or that the wetness was making her shiver. "That was kind of you."

"She'll take care of it. I trust her. I'm sorry I scared you. It was foolish of me to think I could help you by taking myself out of the equation."

"You are my protector."

"I'll defend you with my life, lover mine."

"I like it when you claim me like that."

"Lover mine?" He kissed her head and lifted her into his arms. "Let's fly."

She snuggled against his chest, and as they took to the air, she wished he really could fly and that, together, they could leave this earth. And then she abandoned the wild wish, because she knew she'd already had it once, wrapped in Sam's arms as they had made love.

Another hot shower was what she needed to wash off the strangely sticky blue angel blood and restore her body to normal temperature. The hotel bathroom mirror was steamed and Cassandra drew a circle on it.

She tilted her head, wondering why she'd done that. Then, without thinking it through, she drew a spiral in the middle of the circle, a match to her sigil.

"The muse protected by her angel," she whispered. "His halo surrounds me. I'm not going to let him go. He's mine."

Naked, and still wet from the shower, she stalked from the bathroom to the bedroom, where Sam sat on the bed. Tearing open his blood-soaked, tattered shirt, she kissed his chest.

"Whoa! What's up?"

"I want to have angry, end-of-the-world sex," she said. "Got a problem with that?"

"No. But it's not the end of the world."

"It's not the apocalypse, either, but it feels pretty close right now. Don't harsh my angry sex vibes, Sam. Give me some of this angel flesh. Right now."

She shoved him hard and he fell back on the bed, arms splayed. But he wasn't going to play shy. He wrapped his legs about her hips and pulled her onto him. The possession racheted up her desire tenfold.

Unzipping his fly, she didn't bother to pull down the pants and instead slid her hand inside to grip his erection. "You saving this for something special? Or can we get some use out of it?"

He heeled off his pants and lifted her thighs to position her directly over his cock. "You want it angry? I'm not angry with you, but I can give you dirty and needy."

He lowered her onto his shaft, and the hot width of him burned her sweetly as she slid onto his hardness. Holding her hips, he moved her up and down. She followed his direction, slapping a palm to his chest where the halo had cut but had not left a scar.

"If this is why I Fell," he growled, jaw tight, "I'd do it again and again."

"You like sex with mortal women, big boy?"

"Just you, Cassandra mine. Only you. Ah!"

He came, his shoulders shuddering and a throaty growl vibrating against her fingers. He shot hot inside her and one sweep of his fingers across her swollen nub brought her right along with him.

Cassandra swung back her arms and gripped him below the knees as her loins contracted and frenzied the exquisite high of orgasm through her muscles. It had happened so fast, so perfectly.

"Oh, God."

His surprising utterance made her swing upright and bracket his face with her hands. "What did you just say?"

"Now I know why everyone gives a shout out to Him while in the throes of orgasm. It truly is something worthy of thanks."

"Angel boy, we're just getting started."

He tilted his hips, turned her onto her back on the bed, and slid his hands down her torso and thighs, spreading her legs wide. Bowing to her mons, he pressed his mouth against her heat to taste her.

Chapter 18

Cassandra held a coffee cup in each hand, and still managed to push the elevator button with her elbow. Normally, she didn't begin to function until after sunrise, and pushing buttons with her elbows? So talented!

An incredible mood had fixed into her bones. The past few hours had been perfect, wrapped in an angel's arms. And though the day promised Really Bad Stuff, she wasn't going to worry about it until after she'd had her coffee.

The elevator dinged, and she was startled to see two men from inside walk toward her. Must be morticians from the conference.

As they paralleled her, one grabbed her about the shoulders, and the other slapped a palm over her mouth. One of her hands crushed the paper coffee cup, spilling hot liquid down her pants leg. She tried to swing the other cup toward one of her attackers, but the coffee only splashed the inner elevator wall.

They carried her, squirming, around the corner and outside to a waiting black van.

A black van only meant one thing.

What the hell were vampires doing up so early? Or were they getting ready to tuck in for the day?

What was she thinking? Vampires had kidnapped her.

"Cassandra? Ah—yikes! Oh. Oh, dear."

Eyes closed, Sam heard a female voice somewhere in the room. His skin was cool, but whispered with memory of Cassandra's tongue laving its entirety.

Mmm, he wanted more. And wished he could lick her without giving her the itchy angelkiss. Soon, he'd claim his soul, which would grant him mortality—and the ability to lick his lover in return. Above offered nothing when compared to lying in Cassandra's arms.

"Sorry. Is my sister in the bathroom? Er, are you awake? Oh, dear."

That wasn't Cassandra's voice. Must be the sister. Of course, Cassandra was lying right next to him. Sam slapped the empty side of the bed.

He came awake with a start, sitting upright, noting he lay naked on top of the sheets.

Coco stood near the door, examining the ceiling.

"Sorry." He dragged a sheet up from the floor and wrapped it around his waist.

A knock on the door sounded just before the door opened. The vampire walked in, took one look at Sam standing in nothing but a sheet, and turned a scornful look on his lover.

The trio quickly realized something was not right. Zane had returned from the coffee shop and hadn't run into Cassandra while there. After Sam dressed in jeans and a thin T-shirt Zane had lent to him and led them to the elevator, they discovered traces of spilled coffee. They reached the ground floor and saw the empty coffee cups abandoned near the door exiting to the parking lot.

"Someone has taken her," Coco deduced. She clung to Zane, who kissed her forehead and reassured her they would find her sister. "But who would do this?"

"Vampires," Sam confirmed. "I can smell their acrid scent."

Zane cleared his throat.

"It's an aggressive scent," Sam clarified. "I'll wager they've taken her to the warehouse where they're keeping the nephilim."

"For what purpose?" Coco asked. "They don't need the muse now they have a nephilim."

"What if their experiments with the nephilim

continue to go awry?" Sam conjectured. "They can use a muse and another…" He swallowed, realization hitting hard. "They've taken her to lure me to them. That must be it."

And yet, something didn't feel right about that, either. The vampires could summon any number of Fallen now they had the book of sigils and names. They didn't need Sam.

And that made Cassandra's predicament ten times worse.

"You can't go after her," Coco said to him. "You won't be able to keep your emotions in check. You'll get angry. What if you shift?"

"Then Sam will stay far away," Zane suggested. "I can go in after them."

"No. They don't need me." Sam started toward the outer door, fury pushing his steps. "They stole the book from Cassandra's loft. They're going to summon another Fallen."

"But I thought you had to be dead for another Fallen to go after Cassandra. Oh, dear." Coco melted into Zane's arms, but thankfully it was not a faint.

"No, the other Fallen merely has to have lost his muse or already attempted her. I'm not sure, really. Whatever their plans, Cassandra is in trouble. And I won't stand around talking about it."

Cassandra wrestled with the manacles about her wrists. The heavy iron tore her skin making it bleed. It hurt, but she couldn't feel the pain beyond the initial tear of skin. Because she was distracted by *its* heartbeat.

In a cage not twenty feet away from her, the nephilim sat, its bare shoulders rolled forward, and legs bent and clasped against its torso. The thing's heavy round head was bald and distorted, as if the skin had melted to a sloggy pile around its jaw. The ear was placed low and was pointed and tiny. On its back a small set of wilted wings, atrophied and pink, flapped, but could not lift a kitten from the ground, let alone the giant.

Every so often it would give a mournful howl and bang the cage bars with its head. Impressions of the bars remained on the skull as if the bone were soft enough to be molded.

Perhaps the bones were. It was still a new-born. She guessed it must stand over nine feet tall. Naked and deformed, hideous was the only way to describe it. Until it turned to look at her.

Now Cassandra gazed into the perfectly round eyes. The irises boasted the kaleidoscope colors all Fallen possessed, except these irises really did move and shift, changing colors and creating gorgeous new designs. And they were watered with tears.

Falling deep into the nephilim's sorrowful gaze, Cassandra felt its pain and fear. It had only been on earth a day or two, a new and strange world where it should not even exist. It was merely struggling to survive the only way it could—on flesh and blood. The creature couldn't understand why it had been caged, held captive and tortured.

It was a baby. It needed what all children required—someone to offer reassurance, care for it, to…to hold its hand.

All I desire is someone to hold my hand.

Swallowing her sobs, Cassandra whispered, "I'm so sorry. This never should have happened."

The nephilim blinked, releasing copious tears. Then it opened its jaw wide, revealing sharp, double rows of fanged teeth and yowled so loudly Cassandra caught her head in her palms to cover her ears. Myriad tongues screamed out in that yell, like centuries of battle cries from all races and breeds. It pounded in Cassandra's veins, and she bent over, curling into a ball.

"Shut that thing up!"

A pair of well-shod legs and feet stopped before her. Pricey loafers and tailored trousers. The man squatted and, able to ignore the whimpering yowls from the nearby cage without a wince, he angled his head to look her over.

A black business suit and black shirt sported the glint of hematite at cuffs and neck. Hair as dark as the metallic stone was combed into a slick queue. His black eyes held centuries of knowledge, though no wrinkles creased his face. Those dark eyes touched her with a strange kindness.

"Antonio del Gado. Vampire," he offered by way of introduction. "And you are Cassandra Stevens. Muse." He lifted a chain from around his neck and popped out the silver medallion from behind his shirt. "This was very clever."

It was one of her sigil necklaces. *Her* sigil. She'd only made one of them, and it had sold for a ridiculous amount, enough to pay her rent for a year.

Sam's sigil, too.

The vampire could summon Sam here and— no, Sam would not shift to half form. He had sworn to her he would never shift again.

Unless he was taunted with a Taser, which would steal his control.

"I don't need your Fallen," the vampire purred wickedly, his voice softened by a Spanish accent. "I've the book and have summoned another Fallen, Kambriel, to earth. My men have located him already and soon he'll be here. For you."

"You bastard. You have what you want."

Antonio glanced over the cage where the nephilim sat with its head smashed against the bars, quiet for now, tears rolling down its melted face.

"That thing may not survive our initial run of experiments. Apparently it's not so easy as drinking the blood. I don't know what we are doing wrong. But we'll figure it out, even if we have to tear the thing apart."

"What's so important about being able to walk in the day? You've obviously survived for decades—"

"Centuries," he rolled off his tongue. "After

centuries of darkness I want the light. And the strength that comes from the nephilim's blood."

"You're endangering innocents."

"You're not innocent."

"I'm talking about the humans the nephilim may have harmed while it was walking free."

"But we've contained it now. No more danger. You should be pleased, Cassandra."

"Pleased you're going to sic a Fallen on me and make me give birth to one of those? Pleased I'll die after giving birth? Go screw yourself."

"There is a possibility you may survive the birth."

"Unlikely."

"If you were vampire, you would."

The suggestion, so out of the blue, struck at her as if he'd stabbed her in the heart with a stake. And when Cassandra looked up at Antonio del Gado, long ivory fangs slid over his lower lip and his devious grin widened.

Chapter 19

Sam wanted to use his ability to walk swiftly to get to the warehouse, but Zane strode alongside him, and he did need all the extra help he could get. He was one angel with the strength of twenty men, but that didn't mean he'd the dexterity to fight off twenty vampires coming at him at once.

They'd made Coco stay behind at the hotel. To bring her along would only put her in danger. The vampire had kissed her quickly and calmed her frantic gibbering, probably with his innate persuasion. An example of love, the duo gave Sam hope that he and Cassandra could have the same love.

"You've got your halo, I've the demon blade," Zane said as they walked swiftly across the bridge toward the warehouse. "You sure you won't take this extra halo? I can't use them both at once."

"I will not touch another Fallen's halo. If you've wielded it against a Fallen one, you should be able to use it again."

"Right then. Sure wish we had an entire gang of vampires to help us. Or werewolves. Those hairy blokes would be great help in a pinch."

"Ivan Drake had none to offer?"

"The vampire population in Berlin is nearly nil at the moment. Tribal wars have led them south where the vanguard lies. I don't get vampire politics, so I didn't ask. I'm glad to be unaligned."

"But you were Anakim. Did you not have designs to capture the Fallen?"

"Me? None, whatsoever. I left as soon as Antonio suggested the devious plan. I'm not about hurting innocent women."

"You are not like most vampires, then."

"Apparently, you don't know a lot of vampires. We come good, evil and somewhere in between. Just like your standard human. Don't judge, bloke. You'll notice I haven't gone ninja on your evil Fallen arse."

"I am not like my brethren. Forgive me, Zane. You've made your point. I'm focused on freeing Cassandra."

"I know. She's your girl. I understand completely. But while you're charging in to her rescue, vampires are going to flank us. And if they have the book they may have summoned another bloody Fallen."

"I've got it under control," Sam said harshly.

He smacked a fist in a palm, feeling his muscles tense to a hardness that rivaled his silver wings. He'd like to shift to half form and take the vampires out with fierce wings, but he could not risk the peril he would introduce to Cassandra were he in that form. He'd made a promise to her; he would keep it at all costs.

If the vampires had harmed one inch of her soft skin he would flail the flesh from their bodies before shoving his fingers into their chests and ripping out their beating hearts.

"We have the advantage of daylight," he said.

"Del Gado has minions who can go out in daylight. Look at me. We all are affected by some level of sun exposure, but I'm good for half an hour in indirect light. And it's cloudy, which doubles my exposure time. Besides, his men have special UV protection suits."

"Won't matter. I'll kill any vampire in my path."

"Then I'll stay clear of your path. And what if they zap you with a Taser? Think about that. If they take you out, then I'm on my own. We gotta work together, bloke. Or you'll never see your bird alive again."

Make that his bunny.

"You offer a good argument. Let's work on the plan of attack before we arrive."

* * *

Cassandra kicked Antonio del Gado in the gut. His fangs grazed her jaw before he stumbled backward and landed sprawled.

In the cage, the nephilim stood and shook the bars. One bar, as thick as her arm and fashioned from iron, loosened at the bottom.

Granny had not given her any advice or spells against a nephilim. The idea of such a creature walking the earth had always been an *idea*.

"You're frightening it!" she said, admonishing the vampire who stood and brushed off his suit sleeves.

"Me? That thing is an abomination! It cannot be anything but monstrous."

"It's just a baby. Leave it alone. Quit poking it with needles and just…"

"Just what?" Del Gado leaned in, but not close enough for her to kick him again. The silver sigil necklace dangled close enough to grab. "Just let it go? Very well, I will do that. I will take great joy in watching the creature terrorize the city of Berlin. And while we're enjoying the mayhem, I will slay your Fallen, and the other Fallen—"

"Antonio!"

He turned. A crew of four vampires dragged a naked man across the cement floor in the massive warehouse, and dropped him halfway.

"The new Fallen," one of them said. "Kambriel. The Taser knocked him out, but he should be coming to real soon."

"You couldn't have offered him a pair of slacks?"

The vampire winced. "It was kind of creepy carrying a naked dude here."

"Give him your clothes."

The vampire gaped.

"Now!"

The shaky underling pulled off his leather jacket, and stripped to his striped boxer shorts.

Antonio twisted a wickedly gleeful look at Cassandra. She could imagine him rubbing a palm over a dastardly fist.

"The party soon begins," he said and winked at her. "Pity you wouldn't allow me to transform you to vampire first."

"I'd rather be dead," she said flatly, and knew that was the only other option.

With the warehouse in sight, Sam charged, his feet leaving the ground and the superfast walk angels were capable of taking him to the door in seconds. The vampire followed at a distance, as they'd decided. Sam would reconnaissance, and by the time Zane arrived, he'd have the layout and details of how many were inside.

Marching toward the two-story steel door, Sam was bodychecked from the side by a massive form. He and his attacker soared through the air and ended up in a snowdrift higher than a car.

A metal-armored fist punched Sam's jaw. He shook off the bone-jarring pain and blinked. "A bloody Sinistari. I don't need this now! Raphael, call off your troops!"

A kick sent the demon stumbling backward. Sam raced after him, pummeling him to the ground before the door. The two exchanged punches, kicks and curses. He didn't see the demon's blade, which could be his end, yet Sam knew it must be on the demon somewhere.

"You've got the wrong Fallen," he barked, and smashed a fist into the demon's chest. He wore armor, which was cheating, because in demonic form the Sinistari were already solid metal.

The demon jumped to stand, surprisingly agile in the heavy armor. "All Fallen are wrong."

"Yeah? You come from Fallen stock, buddy."

The demon tilted its head in wonder. "Buddy?"

"Right. You probably just arrived. Haven't had a chance to walk the world and learn slang, phrases and facts. You were once like me." He unhooked the halo from his hip and slashed it in the air.

The demon reached behind one shoulder and drew out a two-foot-long blade.

"Seriously? Doesn't look like a standard-issue Sinistari blade."

"I've modified it," the demon said with a hematite grin. "A millennia spent Beneath grants one time to develop a hobby. Say your prayers, Fallen one. I'm sending you home to daddy."

Sam dodged the swinging blade. "He's your father, too!"

"You lie!"

Sam released the halo, which cut around the demon's neck, through the armor, and circled back to Sam's hand.

The demon's helmet broke away and he shook it off to reveal a black, horned skull. The tips of its horns, curled along its head, glowed red. No damage to his metallic flesh. It charged, catching Sam at the shoulders and pushing them against the steel door. The entire door shook and clattered.

The Sinistari's blade, aimed downward at Sam, paused. The demon tilted its head, listening. It sniffed. "There's another Fallen?"

Sam's hard glass heart expanded a beat and dropped. In the moment of silence, enemy clutching enemy, he sensed…Cassandra. She called to him from inside his heart because that was where she lived. But he also sensed what the demon sensed.

"Another Fallen? That means—" He shoved at the Sinistari. "He's going to hurt her! You've got the wrong angel. The muse is inside!"

The demon redirected the blade toward the door, wedging it in the crease between both doors, and popped it open. A dozen vampires rushed them.

Zane arrived, huffing, and dashed in behind the demon and Sam. "You go after Cassandra," he directed at Sam. He eyed the demon, who took in the situation with a seething hiss.

"Wanna kill some vampires?" Sam said to the Sinistari, not expecting an answer. "Hold them off, while I get the girl!"

"You will not attempt her!" the demon roared.

"He won't," Zane said to the demon as they met the oncoming vampires. "He's in love with her, see." First slash of the demon blade Zane owned took out one vampire, but didn't reduce it to dust. "Gonna have to cut off some heads, I see. Help me!"

The Sinistari, who considered the crazed vampire beating with futile result against his armor, glanced at Sam, who raced toward the dais where a muse had been chained and another Fallen stood. The running Fallen repelled all approaching vampires with a gesture of his hand.

A thin chain wrapped about the Sinistari's wrist and tugged. The vampire, who appeared to be Samandiriel's cohort, nodded and released the chain from his wrist with a flick. "You helping?"

"Fine." The Sinistari grabbed the vampire beating his chest and snapped off its head. "This won't take long."

Chapter 20

The Fallen angel standing above her brandished wings of startlingly beautiful binary code. The green, digital code was ordered in the shape of wings, and moved as if wind dusting through the feathers. Across his chest a sigil flashed blue, though why it did baffled her. His sigil shouldn't glow unless he was near his muse. And she was most definitely not his muse.

· Then another idea occurred to Cassandra. She prayed that none of the muses Coco had put on flights away from Berlin had changed their minds about leaving.

None of that mattered. What did was the angel who approached her with a lascivious grin and lust in his multicolored eyes. He was focused on one goal: to mate with her.

Cassandra screamed as a wing of seemingly intangible substance swept forward and brushed her cheek. It felt like fire and she smelled burned hair. The coded feathers slipped around behind her neck, burning a trail in her flesh. He leaned in, sticking out his tongue to stroke across her face—and then the creature was gone.

The Fallen was flung up and away from her. And in his place stood Sam. Unwinged. Shirt torn away and muscles flexing as tensely as his jaw. He reached for her, but the other Fallen—Kambriel—collided with him, and the twosome flew across the warehouse.

In the cage, the nephilim yowled and worked at the bar, which had become even looser.

At the far end of the warehouse, vampires battled with what looked like a Sinistari and Zane.

"Coco? The vamp better not have brought her along."

Standing and straining against the manacles, Cassandra searched the upper catwalk where she'd seen Antonio enter and leave the warehouse. The key to unlock the manacles was in his trouser pocket. She bet he wasn't going to stick around with all Hell scattered loose below.

Above and Beneath, she corrected. The demon and the angels had come to heads. Toss in a few earthly bloodsuckers and—

An ear-shattering screech felled her to her knees. The nephilim banged the bar it had wrenched free from the cage against the other bars.

The space was yet too small for it to fit through. But that didn't stop it from jamming a shoulder between the bars and pushing. It wouldn't take long for it to bend the other bars.

Zane dodged to avoid the Sinistari's arm as it slashed around the long demon blade and cut off the heads of two vampires. One Anakim minion left standing.

The Sinistari could handle it.

Zane leaped over the piles of ash, only a little disturbed that he could have ended up the same. Ahead, the Fallen ones went at it up by the caged creature—and Cassandra.

His first objective was to keep Coco's sister safe. But those cage bars were beginning to bend. Bloody hell, that creature was ugly.

The two Fallen clashed and their momentum sent them soaring to the top of the cage. The new Fallen used its odd, glowing wings as weapons, cutting deftly across Sam's body, and using them to trip him or punch as if a multitude of extra arms. Sam appeared to be tiring, losing the battle as he teetered at the edge of the cage—until he was not.

Growling and thrusting his shoulders back and forth, Sam shifted, shaking out wings of silver.

"Not bloody good. No wings! You forgot, no wings!"

Zane raced for the cage. In his peripheral vision he sighted Cassandra. She was safe for now.

It seemed the Fallen could go at it forever, sweeping wings and tearing at muscles. They were an equal match. Yet Sam's halo, dropped during the fight, lay on the ground near the muse. He had no means to destroy his opponent.

"This better work." Swinging the chain out wide and in a circle, Zane aimed high. "Sam! Catch!" He released the chain and said a prayer to any God who would listen.

Kambriel's wings of code swept across Sam's thigh, burning deep into his mortal flesh. Damned wings were like laser beams. He folded a wing forward and cut across the Fallen's throat, but the gaping line of blue didn't slow down his opponent.

Below, he heard Zane call out to catch. Sam saw the glint of blade soar high. Yes, the demon blade. Just what he needed.

Clutching, he leaped out from the cage top and grabbed the blade. As he began to free-fall, the Fallen grabbed Sam by the neck with a wing and squeezed. The vise grip cut through his mortal flesh and muscle. He could cry out, but he didn't need to.

Using his last bit of strength, Sam swung an arm backward and embedded the Sinistari blade into the Fallen's chest.

Sam had slain the Fallen intent on mating with her.

Sam had shifted to half form during the battle.

Which meant only one thing—she was not safe from him now.

But Cassandra couldn't reason beyond what she witnessed. As Sam held the blade deep inside his brethren Fallen, the few standing below gathered. The Sinistari stomped across the floor, seething but apparently content to wait and see which Fallen remained whole for him to slay next.

Zane, head back and jaw gaping in wonder, let out a cry as the first crystals of angel ash began to fall.

Like winter snow, the crystal remains of Kambriel fluttered from above the cage where Sam stood, silver wings outstretched magnificently. The ash caught the harsh fluorescent light and glinted in all colors, much like the Fallen's eyes. So beautiful.

The nephilim had noticed, too. Cage bar held in one stubby pink hand, it opened its mouth to wonder at the substance falling directly above it.

"No," Cassandra whispered, and caught her fist against her chest. "Don't stand under it. It'll…"

But she could not stop what had already begun.

Angel ash fluttered onto the nephilim's bare, distorted head and spilled over its sloggy eyelids. The creature lapped at the substance, gulping at it as if starved. Its entire body seemed to soak in the crystal, drawing it into the pores.

And when it was completely covered with

angel ash, a brilliant light spread over the entire creature, and a flash beamed out from the nephilim, as if from divinity. Cassandra had to shield her eyes. Zane bent and twisted away from the brilliance as if it were sunlight.

The Sinistari plunged onto one knee, reverent as it bowed its metallic head.

The nephilim released a great howl that shook the walls and roof and shattered a few windows. Limbs outstretched, it cried to the heavens from which it could claim no home.

Cassandra choked back tears.

The brilliance flashed out.

A few flakes of angel ash sifted down from above.

Cassandra approached the cage, but was abruptly stopped by the chains. The cage was empty. Not a trace of angel ash or nephilim. It had not escaped; the ash of a Fallen one had simply consumed it.

Gone. Accidentally slain. An innocent condemned by the need for bloodshed to survive.

Someone grabbed her from behind. "We need to get you out of here, love. Boyfriend isn't looking too friendly right now. Rather, I think he wants to get friendly, if you know what I mean."

Above them, Sam peered down from the top of the cage. His wings flexed out, and his body shone under the lights as if he were a life-size silver sculpture.

Cassandra had never seen anything so beautiful.

"Sinistari!" Zane shouted. "Come here and help me get this pretty muse out of these manacles."

"I'll do better than that." The demon brandished his blade and looked up to Sam.

"No!" Cassandra shouted, but the demon paid her no heed. It stepped forward, but the vampire put out a foot and tripped it.

Zane flashed a wink at Cassandra. "That's not going to do us any good—he'll be up in a jiff. But I know where your head is at, love. Maybe I can pick these locks."

She gave him her wrist, but couldn't take her eyes from Sam. The outlaw angel held her gaze. Outstretched behind him and to his sides, his wings gleamed. Was he considering whether or not to jump and approach her? He must know, even in half form, that he could harm her.

Did it matter to him while in that form? Could he distinguish between right and what was deemed wrong according to human morals? He'd said the compulsion focused him. All he could see was he and the muse, together. And she suspected such a coupling would not be like the sweet love they had shared only hours earlier.

One manacle fell from her wrist. Zane started on the other.

The angel standing upon the cage jumped, wings stretching out to slow its descent.

The Sinistari lunged, blade aimed for Sam's heart.

Cassandra swept low and grabbed the halo. She had but a moment to aim, and knew she could never get it right, but had to try. She released the circlet in a *whoosh*.

The halo cut through the demon's wrist, severing the hand that wielded the blade and dropping it to the floor. It yowled and spun, spattering black blood across Cassandra's legs. It burned, but she'd withstood far worse.

The angel dodged to avoid the demon and in doing so, its wing tipped the halo and reset its trajectory. The halo soared over the top of Sam's head—and stopped.

The Fallen landed on the floor before the cage with a thump that stirred up the dust and minute ashes of angel. His halo, affixed above his head, glowed blue, yet it was growing brighter, much like the nephilim had done before dispersing into nothing. Sam whipped back his wings, but his movements did not dislodge the halo.

The other manacle dropped from Cassandra's wrist. She shoved away from Zane and ran to Sam.

Ignoring the fact she rushed into the arms of a winged angel who could harm her, she plunged into his solid form. It was as if she collided with destiny. He was warm. Heaving. She felt a pulse against her chest.

Was his heart beating?

Silver wings slid down her back and along her legs. The feel of it was like hot metal, but it didn't hurt. It felt as if sunlight moved through her veins.

That sunlight rained over her body in the form of silver ash as the wings dispersed around her.

Sam's body went limp, and he dropped from her embrace.

Chapter 21

Sam lay sprawled on the cement floor, nestled upon the silver ash that had once been his wings. He didn't move, no matter that Cassandra shook his shoulders.

Beside her Zane stood guard. "Stay back, Sinistari. You're after the Fallen. This one is…no longer."

No longer? Cassandra's heart fissured. Could it be real?

Sam's halo was nowhere visible. She hadn't seen it fall away from him as he'd collapsed.

What was going on? If he was dead the rest of his body would ash. Or maybe it just took longer. Usually the Fallen's wings ashed first and then his body.

"No." She pressed an ear to his chest. "It's beating. His heart is beating. He's alive. He has to be."

"Impossible," intoned the demon deeply. He clutched his wrist where the hand had been cut off and black tar oozed.

"Not impossible." The vampire stepped closer to the demon, keeping him back. "Your bloke going to be okay, love?"

"I'm not sure. I can't bring him awake. Oh, hell, why not?"

A swirl of dancing lights suddenly rose from out of Sam's chest. They dipped and flickered, hazing the air. Was that the beginning of his end?

Cassandra clasped at the intangible lights, trying to force them back into Sam's chest.

A man shimmered into view and tutted before saying, "Won't work, Cassandra Stevens. Those are mine." He gestured the lights toward him and they giddily wavered up to his dark figure.

The Sinistari took a step back. "Soul bringer."

"He's not dead!" Cassandra pleaded with the soul bringer, helpless to stop what she couldn't comprehend.

"Is that so?"

"No! He's…he's got to be alive. He just doesn't need these souls anymore. They belong to the souls of all the mortals he taught the craft of silversmithing. Go ahead and take them." She swished the lights away from Sam's chest, then pounded a fist upon his hard pectoral, right over his heart. "No! We were going to be there for each other. He was going to sacrifice Above to stay with me. I…I love him. I…I thought we could have a happily-ever-after."

Much as her idea of happily ever after had never seemed real, she wanted it now. She'd fought angels and demons, and vicious vampires. Didn't she deserve a happy ending?

You're not a princess, sweetie.

No, but she was someone's bunny, and she wasn't about to let this be the end.

With silly fairy tales dancing in her brain, Cassandra bent to kiss her lover's mouth. The stories were always better than reality. A kiss could never bring a person back to life.

It was always and only true love that could breathe life into a loved one.

"I do love you," she whispered against Sam's lips. "I have loved you before you came to earth. I sculpted you, knowing you were the enemy, but wanting you to be mine. Come back to me, Sam. Love me. Let me love you."

She clasped his hand and held it to her heart. "I promised you I'd hold your hand. Well, I'm doing it now. Can you feel me, Sam?"

She kissed him hard, clasping his head between her hands and straddling him to lift his head. A shaky hand slid over her hip, and she thought it was the vampire, until she noticed Zane ran past her.

"Be right back, love. I see a sneaky master vampire I need to introduce to my blade."

"I'll go along," the Sinistari growled.

And the hand at her back pulled her down to embrace against his hard chest that housed a beating heart. Sam pushed fingers through her hair. "Entwine me within your ribbons forever, love." He pulled her to his mouth to kiss.

Cassandra had dreamed of this kiss. She'd never thought to know it. Had hoped. Had aspired to such a selfless connection. And now she felt it become reality.

The divine light she'd witnessed in the nephilim and in Sam before his wings had dispersed now grew between the two of them, blazing through her system. His heart beat against her palm. And Cassandra knew the light was really his earthbound soul coming alive inside him.

"Love you," he murmured. "Always have."

"You're alive."

"Yes. And...mortal?"

"I think so. I'm sorry, I wasn't trying to put the halo above your head. I just wanted to take out the Sinistari. My aim was horribly off. Can you forgive me?"

"For giving me mortality?" He pushed onto his elbows. Azure eyes studied hers. Not multicolored, but instead a clear, liquid blue. "For loving me? I will never forgive you. It's what I want, Cassandra. You and me. Together."

Epilogue

Coco and Zane married two days later in the AquaDom elevator as the fish swam about them and Cassandra and Sam stood by as witnesses. The newlyweds planned to return to London after a cruise around the world. Zane wanted to learn scuba diving, and Coco would finally have her world adventures. But Zane intended to be over-protective for the next few months. They'd figured out why Coco had been fainting; she was three months' pregnant.

After the book had been retrieved from Antonio del Gado, the Sinistari stalked the world to ensure no more Fallen existed. He found but one, slew it and claimed its feather. He then handed the book over to Raphael with Sam and Cassandra's blessing. The demon, whose name Sam had never gotten, was never seen again.

The Anakim leader escaped capture, but his lairs in Berlin and Paris were looted and destroyed under Ivan Drake's command. If the tribe leader showed anywhere in the world the Council would snatch him and administer just punishment.

The silver sigil necklace del Gado had worn was found in the warehouse, and Cassandra tucked it in a jewelry box at home. She still bore the sigil on her wrist, but it was a soft brown now, much like Coco's faded mehndi designs, and she knew it would never glow again.

Cassandra thanked the moving men who had dropped off a new couch and tipped them on their way out of her loft. She'd redecorated and repainted, and now felt sure no one would ever guess five vampires had been slain in the living room. She still intended to move back to London, but the new paint job could not be avoided.

The shower stopped, and she sauntered into the bathroom to snuggle against the steamy man who stepped out and groped for a towel in the fog.

"I like you wet," she said, and playfully licked his nipple.

He swung her over a shoulder and stalked into the bedroom, wet feet slapping a trail across the hardwood floor. Tossing her onto the bed, he leaped and landed beside her and curled her into his arms.

"I love you," she said, and kissed his wet cheek.

"I love you, too. Weird how the accident took away all memory of my past but left my memories of you."

"Weird, but good."

"Yes, very good."

He rolled on top of her, lifting her nightgown, and slipped inside her to slowly move in and out.

After Sam had gained his earthbound soul, his memory of being an angel quickly vanished. They had barely made it to the flat when she'd found him standing in the doorway, unsure and wondering why he couldn't recall where he'd been or where he had to go.

Thankfully, Sam had known her. Had trusted her when she'd conjured a story about him being in a car accident, which had left behind the weird burn in the shape of a spiral at the back of his hip—because he'd had the necklace in a pocket; which was why it matched her tattoo (he believed hers was a tattoo)—as well as altering his memory.

He'd wondered where he worked and if he had to get back to the job. Cassandra had made an excuse he was an artist's model and that's how they'd met, when she'd created the silver sculpture of him. Right now, he was between jobs and had been looking for an agent.

It worked for both of them—for now. She didn't like lying to him, and planned to someday tell him the truth. She just needed the right words, and a little time to work it out. More Fallen would come, now, or maybe decades or centuries later. Right now, she wanted a breather from doom. They had both earned it.

In the weeks since Sam had saved the world from the apocalypse—or at least a small catastrophe—they had spent most of their time making love, and some of the time eating and making plans to join Coco and Zane on their cruise. She'd explain Zane being a vampire to him later, as well.

Reaching aside, Cassandra picked up the silver feather from the nightstand. She'd found it on top of the silver ash left behind from Sam's wings. She drew it across her cheek and then down her lover's chest.

"I like it kinky," he purred deeply.

"Do you now, Mr. I Don't Remember Anything?"

"I think I do. Give me that."

He grasped the feather with his teeth and began to tickle her with it. Together, they now enjoyed heaven on earth.

* * * * *

Want to learn how Zane and Coco met?
Turn the page and read their story,
THE NINJA VAMPIRE'S GIRL,
published in ebook form by
Nocturne Bites!

Chapter One

London

I glided down the vast marble hallway, which was trimmed in gilded and plaster frieze, relieved to be away from the ballroom tucked amongst the wigs and damasks, satins and frockcoats. The party was to die for, the people gorgeous and the champagne and chocolate endless.

But I was not here for drink or flirtation.

Veering toward the lone ottoman placed in the center of the grand hallway, I plunged onto the tufted velvet and turned onto my back. The tight corset squeezed my ribs but I liked the snuggly feeling. And it pushed up my breasts nicely, making me feel sensual and womanly.

Alençon lace at my elbows hung over my

wrists, and I blew it aside to inspect the mehndi stained onto the palm of my hand. It was traditionally worn for weddings and celebrations, but I had hopes the sigils worked into the design would provide protection.

Scanning the three-story room with a vaulted ceiling that looked as if Michelangelo had set up a scaffold beneath, my eyes took in the elaborate gold frieze, gaudy paintings and portraits and crystal chandeliers. So much artwork in this hall, it resembled something from the British Museum.

"It could be anywhere," I muttered, sliding my hand down the black satin corset.

The red damask bodice was sown to the corset, but the red ribbons tying down the front of the corset were for show. Too busy for my taste, but the whole costume worked for this adventure.

I did like adventure. Adventure was my middle name.

Along the ceiling, plaster angels had been worked into the cornices, but they were all pudgy cherubs. Nothing so bold and virile as what I had hopes to find.

A musical jingle sounded in the stillness. I tugged a cell phone out from the side of the corset where it nestled against my breast, and answered.

"Cassandra? Yes, I'm here at the party. No, haven't found it yet. You're sure Leonard Marshall has one?"

My sister shuffled papers on her end—that would be a sweet little flat in Berlin—while my eyes strayed over the painting of a grazing horse, and then to the more modern and, frankly, groovy canvas that featured bright-colored rings dancing over a black background.

"It's got to be there, Coco."

"Wait." I sat up, wincing as the corset dug into my ribs. "I think I found it. Talk to you soon, Caz."

Tucking away the phone, I approached the groovy canvas hung above the right corner of the doorway. I squinted discerningly. One ring on that painting was most definitely not like the others.

"Score."

There was enough fancy plasterwork and wood chair railing on the wall to facilitate a makeshift rock climber like in the gym I attended.… Okay, so I paid membership fees, but the last time I worked out was too long ago to remember.

Pushing aside the bothersome poufy skirts to reveal my legs, I fit my ballet flat above the base-board plaster decoration, found finger-holds above a cherub's head and started to climb.

I'd left the hallway door open about a foot and the music from the ballroom—eighteeth-century harpsichord fused with techno thump—promised the revelers would party all night in celebration of Midsummer. I wasn't much for parties. My adventuring kept me pretty busy. And I could hardly think to celebrate when my sister was in trouble.

Securing my fingertips along the top of the door frame, I managed to boost up with my toes. The ring secured onto the canvas was a reach away.

My toe slipped on the satin hem of the dress. I slapped my free hand high, clasping the ring… and teetered backward into a free fall.

The woman landed in my arms, a flailing scatter of limbs and swishy satin. I caught her easily, her huge dress disguising her fey weight.

"It's not every day a bloke catches an angel," I said. "And looky here, this angel comes complete with halo."

She kicked and struggled so I let her stand and shuffle away. She shook the halo at me, prepared to spout some nasty reply, but she did not. Her jaw fell, and her bright brown eyes fixed to my face.

"It's not polite to stare, love." I stroked my cheek. "It's just a scratch."

She summoned courtesy, and straightened her delicate shoulders. "Sorry. I, uh…" She held the halo before her, momentarily marveling over it, then quickly tucked it behind her back.

The corset cinched her breasts high and firm. I licked my lips. I could go for some of that.

"You going to share?" I queried, cautiously pacing toward her, while she stepped backward, *away* from the door. I reached out with my mind to touch hers. The persuasion innate to my kind would serve my means to success. "Hand it over, love."

"I'm not your love. Who are you? What do you want?"

"I want that pretty halo your daring adventure has earned you."

"Well, as you said, it was *my* daring adventure. That makes it mine. So bug off, creep. Er...I, um..."

Her bright red lips parted. The hand holding the halo out of sight slid across her skirts, displaying the cheap-looking silver ring of ineffable metal.

I focused the persuasion. Just a little deeper...

Her long, dark lashes fluttered. Any moment now the halo would be mine.

"Wh-what are you doing to me?" She put up her free hand to block the unseen intrusion. "I can feel you trying to control... Are you a—? Are you a vampire?"

Ouch. This woman was in the know. My persuasion scattered and dropped. She turned to run.

"Guess I'll have to do this the old-fashioned way."

I beat her to the ottoman center of the hallway, and wrapped an arm about her shoulders as I landed on the big comfy island. Pulling her shoulders against my chest, I bent to sink my fangs into her juicy, thick jugular.

Blood oozed down my throat. Sweet mercy. When was the last time I'd sipped so fine a vintage? Mortals tended to be polluted with fast food and pharmaceuticals. This woman tasted pure, sweet and a little like chocolate. Delicious.

But I had a task to tend.

Reaching about with my free hand, I groped

for the halo, but she flailed madly, and it was hard enough keeping her neck at my mouth.

A kick from beneath her fussy skirts proved ineffectual. I clamped my hand over her mouth just as she screamed. Her wide eyes did not look at me, but instead, over my shoulder.

The door behind us slammed against the wall.

We both turned to spy the hulking angel, with wrought-iron wings extended out thirty feet behind him, smack a fist into his palm.

"Bloody hell."

Chapter Two

I recognized the man with shoulders wider than an armored truck as an angel even before I saw the wings spread out behind him and creak like the black iron they resembled.

An angel's wings are forged from the materials of their innate skill—the craft they'd taught mortals after Falling and had been punished for because supposedly *the Arts* had been sinful back then. This one must have been an ironsmith.

I clutched the halo until I thought surely my palm would bleed. My neck hurt. The vampire had torn his fangs from my vein when the angel walked in.

I had not expected to encounter a vampire tonight. Most especially, not a vampire sporting shocking white hair and a scar cutting from his forehead, through eyebrow and eye, and ending at his jaw. His scarred eye was cloudy white. Creepier than fangs, let me tell you.

But right now the vampire was the one thing standing between the growling angel and me, so I wasn't going to be picky about appearance. I tucked myself behind the ottoman just as a blade swung through the air.

Freaky appearance aside, the vampire was tall, lean and wore a sleeveless shirt that showed off sculpted muscles only seen in the movies. He was ripped, and yes, I had to slap a palm over my heart. Be still, pitter-pattering heart. Vampires are *not* sexy.

He swung some kind of chain that sported a nasty scythed blade on the end of it. And did he have the moves. Twirling it overhead in a whir of silver, he then slashed it down before him to detour the charging angel.

The vampire dropped to his back, rolled and came up with a slash of the blade that cut through the angel's thigh. Blue blood spattered the air.

Granny Stevens had taught Cassandra and I the lore on angels, so the blue blood didn't surprise me. But this was the first time I'd seen a real Fallen one in the so-called flesh. I wasn't about to shake its hand or offer to do lunch with it.

The Fallen wanted what I had.

Now I noticed the halo clutched to my chest glowed blue. "Damn." Blue meant one thing; it belonged to this particular angel.

I thrust out my hand, displaying the palm with the mehndi sigils on it. Not sure if it would work as a repellent but I wasn't going to take any chances in case my protector failed.

The vampire soared through the air and landed the ottoman with an *oof!* He flipped over backward, landing behind me on the floor, crouched and sported a ferocious sneer.

Then the bravery struck. And don't ask me where it came from.

"I'll get it!"

I popped up and wielded the halo like a Frisbee—I had been Frisbee champion in twelfth grade. Just as I sent it soaring toward the angel's neck, the vampire landed on my back, slapping my arm down.

"What the bloody hell did you do that for?" he gasped hotly against my face.

"Don't worry, it's supposed to come back like a—"

"A bleedin' boomerang. Love, that only works for the *original owner.*"

"Oh, no." Really? I don't think Granny ever told us that little detail.

"Duck!"

The vampire shoved me to the floor. I caught myself on palms and stomach, cell phone skittering across the hardwood. His body landed on top of mine, flattening me.

I heard the whooshing skim of the halo over our bodies, and saw it turn in the air at the opposite end of the hallway. It nicked a painting of naked nymphs and soared back toward the thrower. The angel caught the halo, gargled out a wicked chuckle and stomped out of the hall.

The vampire's fist beat the floor next to my face. "Damn it!"

"Sorry," I muttered and kicked at him to get off me. "I didn't know. I've got to go after it."

Grabbing my phone, I started toward the door, but my skirt caught on something and I went down, ungracefully landing on all fours.

The vampire released my skirt. Of all the— Blood puddled on the floor near my hand. Sitting up, I noticed the bleeding wounds on his back. The halo had cut through his shirt and sheered him from hip to shoulder.

"You're hurt!"

He snickered and pushed up to kneel. Easing back his wounded shoulder, he winced. "Guess I've you to thank for losing both the trophy and my skin. What's your name, love? So I can burn it from my memory. No, wait. No name will suffice."

"Coco," I blurted. Screw him for blaming me for his inability to dodge low enough.

Oh, Coco. He saved you!

"Coco. As in Chanel?"

"No, as in Rococo. My parents had a thing for Louis the Fifteenth. Now, I'd love to stick around and chat, but I have a halo to go after."

* * *

The bird had spunk. I liked that. But she wasn't going to cock up the nab for me again. I'd been so close!

"You're not going anywhere." I coiled up the chain.

"It's my halo!"

"Yeah?" Pretty, the way she held her tiny fists like that. It would be too easy for an angel to break her. "Fine. I don't need the halo, but I do need the angel attached to said halo. I almost had him."

"Oh, right, I noticed you had him when you were dodging the halo from hell."

I gave her the mongoose eye; it wasn't quite evil, mostly admonishing with a trim of evil.

Hooking the chain at my hip, I slicked the blue blood off the blade. Nasty stuff, that. I had no desire to taste it because I liked all my bits the way they were currently configured. Vampire drinks angel blood? Kaboom!

On the other hand, the blood from a Nephilim...

"What are you?" She followed as I stomped out of the hall, veering away from the ridiculous music. "Some kind of ninja vampire?"

How did she—? Right. I'd forgotten about the bite. I was in too much pain to care about such a tasty lick right now. I'd just had half my back flayed off, no thanks to her.

The side of her neck bled, and she was tripping on her torn skirt, but she managed to keep up with me as I angled toward a door I knew opened onto a private alley.

"Name's Zane," I offered. "No ninja blood in me." Not lately, anyway.

I kicked open the door, ignoring her stupid quest to follow.

"Wait!" She managed to catch up and shoved me. Hard. "Sorry," she offered, rubbing my blood off on her red skirts. She'd slapped me firmly on the abraded flesh, which was only half-healed.

"No problem, love. Hurt me all you like. I favor the rough stuff."

"I'm going with you," she said in an unsure voice that belonged home polishing furniture and cooking up dinners, all with a bouffant and manicure.

"You are not."

I let my eyes roam over her ridiculous attire. Hardly angel-tracking wear. And yet the fantasy of pushing up those skirts and kneeling beneath them to lick her until she moaned popped into my dirty little brain. I'd tasted her once. I did favor sweets.

Coco held up a finger to request my pause. I almost turned away, but the tearing seams proved more tantalizing than tracking the angel blood spotting the blacktop.

She tore away the red bodice from the sexy black corset. Ripping methodically, she removed the skirt, beneath which she wore slim-fitted black leggings. "Besides," she said, "I have information you need. I know where the muse lives."

I tilted a nod of appreciation, both for her attire—from eighteenth-century princess to sexy, modern cat burglar—and her knowledge. Then I slammed her against the wall.

Pressing her shoulders back, I moved in. Hip to hip. Chest to oh-so-luscious chest. "I've changed my mind about you, Coco. I like you."

"Is it my sparkling personality or my knowledge about the muse?"

"Actually, it's your gorgeous tits and sweet blood. I haven't tasted anything so smooth since that bottle of 1870 whiskey that went down in one night. Do you know you taste like chocolate?"

"Really? Must have been the mousse I snagged from the buffet earlier. Okay, so I went back for seconds. Sue me. You're very close—"

I lunged to bite again, but her palm smacked my mouth hard. Ouch, that hurt the fangs!

"Not so fast, vampire. You want to get all up close and personal? The fangs gotta stay out of sight."

"Is that so?" I hooked my fingers behind the corset, between the tempting warmth of her breasts, and tugged her closer. "Fine."

She didn't expect the kiss. Hell, I hadn't expected it, either. But it was as unavoidable as a bomb ticking down the last two seconds.

I crushed her lips, bruising them with the frustration of having lost the halo. How dare she steal from me? Miss Coco in her sexy corset and chocolate-mousse kisses. Lips covering my teeth, I sucked in her lower lip. Her body melded to mine, matching curves to hard planes.

And then I pressed a soft kiss to her mouth because she demanded it with a whimper. That wanting sound seeped through my pores and shocked my system with some kind of persuasion I'd never been privy to. Vamps can't be persuaded. And yet…

I surrender, precious mortal. What do you want from me?

Chapter Three

I had never kissed a man like this before. Standing in a dark alley, outside a fabulous estate, having purloined a valued object from a hideous modern artwork. Bodies crushed to one another in subtle desperation. Fingers moved over clothing, seeking the warmth of flesh, the promise of connection. Breaths inhaled. Mouths dancing. Teeth daring.

He thought he was forcing himself on me, the ineffectual little halo thief who had fallen into his arms. But I liked his powerful manner, his aggressive stance. His macho threat to control. This man—this *vampire*.

Wait.

I shoved him from my mouth. He winced and shook his head. A smirk revealed sexy white teeth—and fangs.

"You bit me!" I protested.

"Right, love, thanks for reminding me. I almost forgot that I didn't take time to seal the wound. Don't want you vamping out before the next full moon. Better fix that."

The intrusion of his fangs in my neck hurt because he sunk them into the previous bite marks. I nudged up my knee, hoping to hit the family jewels, because this time his aggression was real, and not a play at romance.

I thought the vampire's kiss was supposed to be so sexy, so erotic, so…

My arms dropped at my sides. As did my apprehensions.

Okay, so maybe there was something to this being bitten thing. My body hummed. I could feel the blood gush through my system, pricking at my nerve endings with a soft, sensual zing. All parts of me grew warm and tingly. Was that a moan? Oh, yes, that felt so…right. I pressed my legs together because I felt it in my loins. That sweet, sensitive spot felt as though he were tracing it with his tongue.

Oh, mercy…

Zane stopped sucking at my neck and dragged his tongue over the punctures. "Whew! Your blood makes a guy wish he could fall in love."

He stepped back, shaking his fingers out at his sides and bouncing a bit.

I exhaled, lost in a heady spin of sensations.

Tentatively, I touched the twin wounds. "You can't?"

Cocky now, he swaggered up to me and whispered aside my ear. "Monsters don't get to fall in love."

"Maybe I like monsters." Yikes. Where had that weird confession come from?

I trailed my fingertips down his face, aside the nasty scar. I wanted to ask him about it, but really I wanted to get to the climax his bite had almost brought me to.

I lunged in for another kiss. His arms didn't wrap about my hips, instead I sensed he held them up as if being robbed.

"I'm not going to steal from you," I murmured against his firm lips. They were beautiful, made for my mouth. So I kissed them again. And again. And I dashed my tongue inside to trace his lower teeth, but daren't flick it up for fear of his sharp fangs.

"Whoa, love." He pressed me against the wall, but did not hold me there with his body. "You're acting kind of silly now."

I teased a fingertip at the corner of my mouth. "It's called flirting."

"It's called the swoon. You get giddy from my bite. Orgasmic, even."

"Not quite. I need more giddy."

Encircling his neck with my arms, I rubbed up against him, angry that the stupid corset was so rigid and while I could feel his taut muscles, he probably couldn't feel how hard my nipples were. Oh, but they ached for his tongue.

Now he kissed me, and this time it was deep and lingering and laced with our throaty moans. I hooked a leg up along his hip and he lifted, holding me there, so strong, so dominant. I devoured what he gave me. A stolen sigh. A pulse of muscle against my thigh. A desirous moan in his deep, British tones.

"There's no time to waste," he said against my mouth. "We find the angel, and I promise we will finish what we started here. But you gotta take me to the muse's home, love. You don't want the angel to beat us there, do you?"

Shocked out of the giddy, I nodded. "Right. Must protect the muse."

Man, the guy had some kind of powerful pheromones. I wobbled and pressed a hand to the brick wall so he wouldn't think I was drunk.

Deep breath, Coco. Ahh...

"That way. About ten blocks."

Twice now I'd sipped from Coco. She was sweeter than I remembered cocoa being, and I did remember it. I'd only been vamp about ten years. Hot chocolate had once been a favorite drink. Her skin was the same color—cocoa satin—and it begged to be licked.

What the hell was I doing, allowing this bird to accompany me on what could prove the most dangerous encounter I'd had in years? Though it had healed, my back still ached. New scars always did pull a bit. I knew it would scar permanently. Wasn't like a normal injury that would heal up with fresh skin. That halo was divine—it left an indelible mark. And while religious objects could fatally wound baptized vampires, I had not been baptized, which I was thankful for right now.

I had my own divine weapon, and I wished I didn't have to use it up close and personal. *Thanks, Coco, for tossing the angel the halo.*

Ah, well, it made for a more interesting evening.

"So how's a pretty bird like you know about muses and angels and vampires?" I prompted as she strode down a cobbled street beside me. This neighborhood in Bayswater was ritzy, but a man didn't have to walk far to hit a scruffy spot.

"My sister is a muse." Her voice was unnaturally bubbly. She shouldn't be so enthusiastic about this adventure. And when she slipped her hand in mine, I almost jerked it free, because I did not do Sunday walks in the park.

I clasped her fingers. It wasn't Sunday, and we weren't headed toward a park, that was sure.

"Granny told us all about muses and the Fallen. We didn't learn about the vampires' involvement until recently. Oh, hell."

She stopped abruptly, tugging her hand from mine as if it were coated with acid. "Are you...? What was the name of that tribe...?"

I cocked my head to the side, marveling over

the dimple that formed at the corner of her eye when she squinted in thought. A bloke could lose himself in that sweet spot.

"Anakim?" I suggested.

"You are?" She looked about for escape, so I grabbed her shoulders and forced her to see me with a trace of persuasion to calm her panic. "But that makes you—"

"I didn't say I was Anakim, love. And I'm not going to say. I'm just Zane."

"The ninja vampire?" Her nervous, yet hopeful smile beamed through my chest and warmed my heart. Silly girl, I'd meant it about us monsters.

"Right, the ninja vampire." It sounded like I should be sporting tights and pow-banging my way through a comic book. I was not ninja, but why spoil the fun? "So you're trying to get this halo for your sister?"

"Yes. She may be able to use it as a weapon against the Fallen, should one come for her."

Fallen angels were attracted to a muse, one particular mortal female matched to one particular angel. The Fallen had sex with the muse—usually not consensual—in hopes of creating Nephilim progeny.

And a whole lot of nothing good happened after that.

"I don't think the halo works as an effective weapon unless wielded by a Fallen," I said.

"Maybe. It's worth a try, though," she said. "And it gives hope."

"The halo? Hope seems a flimsy weapon, you ask me."

"You of so little faith."

"You got that right. Lacking faith has kept this vampire in one piece, let me tell you." I absently stroked the scar dashing my cheek.

"We're here."

I scanned up the apartment building, following Coco's gesture to the second floor. All the windows were dark, but then, it was after midnight.

"I'll go up and have a look-see."

She grabbed my arm, holding me back. "You're not going to trick me, are you? Take the halo and run?"

"If the halo is up there, that means the angel is, as well. I only need the halo to attract the angel," I said. "After that, it's yours."

"Oh."

"Surprised I don't have plans to go all evil-bloodsucker on you?"

She shrugged.

Yeah, she was surprised.

Chapter Four

The vampire walking toward me had the sexiest stride. A bit of a swagger, his arms gliding sinuously at his sides, but sleek, lean edges that could blend into the shadows and emerge to wrap about you like a dream come to life.

Oh, hell, Coco, what are you thinking? I was not letting this guy get under my skin. He was a vampire.

I prided myself on free thinking, being nonjudgmental. "Love your neighbor and peace to the world" and all that jazz. Born a mix of British, African-American and French, race never registered on my radar. Wasn't vampirism just another race?

And really? He'd already gotten under my skin and into my veins. Too late to turn back now.

"She's dead," he said curtly, shoving his hands in his pockets and paralleling me.

"The angel has already been here?"

"No, I mean dead, as in cancer or some such. Her flat was empty. Talked to a neighbor in his PJs who said she spent the last three months in the hospital. Her death was completely unrelated to being a muse. So now we've an angel, armed with his halo, stalking the streets of London in search of another muse."

"Oh, my God. My sister!"

"She lives in town?"

"No, Berlin, but she could be in danger. Can't angels like fly or walk the world swiftly?"

"No flight, but indeed they do that fast-walking bit that tends to impress me, despite their nasty nature."

I tugged out the cell phone and tapped in Cassandra's number.

Zane leaned against a street post, ankles crossed and eyes taking in the surroundings like a panther on the prowl.

When had that scar become sexy? It cut over his dark brow and right through that funny-looking white eye, then tore through a high cheekbone *GQ* models would have killed for. I wanted to touch it, trace it softly, maybe even dash my tongue over it, instilling a hint of kindness where he'd only felt rage. I didn't think vampires could scar—

"Cassandra? You okay?"

I explained to her we'd lost the halo, and didn't

mention my accomplice happened to drink my blood twice already. She did not want me to come to her, but I insisted. I'd book the next flight to Berlin.

"Why are you defying your sister?" Zane asked as I started down the street toward an Underground station where I could take a subway to my flat, pack and catch a cab to the airport. "There's nothing you can do without the halo. You're not an angel slayer, love."

"Nor are you!"

He flinched, but shook out his shoulders and gave an abrupt twist of his neck. "Right, then. So I guess this is where we part ways."

Seriously? He could walk away from me *like that?* Without another kiss? Without even asking for my phone number?

Coco, you are not falling in love with this guy!

No, I was not, but serious like was very probable.

He grabbed my arm and tugged me into the shadows. Before I could protest his insistent need for the rough stuff, I followed his gesture, pointing down the street. I recognized the hulking frame and the menacing air.

"Gotcha," Zane whispered. "The angel comes to us."

And like that the sky opened up and doused us with rain.

It was more than rain, it was Noah's bloody flood pouring from the heavens. I grabbed Coco's arm and hustled her across the street to find refuge under the tin overhang of a sweet shop. But I wasn't about to lose the angel this time. She followed as I tracked around the corner and spied the angel entering a warehouse.

I could go in, kill the bastard and take what I needed. But he was armed with a deadly weapon, and me and my aching backside were a little skittish of that damned halo.

"We're going to wait it out," I decided, shrugging a shoulder that tugged at my scarred back.

We slunk along the shadows and the opposite buildings, until I found an abandoned warehouse across the street. The second floor provided vantage of the angel's hiding spot. I spied the tiny blue glow from the halo.

"He's not going anywhere," I reported.

Coco sighted in on the halo. "Why not?"

"Your granny didn't teach you that angels don't like water? They can drown in less than four inches."

"I don't understand. Why don't they just fly off?"

"I told you, the Fallen cannot fly. It's something to do with Noah's flood. First time God wiped them from the earth in punishment for Falling was with the great flood."

"Wow." She leaned against a Sheetrock wall, punched out in places and scrawled with graffiti. "You're all up on your Biblical lore. I wouldn't have expected—"

"That a monster would have such knowledge? I haven't always been a vampire, love." I squatted to the side of the window so the angel wouldn't spy me.

"Ninja first, then vampire?" she inquired, and knelt before me. Her knowing smile let me know she was in on the ninja joke.

I was uncomfortable with her being so close. But why? We'd already kissed and groped. Hell, I'd been inside her thick vein, had penetrated her so intimately. It doesn't get much better than that.

Very well, it could...

Thunder rumbled across the rooftops, but she held my gaze, unflinching. She was either very brave, or too stupid to know her own peril.

And look at me. Peril? Sod me, but I wanted the woman, naked and moaning beneath me. The only peril that involved was that of the— No, I wasn't going there. Not some bollocks about the heart and all that love mush.

"Tell me about this." She stroked my cheek over the scar tissue.

I jerked away from her tenderness. "No."

"Fine. You know you're not a monster, right?"

Oh, the poor beguiled little bird.

"What part of bloodsucking fiend does not re-semble monster-ish to you?"

"The part where you care enough about a stranger to protect her. I'm not sure why you're after the angel, but I sense that's not so evil, either."

I blew out a breath, not sure how to reply. She

had me pegged wrong. Guess it was up to me to set her straight.

"Monsters attack innocent women in alleyways and leave their necks torn open, the carotid spurting until they die. That monster, when he saw me approaching to see if the woman needed help, turned on me and did the same. Except, I survived."

I tilted my head at her. "So you see? I'm from sturdy monster stock. It doesn't get much worse than taking life from others to sustain your own."

"You don't kill." She insinuated herself upon my lap with an ease I wouldn't have managed even with persuasion. "I know you don't."

I'd killed many while serving the British SAS only a decade earlier. But that was neither here nor there.

Her touch along my brow was too gentle. I wanted to drown in the tenderness, just…surrender to what I desperately wanted. It had been a long time since this monster had experienced such intimacy.

"Sounds like the storm is a doozy," she said. "We're going to be here awhile. So let's make out."

"Er…okay, love."

I let her kiss me because she was right. The angel was trapped until the storm let up. And I wasn't much for standing stakeout, staring across the way at our prey for endless, spine-breaking hours. Had to pass the time somehow.…

"Wait." I pushed her from my mouth, regretting

the loss of her warm neediness. "I get it. Tough guy shoves you around a bit, bites you and treats you badly. You're chasing the bad-boy fantasy, eh?"

"If that's how you want to call it." The twinkle in her brown eyes told me she wasn't that stupid, and was also smart enough to play along with me to get what she wanted. Apparently, what she wanted was me.

That was a bit of all right.

Oh, but she knew how to give a kiss. And me sitting there, drowning in her sensual taste, the press of our bodies, the happy wonder of her—

"Wait."

She sat back with a frustrated sigh.

"Can't do it," I muttered. A lie. What was up with that? Free kisses and all the other good stuff that would follow? What kind of sod was I to refuse?

"Why not?" She toyed a finger along the curve of her cocoa-and-cream breast. Pouty lips teased my defenses. "Am I doing it wrong?"

"No." *Don't pout those kiss-bruised lips. Just... ah, bollocks. Must. Resist.*

"Don't I appeal to you?"

"You do. But, love—"

"I have bad breath or something?"

"I'll bite you," I snapped out. It was a good excuse, not necessarily true, but it should serve.

"Don't you need my permission to bite me?

How *did* you manage that without first asking me—?"

Glass shattered, and a disk of blue light sheered the soft dark hair tufting Coco's ear. I grabbed her against my chest. A drop of blood hit my forehead. She'd been nicked; the top of her ear bled.

The halo circled around and soared back through the broken window at supersonic speed.

"He's spotted us." I shoved Coco to the floor. "Stay down."

Chapter Five

Again the halo burst through a window, spinning
like an insane 33 1/3 rpm flung off the turntable.
It reached the back of the warehouse, and spun out
through the window.

Zane lunged a look through the window and
managed to dodge the return path of the deadly
thing.

Now I got it. Granny had told my sister and I
that the halo always returned to the thrower. She'd
forgotten to mention the part that the thrower must
be the original owner. We wouldn't be in this situation if I'd known that.

My ear burned but I resisted touching it. I didn't
want to know how badly I'd been hurt, but suspected it was just a nick.

I shuffled against a wall, my hand slipping on the bits of crumbled Sheetrock and rubble. I wasn't about to get in the way. I had a ninja vampire to protect me.

A flash of silver caught my attention. The vampire swung the chain at his side, the brilliant blade catching the moonlight like a beacon. It had something to do with the scar on his face, I guessed. A battle prize won for the price of a devastating wound?

"Watch out, love!"

I ducked to the floor, grinning ear to ear, because I foolishly believed he meant it when he called me *love*. It was an endearment, nothing more. I think the heady rush of danger, adrenaline and blood loss was making me a little loopy. If not fatally attracted to the baddest of the bad.

Another window crashed. Glass shards rained over my back. The chain *swooshed* overhead. And the clink of metal against metal. He'd snagged the halo!

I wanted to jump up and hug him, slobber him with kisses and congratulate him on being the hero—

"Don't move," he commanded.

—or not.

His boots cracked over the glass. His fingers moved over my back, carefully removing the shards and brushing through my hair and over my skin. "Okay, you can stand now."

"You got it." I hugged him, and he allowed it. It

wasn't a return hug, I knew that much. He was just letting it happen. He really believed the monster bit. Poor guy. "You got what you wanted."

He sighed and pushed me from his embrace. "Not quite yet."

We eyed the warehouse through the insistent downpour. The angel stood at the broken window. Zane waved the halo mockingly, which earned us a nasty gesture I didn't think angels were allowed to perform.

Noting my surprise, Zane said, "The Fallen are not like the angels you believe in, love. Nothing fluffy or divine about them. This is yours." He handed me the halo. "Now that he's without a weapon, I can go after him."

He swung up the chain and grabbed the blade. "Got this pretty slicer from a Sinistari demon. The tip is coated in some kind of angel poison. It's the only thing that'll kill a Fallen. Gotta shove it up into his glass heart, though, which means I'll have to get real close. Wish me luck."

"Wait." I leaned in and kissed the scar cutting his cheek. "It's from the blade, right? You went up against a Sinistari?" Granny had told us they are a breed of demons forged specifically to slay the Fallen. "I don't understand. Why do you need this angel dead?"

"Doesn't matter what angel, as long as it's dead." He huffed out a sigh. "Do we need to do this now?"

The rain beat relentlessly. The angel across the street wasn't going anywhere.

"Yes, now."

Why was this bird making it so difficult to like her? She wanted too much. We'd just met. Hell, we were soon to part. I didn't do attachment. It wasn't easy when one needed to snack on their partner every once in a while. Made for mistrust and fear, and that's never good for a relationship.

"You are Anakim," she said. "They're the vampire tribe after the angels right now. They think if they can capture a Nephilim, they can drink its blood and strengthen their bloodline. Make it so they can walk in the day like most other vampires."

"You know your stuff," I said, stalling, shaking the chain loosely in my grip. The blade banged my leg above the combat boots.

I noticed a fine line of crimson at the corner of her eye and my instincts put me up close to her before I had even decided to move. I tongued the cut. She sighed and bent into my embrace. Giving. Wanting. So vulnerable.

Had my persuasion taken away her free will? I hadn't used that much on her earlier, and I certainly hadn't used any right now.

"I like you, Zane," she said, her fingers finding the vein on my throat and holding over my pulse. "I want to know you."

"It's the persuasion. Nothing but."

She gut-punched me. I doubled at the surprising force of her right hook pummeling below the kidney. Mother of—

"You call that persuasion?" she challenged.

"Apparently not," I croaked.

"I do what I want, when I want, with whomever I want. You're not making me do a thing, vampire. So get over it."

I smirked, loving that if I had to go a few rounds with anyone tonight it was this particular hotheaded chick with the chocolate blood and sinful kisses.

So she wanted me, scars and all? Made a bloke's shoulders straighten and I lifted my chin a notch.

"Fine. I'm Anakim, or was. After the vamp bit me I joined the tribe because I didn't know what else there was to do. Besides, I needed some direction on the whole avoiding-the-sunlight thing."

"The Anakim tribe is weak," she said. "They won't stop until they get a Nephilim."

"Exactly. They—we—got our hands on an angel and his muse recently. It wasn't pretty. They are trying to breed helpless mortal muses to vicious Fallen. Much as I want to walk in the sun, I won't do it at a woman's expense. I'll stick to the shadows, thank you very much."

"Noble."

I shrugged. Monsters didn't do noble, either.

"So what are you going to do with the dead angel?" she asked.

"One less Fallen is one less horror for all the muses, wouldn't you say?"

She narrowed her eyes, seeing into a part of me I barely knew. "But you want something more."

This bird was not stupid.

"Yeah? Well, that's the part you don't get to know about. So you take the bloody halo and bring it to your sister. Give her a kiss for me, and I wish you all the luck avoiding her Fallen. Best advice I can give you is to run if you ever see another. Meanwhile, I'm going to trip on over to the angel across the way. He's only got iron wings and steel muscles to fight me now. Wish me luck."

"I'm coming with you."

"This is no longer a partnership, Coco. I let you toddle along—"

"Toddle along! You wouldn't have found the angel if I hadn't led you to the muse's place."

"A dead muse. Luck happened us upon the angel."

She did not pout, nor try to cajole my tender slice of heart with big sad eyes. But she did thrust back her shoulders and stare me down. Ninja vampires were supposed to be impervious.

I wasn't ninja. I possessed some wicked martial skills, learned during my military service. But who'da thought I'd need emotional skills to fend off my most challenging opponent yet? Unfortunately, I hadn't received that particular training.

"Fine." I had a feeling I was going to regret this, but it was a better option than simply walking away and never seeing this lovely bird again. "You can stick around, because arguing with you will only piss me off. But you are not going in that building. You stay outside and keep watch, okay?"

She touched me before I even saw it coming. Her palm flattened over my heart. A heart that beat and wasn't as black as I thought it should be, and a heart that remembered what it was like to be mortal. Mortality had been tough—I'd served the British army a decade in combat and secret black ops missions that had brought me to the brink— but I'd never lost the capacity to need, to want, to pine for love.

Monsters don't get to love.

Right. Almost forgot.

"Let's go."

Chapter Six

The evening had taken an odd turn. I'd thought to find the halo, stick it in a brown padded mailer and send if off to my sister, Cassandra. Task complete. Back to the grind. The grind being nine-to-five detail behind the desk at a travel agency.

Adventure being my thing—albeit, on the glossy pages of a travel brochure—I preferred this altered version of the evening. Land in the arms of a scary-looking man, who happens to be a vampire, who happens to bite me—twice. Chase an angel. Dodge angel's deadly weapon. Win back the halo. The day is saved and the girl gets the guy!

Except whatever was going on in the warehouse across the street right now didn't sound, or look, like day-saving.

Zane was in there, and that made me antsy. I didn't want him to get hurt. I doubted the angel would leave him scarred this time around. No, the Fallen was out for blood after we'd stolen his halo.

Halos were supposed to hold the Fallen's earth-bound soul. The angel could take that soul and become mortal. But Granny told us most Fallen didn't want to go with a pitiful human existence and eventually die a mortal death. They preferred to remain something more than mortal—and to go after their muses as their twisted libidos demanded.

Things crashed, maybe boards, windows and interior walls. Every so often a brilliant flash of blue would mimic the glow of the halo I held. A man cried out in pain—Zane. I'd developed a twitch, wanting to rush in every time I heard his miserable shouts.

Like that would do any good. Go, super travel-agent lady! Not to be. Actually, my middle name is Marie, not Adventure.

Squatting against the wall, I huddled, protecting the halo between my legs and chest, and kept one eye on the second-floor window. Had something just been thrown across the room? Something man-sized?

I ducked my head against my knees.

"Don't look, Coco. He'll be fine. He said he had a good chance now the angel had been disarmed."

Clicky footsteps set up the hairs on my arms. I

recognized the pitter-pat of high heels. One person. Coming up around the corner from where I sat.

I swung up and almost did a chest bump with the woman who was preoccupied with scratching her wrist. A wrist that glowed blue.

"I don't know what it is," she muttered, boggled and obviously more worried about the glowing sigil than a complete stranger who bowed over her wrist to inspect. "It's always been there, but it just started to glow. It's like some kind of alien implant. Oh, my bloody hell!"

"Don't worry." I cringed. *Not the truth, Coco.* But I needed to calm her, and make sure no one nearby—like the Fallen—saw her.

I walked her back around the corner and hugged her. She allowed it. I sensed she was in shock for she shivered minutely. "It's an angel sigil," I said. "You were born with it, right?"

She nodded. Wisps of blond hair that had dried about her hairline teased the air. The rain had stopped, but it was dark, murky and more humid than a steam room.

"It's very pretty." I traced the square shape that had a triangle in the middle. I hadn't seen the Fallen's sigil, but I knew that this muse matched the angel Zane was fighting. That's the only reason it would glow. "And it itches?"

She nodded again. Her skin was red and I worried she'd tear it with those press-on nails. "Stop." Itching turned the sigil into a beacon the angel could follow right to the muse. I clasped both hands about her wrist. "I'll explain things. You won't like what I have to say, but you need the information."

"Sure, whatever, lady. Wait."

We both studied her inflamed skin, the sigil now a soft brown against the redness where she'd scratched. It had stopped glowing. I cast a glance over my shoulder. Darkness in the second-floor window.

Had Zane accomplished the task?

Or would the muse and I be dodging a furious angel intent on claiming the halo and his muse?

I strung the halo on a forearm, and then sheltered the woman from whatever might come our way.

The air glimmered before me. I staggered, bloody blade held back and out with one hand. The cuts on my body hurt like hell, and the blood drooling out soaked me in crimson. Those damned iron wings had been sharp.

Had been. Heh.

The angel's body burst into a brilliant nimbus and shattered. A glamorous wall of sparkly bits hung suspended before me momentarily. The wings dropped in flakes of black iron, the crystallized body fell in a man-length pile of ash before my feet.

This is what I'd been stalking the streets for tonight. What I'd been striving for over the months since witnessing the Anakim tribe's macabre machinations.

And yet, I looked over my shoulder, out the window, but could not see street level. Did she wait for me? *Didn't the hero deserve a kiss?* Or had Coco wisely fled?

For a moment of utter wimpy wistfulness, I thought I saw her bright brown eyes flash at me. And then I blinked, and the sexy princess turned cat burglar was running toward me. Her eyes weren't as happy to see me as I'd hoped, rather wide and unbelieving, actually.

She deftly avoided the angel ash and slammed into me, setting me off balance, so I clung to her. Every cut on my skin screamed. My right leg, which I'm sure was broken, buckled. I went down, and she fell with me, until we kneeled before each other, embracing.

I buried my face in her hair. Rain-fresh summers and the sensual heat of her skin chased back the pain. Chocolate heartbeats pulsed against my chest.

She clasped my head and whispered something that sounded like, "I'm so glad you're alive."

No one had ever been glad that my heart beat. People usually ran when they saw me coming. Coat me in a quart of my own blood, and I'd really send them running.

Yet Coco clung as if she had found something long-ago lost. And I felt a piece being fit into some greater scene. Her life. My life. We fit together oddly enough.

Damn, I wanted to make this work. Could the pieces stay together?

"I'm getting blood all over you, love. Purple, even. Guess the angel blood mixed with my own."

"I don't care." She wouldn't let go.

Fine with me. Her warmth worked a balm to my wounds, and I could feel the skin knit closed, healing rapidly as vampires are wont. It sizzled a bit. Might have gotten traces of angel blood in my system, but I didn't feel the big kaboom looming.

"I talked to the angel's muse outside."

"What? His muse? Was here?"

"Yes, walking by. Must be why the angel was in the area—he followed the lure of her sigil. She was itching it like a crazy lady. I told her everything, and gave her my sister's phone number. I explained she's still not safe even though this Fallen is dead. He is dead, right?"

I toed the crystal dust. "That's about as dead as dead gets. Two muses in close proximity? London is overflowing with them."

"Let's get out of here."

"Works for me. But first—" I tugged out the folded plastic zip bag I kept tucked in a back pocket and handed it to Coco "—hold this. I'm not leaving without what I've come for."

I scooped up the heavy, glittering angel remnants into the bag. It looked like diamonds, and had the weight of precious gemstones, but held no value for any person unless they were tracking a Nephilim.

"That stuff is gorgeous," she said. "What is it?"

"Angel ash. The only means to kill a Nephilim."

"You plan on killing Nephilim? I thought you wanted to prevent Nephilim from being conceived?"

"I do, but I can't be in all places at once. And I'm no professional angel slayer. Tonight was a fluke. I only won because I had this." I patted the blade at my hip. It had been my first angel-slaying mission. "And the Anakim tribe is huge. I can't stop them from trying to create a Nephilim. This stuff is like an insurance policy. It can be doled out to all who may need it."

"Like my sister?"

"It'll prove a might more effective than the halo, I'll wager."

I shoved the last bit of ash in the bag and followed Coco's fingers as we sealed the zip bag. I admired her enthusiasm, yet knew her real feelings were darker than the positive front she wore. Her sister would ever be in danger. There were dozens of Fallen, and the Anakim were summoning more to earth daily. The only thing that could kill them was a demon blade like I owned, or a real Sinistari demon, of which there were only about a dozen.

The future looked bleak. But I wanted to be a part of the solution. I couldn't do it myself. But I didn't want to endanger this precious woman.

"What's this?" She collected the black feather

that had been uncovered beneath the ash. A splay of her fingers moved the delicate vanes. "It's made of iron? And yet it's soft as down."

"When an angel dies one single feather remains. The Sinistari collect them as war prizes. You take it, love. Stick it in your hair."

She did, and the thing almost looked glamorous, if the fact wasn't that it had come from a murderous angel who'd Fallen to earth intent on screwing mortal women.

"You should go," I said, standing and shaking out my broken leg. "Sun's soon up."

"You need to avoid it more than I do. Will you walk me home?" she inquired innocently. But her tone offered a promise of something much more than urgent kisses and groping.

I chuckled. "Are you making a pass at me, love?"

"Well, you did imply that we would finish what we had started after we took care of the big bad." She splayed a hand over the glittering remains of the angel. "Big bad defeated."

I'd never seen the lash-fluttering move utilized so skillfully. I could taste her sweetness on my tongue. And I wanted to feel the air she moved with her lashes against my lips.

"Can you walk?"

"In a few minutes. Just need to give it a bit to heal."

"Maybe this will help."

Truly, her kisses could be bottled and sold as

medical aid. Coco's mouth against mine chased
off the pain and the horror of standing before the
Fallen and ramming the blade up into its chest. The
agony I'd witnessed cross its kaleidoscope eyes
had momentarily made me question my goal. Who
was I—a true bloodsucking monster—to judge yet
another monster? All of it was now obliterated by
Coco's kiss.

Encircled in her arms, I began to drown, sinking deeper into a bright and wondrous abyss. *Not
a monster.*

And I began to believe it.

I stepped onto my right foot and tested the leg.
Healed. "You're good for me, love. Those kisses
of yours are wicked powerful."

"Come on." She grabbed my arm, and I followed her dash through the warehouse. "We have
to beat the sun. My flat is a good jog away."

I didn't protest. In fact, I clasped her hand in
mine and tugged her into the shadows, hugging
the building walls, yet keeping up the race against
the sun.

Chapter Seven

Clothing fell about our feet. I turned and wiggled my shoulders while Zane tugged at the corset strings crisscrossing down my back. The sun brightened the world outside, but I'd hastily pulled the curtains and Zane helped me throw a blanket over the pale bedroom sheers to darken the room.

The stiff corset loosened and fell. Zane's hands eased along my spine, massaging.

"How'd you know I needed that?" I asked, but the question ended in a satisfied moan.

"You've marks on your pretty flesh, love. Let me kiss them away."

His hot mouth touched me there, where the corset had imprisoned me, and there, soft and tender, a dash of his tongue easing away the aches.

A tickle and then the sizzle as our body heat combined in a wicked dance.

I gasped as his hands glided down my hips and his kisses moved to the top of my derriere. There he licked a zigzagging line over my skin, burning his mark into me.

I reached back, slipping my fingers into his spiky hair, unable to ask for what I wanted, and surrendering to the devastating touches.

"Turn about, love."

He knelt before me, shirt off, and exposed abs and delts that required merciless licking and maybe even a few love nips. I was naked, and had never stood so boldly before a man on his knees before. I wanted to clasp my arms across my breasts.

And then I wanted to be worshipped by the twinkle in his deep blue eyes.

Tossing back my head, I closed my eyes to the first touch of his tongue to my mons. He glided along the V of my thigh and down to tease at my humming center. One hot stroke sent my body to a delicious shiver.

I raked my fingers through his hair and he rose to lift me and lay me on the bed, stretching my arms above my head and across the sheets as my hips rose to his ministrations. Oh, sweet mercy, he could have me in mind, body and soul.

And yes, even blood.

Coco's skin was like silk and had the fine color of milk chocolate warmed by the sun. The closest

I'd ever get to the sun, surely. I could worship her endlessly, gliding my skin against hers and reacting to her subtle movements and pleading moans.

She wanted it all. And I wasn't about to deny her.

Finding my place, a finger against her nub, and trailing my tongue up her stomach, I suckled at each hard nipple, tendering the velvety flesh slowly, prolonging the raging climax I could sense building in her sleek body.

Her muscles tightened and flexed beneath my roaming hands. Her hips nudged mine, the contact rubbing her powder-silken skin against my harder-than-marble erection.

If ever a monster could be worthy of love, then I wanted that chance. In this woman's arms. In her heart. Hell, I wanted to enter her very soul.

"Please," she begged. "Come inside me now, Zane. Give yourself to me."

Sweet mercy, the power of her persuasion mastered me.

I hilted myself inside her and we both came at the same time, crying out, clutching one another and clinging out of desperation and, at the same time, joy. Skin crushed to skin, sighs harmonizing, we became one another. We spoke a silent promise.

Muscles tensing and releasing with climax I bowed my head to her breast, grazing my fangs, which always came down during sex, along her moist skin.

"Yes," she gasped, curling her fingers about my skull. "Bite me again, lover."

This time I pricked her shallowly, fully aware I still pricked her deeply with my cock, and the intense orgasm reignited as her chocolate blood melted on my tongue. It deepened her pleasure, too, bringing up the giddy she'd flirtatiously asked for before. This was the soul-claiming part. And together we dove into the beginning of what felt like love.

"You're mine, love," I whispered.

"The ninja vampire's girl." Shuddering with traces of orgasm, she sighed and kissed my shoulder. "I like the sound of that."

I chuckled against her breast. "Works for me."

* * * * *

A sneaky peek at next month...

NOCTURNE™

BEYOND DARKNESS...BEYOND DESIRE

My wish list for next month's titles...

In stores from 16th September 2011:

❏ Alaskan Wolf – Linda O. Johnston

❏ The Truth about Vampires – Theresa Meyers

In stores from 7th October 2011:

❏ Lord of the Vampires – Gena Showalter

Available at WHSmith, Tesco, Asda, Eason, Amazon and Apple

Just can't wait?

Have Your Say

You've just finished your book.
So what did you think?

We'd love to hear your thoughts on our
'Have your say' online panel
www.millsandboon.co.uk/haveyoursay

- Easy to use
- Short questionnaire
- Chance to win Mills & Boon® goodies

New Voices is back!

New Voices

returns on
13th September 2011!

For sneak previews and exclusives:

 Like us on facebook.com/romancehq

 Follow us on twitter.com/MillsandBoonUK

Last year your votes helped Leah Ashton win
New Voices 2010 with her fabulous story
Secrets & Speed Dating!

Who will you be voting for this year?

*Visit us
Online*

Find out more at
www.romanceisnotdead.com

NEW_VOICES